A Match Made in Mehendi

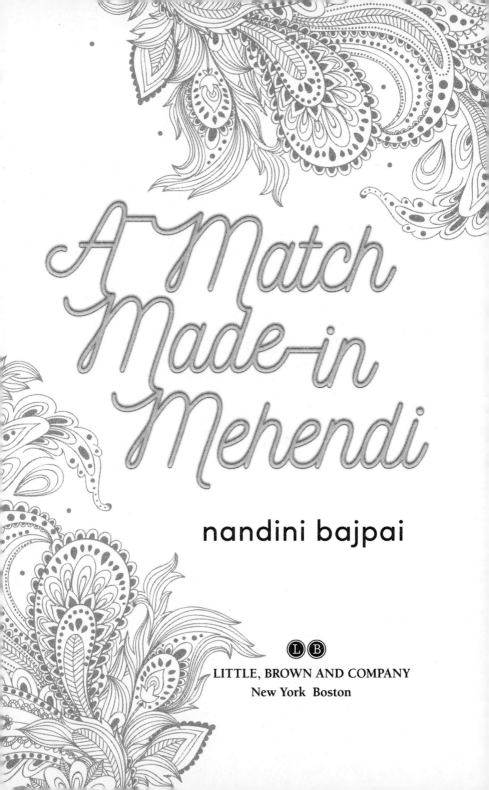

A Match Made–in Mehendi

nandini bajpai

LB

LITTLE, BROWN AND COMPANY

New York Boston

Little, Brown and Company
Hachette Book Group
1290 Avenue of the Americas, New York, NY 10104
Visit us at LBYR.com

First Edition: September 2019

Little, Brown and Company is a division of Hachette Book Group, Inc. The Little, Brown name and logo are trademarks of Hachette Book Group, Inc.

The publisher is not responsible for websites (or their content) that are not owned by the publisher.

Library of Congress Cataloging-in-Publication Data
Names: Bajpai, Nandini, author.
Title: A match made in mehendi / by Nandini Bajpai.
Description: First edition. | New York : Little, Brown and Company, 2019.
Identifiers: LCCN 2018060495| ISBN 9780316522588 (hardcover) |
ISBN 9780316522571 (ebook) | ISBN 9780316522564
(library edition ebook)
Classification: LCC PZ7.1.B335 Mat 2019 | DDC [Fic]—dc23
LC record available at https://lccn.loc.gov/2018060495

ISBNs: 978-0-316-52258-8 (hardcover), 978-0-316-52257-1 (ebook)

Printed in the United States of America

LSC-C

10 9 8 7 6 5 4 3 2 1

For Pushpa and Usha

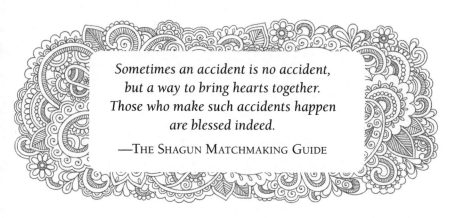

chapter one

*M*atching furniture is like matching couples. There must be balance, harmony, and excitement between the sofa and the side table, the lampshade and the rug—just as there is balance, harmony, and excitement between two people who are perfect for each other.

Sound ridiculous?

Welcome to my life, where this isn't a bit of feng shui or vaastu. It's actually the way my family sees pairing people. My mom and masi are third-generation professional matchmakers, so that's the way they see *everything*. Stuck with them since birth, I can usually put up with this. But today they're making me want to rip the stuffing out of the beautiful silk cushion I'm holding, just like our dog, Sweetie, did when she was a puppy.

"These colors are a great match, no?" Mom thinks maroon and gold are predestined to be together. "The pattern on the cushions has such positive energy. They balance the coffee table nicely, too. What do you think, Simi?"

I tilt my head to squint at the abstract geometric design of the cushion. Someone give me a medal for not screaming. "Can cushions really have energy?"

"Simi!" Mom yells, and I know when she says my name like that she's either going to buy this thing or walk out of Singh's Emporium and start over. Again.

The late afternoon sun spills through the showroom windows of Singh's, a cluttered, comfortable Indian furniture store popular in this part of New Jersey. It's the day before sophomore year starts, and everyone else is probably last-minute speed-reading summer book assignments or taking the final beach trip of the season, but I'm stuck in Peach Tree Mall with my family, picking out couches, chairs, and coffee tables for my masi's new house.

Actually, correction—I'm picking furniture with the *women* in my family. My older brother, Navdeep, got to ditch, along with my dad and uncle. Male opinions were deemed unnecessary, I guess. It's just my mom, my masi— mother's sister—and my cousins Preet and Geet. They didn't want to be scooped up and dragged along, either, but our moms always get what they want.

And they never settle for the first thing they like, or even the fifth. They believe in options. And bargains. And the best deals, no matter how much comparison shopping that might mean. This is legit the fifth store we've been at today. No one needs to go to that many furniture stores just to find a place to put their butts.

"Guys, this is as good as it's going to get." Preet's had enough. "I need to get back to my apartment. I have a package coming later. Will you both please stop fussing and buy it already?"

"You're sure?" My mom puts her glasses on to look closely at the upholstery.

"Sure, I'm sure!" Preet waves a hand, making her armful of silver bangles jingle. She looks fabulous today, as usual, in a white sequined chiffon top paired with dark-wash jeans—which, on me, would be borderline cheesy. She's all silky black hair and the kind of curves I thought I'd get when I started high school. But nope. I got nothing. Sad face.

I run my fingers over one of Masi's potential new chairs.

"Comfortable but not too comfortable," Preet says, rolling her eyes. "Which is perfect because you know that our Punjabi peeps never leave if they get too cozy, am I right?"

Mom laughs and pats her back playfully. "You have a point, Toofan Mail."

"Ugh, Manju Masi, don't call me that anymore." Preet frowns at the childhood nickname my mom gave her—after the super-speedy train on the old Indian Railways.

"You're always straight to the point," Mom says. "And with so much excitement."

Props to Preet: I think she just sold them the couch.

Maybe that means we can get out of here and head to the art store. I don't have enough expandable folders or 2B pencils or Post-it notes, and I'm all out of Venetian Sea blue number 34 in my watercolor set, which is critical. This is so *not* the right way to start sophomore year.

"What do you think, Geet?" Masi asks my other cousin.

She grunts, barely looking up from her college textbook and hunkering down in her oversize periodic table sweatshirt. She calls it her signature I-refuse-to-be-pressured-about-beauty-norms look. Mom and Masi have given up trying to influence what she wears. Her boyfriend—whom the whole family (including me) loves—doesn't care what she wears, either. They met their first year of college during Organic Chemistry and formed an instant bond—no pun intended.

Preet, on the other hand, broke up with That Creep Ravinder senior year. She's here today on the understanding that Mom and Masi honor her strict no-discussing-dating-and-marriage-and-matchmaking rule.

"It checks all the boxes," Geet replies. "Like Preet says, it's perfect. So can we go now?"

"Should I write up the invoice, madam?" the furniture salesman asks Masi, hoping to seal the deal.

"Yes, we'll take it," Masi says.

Finally! I take a big gulp of the milky, sweet chai the salesman served us earlier and sputter because, somehow, it's still hot.

"Careful." Mom reaches for the cup.

"Mom, stop." I set it down without spilling. "Ugh, I'm tired of sitting. I'm going to look around while you finish up."

"Don't touch anything, Simi!" Her warning echoes after me.

"Okay, okay." It's annoying when Mom just assumes I'm going to wreck stuff, though my history with breaking china isn't stellar, to be honest. But I'm older now. She should have more faith in me.

The store smells faintly of sandalwood incense and a lemony wood finish. Carved Kashmiri screens separate the space into various sections—living room, bedroom, kids' room. I catch a glimpse of myself in a gilded wall mirror and strike a pose.

Long, skinny legs, denim shorts that barely stay up on my flat butt, flouncy peasant top, flip-flops, a beaded hemp anklet on my left foot (a new trend), the paisley mehendi pattern I painted along my wrists and ankles yesterday, and lots of bouncy waves in my waist-long hair. Maybe I should've added the blue highlights my best friend, Noah, suggested. Even though Mom would hate them. Which means I should definitely get them.

I give a wooden swing painted with horses and elephants a little push and watch as it glides gently back and forth. There's a tiny painted rider with a flamboyant mustache on one of the elephants. I click a picture of it and text it to Noah.

> Welcome back to Jersey, beach bum.

< Nice mustache!

> Not as nice as your tropical vacation.

< Hey, what are you wearing for first day of school?

> Not sure...maybe a mustache?

< That's not what I meant when I said take risks!

> Fine. Fine. Come to my house in the morning. We can walk to school together.

I wander deeper into the store, dodging a large puddle and an orange plastic cone beside it; glancing up, I see that the ceiling's sprung a leak. I flop into the soft cushions of an armchair nearby. I pull out my little sketchbook and look around for something to draw.

Drawing's *my* thing. And I'm good at it. I'll be a famous artist one day, and all my sketches will be worth millions of dollars. No matter how much Mom complains about art not falling into one of the approved careers for Desi people. I don't want to be a doctor, lawyer, or engineer. And in my family, of course, there is a fourth career category that's 1,000 percent parent approved—matchmaking. But I'm not doing that, either.

The puddle on the floor grabs my attention again. It could be a good subject for a still life. Hmm. I could make it a magic portal leading to somewhere other than this awful furniture store. Or... the vase beside the armchair is probably better. I need a "serious" art portfolio for the start of the school year so I can impress my art teacher, Ms. Furst.

I examine the vase and all its delicate floral motifs and exotic tropical birds. I hum a little as I pencil in the outline of the vase and add swirly paisleys to it.

The voices of Mom, Masi, and other customers hum in the background, a mix of Punjabi, Hindi, and Jersey accents that's typical in this area, but my little corner is peaceful. I hold the picture at arm's length and compare it to the actual vase. I'm missing something, but what?

"That's really good." The comment comes out of nowhere.

I leap out of the armchair and back up—straight into

the orange cone and the puddle. "Yuck!" I jump around and my feet skid.

My sketchbook flies out of my hands and hits the vase. It tilts with the impact. I watch, horrified and frozen, as the vase falls to the ground with a loud crash. It shatters into a million pieces.

Disaster.

And of course Mom predicted it.

chapter two

*I*t takes only a moment for the vase to shatter, but the sound rings on and on in my head. I'm sure everyone in the store heard it. I'm sure everyone in the entire mall heard it. Maybe even out in the parking garage.

Simran Sangha—the high school sophomore who doesn't break things anymore, because being clumsy is for freshmen—just evaporated.

The old blundering me stands there awkwardly, a startled-looking dude staring at the damage all around my feet in endless bits and pieces of pottery. My mind fast-forwards to how Mom is going to react in about a minute when she gets here and takes in this scene—her face embarrassed and apologetic about my clumsiness, shaking her head as she opens her purse to pay for another broken thing.

"Oh no, oh no, I'm so, so sorry," I stammer.

The guy is tall and youngish and wears a neatly

wrapped blue turban, jeans, and a white SINGH'S EMPORIUM T-shirt. He looks about the same age as my cousins. The desk near him is stacked with books with titles like *The Essential Rules for Bar Exam Success* and *Multistate Bar Exam Study Aid.*

"Don't move," he warns. "You'll cut yourself. Stay right there while I grab a broom."

I'm frozen in the middle of the disaster zone. Frustration bubbles like a pot of boiling masala chai. Argh! I make a face at the sign on the wall that warns: YOU BREAK IT, YOU BOUGHT IT. That vase looked pricey. There go my plans for new watercolor markers and sketchbooks. Mom will definitely take this out of my allowance.

I crouch, sitting on my heels to pick up the larger pieces of pottery while the employee returns and starts to sweep the fragments into a dustpan. "Again, I'm so sorry. Was the vase very expensive?" I hand the big pieces to him.

He just smiles and shrugs. Uh-oh. It's probably a five-hundred-dollar vase.

I squeeze my eyes shut briefly, then open them, but nope, this isn't a bad dream. "I better go get my mom."

"You don't have to tell anyone." He points to the orange plastic cone next to me. "It was just as much my fault as yours. I startled you and the floor was slick."

I bite my bottom lip and wonder if he means it.

The sound of footsteps echo. Too late! I cringe. Even if he wants to let it go, they've already heard the crash.

I brace myself and pivot around. But it's just Preet, looking as pretty as any picture.

"Are you okay, Simi?" Preet swoops down, tossing back her long dark hair, and gives me a hug. "We heard the noise! What happened?"

"I kind of"—I screw my face up, embarrassed—"destroyed that vase."

"Never mind that; are you hurt?" She scans me with anxious eyes, and I shake my head. "Thank goodness! We can pay for the damage my cousin caused, Mr....?"

"It's Jolly." The turbaned guy is still holding the dustpan filled with broken pottery. His eyes have gone wide. The tips of his ears are turning slightly red, too. A shy grin tugs the corners of his lips up as he looks at Preet. The Preet Effect, on full display.

But wait. I'm used to how guys react to Preet. What's interesting is how Preet is reacting to *him*. Instead of her practiced expert brush-off, she holds out her hand.

"I'm Preet," she says. "This is my cousin Simran. Did you know that already? I'm guessing you might!"

I study Jolly. He's pretty cute. And he doesn't have player vibes like Ravinder did, with his wannabe-Bollywood-star look. Jolly puts the dustpan in his left hand and wipes his right hand on the back of his jeans before shaking hers, making the silver bangles dance on her wrist.

They've all reached us now: Masi, Mom, Geet, and the salesman.

Mom already has her hands on her hips and her mouth pursed with disappointment. "Oh, Simi, not again! How does such a halka-pulka child cause so much destruction? More bang per kilo than a box of barood! Are you hurt?" Mom pats my back, shoulders, and head, checking to make sure that I am still in one piece.

"I'm fine," I mutter through gritted teeth, wiggling away from her hands. "And it was an accident!"

Mom spots the dustpan filled with shards. "It always is." She sighs, opening her purse. "How much was it?"

"No need to worry," Jolly intervenes. "It really was an accident."

"Your store policy is clear." Mom points at the large sign. "I insist!"

"If *he* says you don't have to pay"—the salesman nods at Jolly—"then you don't have to pay for it, ji."

"Please understand, it's really not necessary." Jolly doesn't raise his voice or anything, but suddenly it's hard to argue with him. "The floor was wet and she slipped. We had only one cone marking it. There really should have been more. So it's our responsibility. In fact, I insist on offering a discount for our mistake."

"Really?" Mom shuts her purse with an excited snap. She can't resist a bargain. "Are you sure?"

"Positive. Raju, take their bill and adjust the payment by fifteen percent."

"I do apologize," Mom says. "I'm Manju Sangha, and this is my sister, Meera. What is your name?"

"I'm Jashan Singh, Auntie," Jolly says, "but most people call me Jolly."

"Both such happy-sounding names," Mom says, smiling. "And such a lovely shop. You see, we just found the perfect sofa set for Meera here. She'd been looking for months. Then I told her—we must go to Singh's! They have the best options anywhere!"

Jolly smiles at them.

"This way, madam." The salesman leads Mom and Masi away to the checkout counter.

"We'll be back." Mom looks over her shoulder. Her eyes find me. "Stay here and...Don't. Break. Anything *else*."

Not even a thank-you that my clumsiness scored them a discount?

"You are so kind," Preet murmurs to Jolly after they leave. Her smile is extra warm.

Jolly waves off the praise. But his ears go even redder.

I raise an eyebrow. I may be in trouble right now, but they're so vibing.

"Simi, you're bleeding!" Preet points to my hand.

"What?!" I look down and, to my surprise, a small trickle of blood drips from my right palm.

Jolly lifts it and examines the cut.

"It looks clean," Geet says clinically.

"There's a first aid kit in my office," Jolly says. "I can go get it. Or you all can come with me?"

"My mom has Band-Aids in the car. She'll be fine," Geet insists.

Honestly, can't she see Jolly's trying to buy more time with Preet? Duh. So obvious.

"It really hurts," I whine, because someone has to help Jolly out. "And I don't think Masi has a kit in the car anymore."

"Let's get one from the office," Jolly replies.

Preet takes my arm and pulls me along. Geet follows close behind, looking annoyed. I try to hide my grin.

Jolly ushers us toward a plush office in the back. There's a big dark wood desk, a carved-wood-and-velvet sofa set, and a coffee table in the middle, covered in more fat textbooks. He pulls a first aid kit from a drawer in his desk. He clears away the books, piling them on the desk as he gestures toward the sofas. "Please, sit."

Preet takes the first aid kit from him and binds up my cut expertly, after cleaning it with an antiseptic wipe. "Oh, you have a cut, too." She points to his wrist.

"It's nothing."

"Here, let me."

I jump up quickly to make room for Jolly to take my place beside her. This time Preet's hands are not quite so steady as she works. Jolly's making her laugh, and her bangles jingle prettily. Their heads tilt close together as she presses the Band-Aid along his wrist.

"It's really nice of you not to charge for the vase," Preet tells him. "And to give my mom a discount. I think you've earned a lifelong customer. She's so going to recommend your store to everyone now."

"It was the right thing to do. The important thing is that Simi isn't hurt," he says.

"I agree." Preet clicks the first aid kit shut. A strand of hair tucked behind her ear falls forward, and she pushes it back with one hand. She gives Jolly an impish smile.

He grins back.

I usually hate this kind of stuff. Being the kid of a matchmaker means you're stuck in the middle of lovey-dovey romantic crap all day long. But seeing Preet like this makes me happy. The sparks flying between her and Jolly could seriously power the national grid. Talk about chemistry. I can almost hear the faint sound of wedding dhols drumming in the distance.

Jolly looks over at me and Geet. "Would you like something to eat?"

She shakes her head, but I pipe up. "Yes, please."

"Ravi, chai samosa lah," Jolly calls out, and within minutes, one of the other salesmen has brought out the tea and snacks.

I reach right over and grab a samosa. The crispy crust is

hot and stuffed with potatoes and peas. I sigh with delight as I dip mine into the spicy green chutney and take a big bite.

Preet and Jolly laugh at me.

"What?" I say with a mouthful. "They're my favorite."

They turn back to each other, chatting away like Geet and I aren't in the room. The scent of fried yumminess, peppery and warm, curls around them on the sofa like an invisible blanket.

I elbow Geet and nod toward the sofa, where Preet has now gently placed a hand on Jolly's arm, her head thrown back in laughter. "Geet Di, maybe we should, you know, look at rugs or something?"

"Why?" Geet says.

I nudge her meaningfully. Is she honestly not seeing this?

She likes him? she mouths at me, and I nod. She can be pretty slow for a onetime National Merit Scholar.

She narrows her eyes, watching Preet and Jolly with a small crease between her brows, as if she's observing an experiment. In her head, she's probably going through the list Mom and Masi use when they make a match:

JOLLY'S CASTE: The turban tells us he's Jat.

RELIGION: Sikh

GENDER: Male

AGE: Late twenties

STATUS: Available? No wedding ring visible.

EDUCATION AND EMPLOYMENT: Needs further investigation.

Eavesdropping reveals interesting details: Jolly's the son of the furniture store's owner. He's looking after it while his father is in India on a buying trip. And he's a lawyer. Or will be soon, anyway.

"Yeah, I'm taking the bar exam in six weeks," Jolly says. "My dad always tells me to leave my law books home—he's afraid I'll end up distracted and knock something over." He flashes a smile at me.

Preet laughs. "Oh, you should see some of the things Simi has knocked over in her life—lamps, gigantic bowls of watermelon, garden ornaments. And then there was that incident with the bike, the day she got her training wheels off; remember, Sim?"

Preet's still laughing, but a glance at my ruby-red face and she shuts right up. "But, I mean, it runs in the family, nah?"

"I'm not listening to this," I say, mock-offended, and sneak out my sketchbook. I roll my eyes and practice drawing random figures while we wait for Mom and Masi to return. I sneak glances at them—moving close, mirrored hand motions, eye contact—all signs of a couple liking each other, at least according to leading relationship experts Mom and Masi.

I do a quick sketch of Preet and Jolly. Not to brag or anything, but it's great. Catches the moment and everything. I decorate the air around them with little hearts and smiles. Yeah, I'd totally ship them if I were the matchmaking type. Which I am *not*.

The door swings open and Mom and Masi scurry over, their arms full of fabric swatches. Looks like the discount has triggered some more shopping.

"All done?" I say, standing, ready to go.

Mom notices the Band-Aid on my hand. "Simi, are you hurt?"

"Just a scratch. Preet took care of it. Can we go home now?"

"Just make sure you don't forget anything," Mom says. "Your cell phone, your book..."

"Here." Masi picks up my sketchbook and turns it over before handing it to me. "What's this?"

The sketch of Preet and Jolly—in all its heart-sprinkled glory!

"Good God," Geet mutters.

"Hai Rabba," Mom echoes in Punjabi.

I flush to the roots of my hair, but I'm pale compared with Preet's rosy cheeks.

"It's just a sketch for my figure-drawing class. I didn't mean anything by it. Just trying to draw from life..." I realize the implication of my words as soon as they're out. Oops.

"Oh, you know Simi; such an overactive imagination. Remember when she was seven and thought Jeetu Uncle was a Bollywood star?" Geet says, trying to run interference.

18

"She's just a kid," Preet says. She turns to Jolly to explain. "Very creative, you know?"

Jolly doesn't say a word, but his face is suddenly serious. He holds Preet's gaze with calm, questioning eyes. Preet stops talking for once. Her lips curve into a tiny smile as a silent exchange passes between them.

Masi sits down on the sofa, wearing a small frown.

Mom pats a hairpin back into her bun and squares her shoulders. Her eyes wander over the wall of the office where Jolly's college diplomas hang, in between framed pictures of the Sikh gurus, hands raised in blessing. Her eyebrows rise. It's finally clicked that Jolly isn't an employee but the owner's son.

Mom exchanges a quick glance with my masi, her expression thoughtful. "Beta, will you tell us more about your family? Perhaps we know them?"

"We're from Kapurthala originally, but I was born here in New Jersey, Auntie." Jolly is quick to respond. "My father is an engineer by trade, but he started an import-export business twenty years ago, including the furniture store. My parents are in India right now; that's why I'm helping run the store."

Mom sits by Masi, taking the sketch from her. "I do know your parents, though it's been a while since we met," she says. "You're related to the Randhawas in Washington, DC, aren't you?"

"Yes, that's my mamaji," Jolly says.

Masi nods approvingly, pulls her reading glasses from her pocket, and puts them on. There's nothing to read. She's shifted gears into dead-serious mode. "It's nice that you're helping with the family business. But where did you go to school, and what have you studied?" She's looking for confirmation of the credentials she sees on the wood panels of his office wall.

"Georgetown Law," Jolly says. "And Penn for undergrad. I'm an attorney." He motions to his desk. "Or I will be, as soon as I pass the bar."

"Beta, we would love to catch up with your parents," Masi says. "It's been too long since we saw them last. When are they returning from India?"

"In a week," Jolly says, smiling. "I'll have them call you as soon as they're back."

My mom and Masi grin, too. That gleam in their eyes means trouble.

They're going to ruin everything by getting parents involved.

I open my mouth to say something but stop at the serene look on Preet's face. She likes this guy, or she would have stopped Mom and Masi in their tracks. Nothing happens to Preet that Preet doesn't want, that much I know.

Technically, no one broke the do-not-matchmake rule, either.

I just broke a vase instead.

chapter three

The first day of sophomore year—I'm hoping it's perfect.

My outfit is Preet-inspired—a slim-fit denim skirt, white embroidered kurti top, and an armful of bangles. Flip-flops and a beaded hemp anklet over my mehendi design complete the look. The blend-into-the-background version of me would never put mehendi on during the school year or wear glass bangles to school—an accident waiting to happen. But the New Me loves bangles and mehendi. This year I'm listening to the New Me.

I send Noah a selfie.

Too much?

Nooo. It's so you!!

I came down with Sudden-Onset Chronic Shyness when I started high school. Thanks to the Mortifying Thing that happened at the beginning of freshman year, I went from doing, saying, and wearing what I liked to second-guessing everything. The few friends I hung out with, mostly Desi like me, branched off into different classes and cliques. But Noah and I stuck together. Two freshmen paddling in the tricky waters of high school, trying not to make waves.

Not anymore.

This year, Noah and I have decided to walk tall and act like we *matter*.

I know, I know. It's easy to say that everyone should matter, but in real life some people seem to matter more than others—people like Amanda Taylor. And it's the Amandas of the world who choose who else should matter. But I'm tired of waiting around for someone to deem me worthy. Nope. This year, I'm taking it into my own hands, and so is Noah.

Our original plan was to start a club—something fun that would make us look good on college applications, too. We were going to think of an idea over the summer, but we couldn't come up with anything worth the effort. Now time's running out.

I text Noah again.

> We still don't have a club idea!

> Yeah. Do it next year?

> Nooo. We'll be too busy studying.

I've seen what my brother, Navdeep, now a senior, had to go through as a junior. Good grades, AP tests, extracurriculars, SAT prep. This is our last chance to take a risk in high school. Next year there won't be any time for mistakes.

> Let's just join one.

> What's left? We tried Earth Club, Model UN, Mock Trial, Spanish Club, FBLA....

> Face it. We're not Future Business Leaders of America material.

> I liked Art Club.

> RIP Art Club.

Figures. The one club Noah and I liked got shut down for lack of members. Most of the art kids have other clubs or activities they need to get to after school—a lot of them are in band, too, like Aiden James, graffiti god, clarinet section first chair, and my art class friend. And the rest are too "antiestablishment," as Ms. Furst would say, to join forces.

> Amanda started a Spirit Club.

WTH is that?

> No clue.

Well, no thank you! Let's keep thinking.

> Okay. Leaving now. Byyeeeee!

I put away my phone and start to pace. Usually my room is where I'm most comfortable—my girl cave, Mom calls it. My drawings decorate the walls. Favorite greeting cards I've saved hang from little clothespins, clipped to a ribbon strung between the lamp and my bedpost. My desk and bookshelf are stacked with stuff I love—my art supplies, the cloth elephant decorated with tiny bells that Nanima got me from India, and a decorative shoe rack with my favorite embroidered kolhapuri juttis. But today I'm on edge even here.

My favorite corner of the room is my henna station, with its little brown packets of mehendi lined up alongside my latest experiments. Which reminds me, I forgot to scrape away the dried mehendi from my ankle. As the dark henna flakes off, the design underneath appears, stained a deep cranberry red. It turned out beautiful!

My nerves start to fade. But then Mom's voice drifts through the vents as she talks on the phone to Masi, who lives right next door.

"Simran definitely has it!"

The sound of my name makes me jump. I crane my neck to listen.

"She's a born vicholi. Flawless instincts—she made a match right before our eyes."

"No one even knew that the Singhs' son was back in town and available."

Apparently, Jolly's one of those local "boys" who flew under Mom and Masi's radar for years—very eligible, but no one could confirm whether he was in a relationship or looking or what.

"He's turned out so handsome and smart," Mom says. "And we thought he was a furniture salesman—imagine! But Simi wasn't fooled. She's the next generation of vichole."

Oooof. I squeeze my eyes shut and grimace as my stress levels shoot up again. If I don't watch out, they'll indenture me into our cringey family business before I graduate!

My phone alarm blares. Only fifteen minutes until Noah gets here to walk to school. I knot my long, wavy hair, still damp from the shower, into a messy bun—my default look for when I'm out of time.

Mom knocks on my door. "Simi, breakfast!"

"I don't want anything," I shout back.

"You will have a cup of chai and an omelet. I'm not sending an unfed girl to school. Especially not on the first day. Now, downstairs in five minutes. Masi is coming over, too."

"Oh no," I mutter.

"What was that?" she says, and I know her ear is pressed up against the door.

"Nothing," I reply.

When I get down to the kitchen, Masi is grinning at me like the Cheshire cat. If I get close to her, I know she'll smother me in a jappi, so I stay an arm's length away.

"Beta," she says. "I'm just so happy!" I swat away her grabby hands trying to wrap me up in a hug. "I was very worried that it had skipped a generation or something. And that none of our kids would be able to carry on the family business."

"I'm not a matchmaker. Can't people find their own matches now?"

My older brother, Navdeep, looks up from his nerdy robotics magazine. "Wait, what? Simi's a matchmaker?"

I shout no, and Masi and Mom say yes at the same time.

"If *they* have anything to do with it!" I explain, flashing him my *help me* face.

"Give it a rest," Navdeep says to Mom and Masi. "Let Simi figure out what she wants, okay? It's like Dad pressuring me to apply pre-med all over again. Just because he's a doctor doesn't mean I have to be one."

I snap a two-figure salute at him for effort. He may torment me sometimes, but we do have an unspoken pact to team up in the face of parental pressure.

"There's nothing wrong with *trying* something new," Masi says. "You volunteered at your dad's clinic, but no one's stopping you from pursuing engineering."

"Volunteering at Dad's clinic was a total waste of time. I can't even use it as an extracurricular for engineering," Navdeep complains. "Don't do that to Simi. Let her be a teen docent at the art museum, or a henna-tattoo artist, or any other ridiculous thing she wants to be."

"But she has the talent for matching, puttar," Mom says. "And there've been matchmakers in our family for generations."

"So what? This is America, Ma. We can be whatever we want, right?" Navdeep looks to me. "Hey, Simi, you want me to drop you at school?"

"I'm walking down with Noah," I say. "He should be here any minute. But thanks."

"Anytime," he says. He grabs his car keys and walks off, but only after making a mock *eyes on you* gesture to Mom and Masi.

"Thappar kha!" Mom threatens, lifting a palm like she's about to swat him. He skips out the door laughing.

"See?" I say after he leaves. "Do you see how unreasonable you're both being now?"

"No one is forcing you into anything," Mom says,

setting a steaming omelet in front of me. "We're just happy you're talented."

"Yes, *so* talented," Masi says, squeezing me.

"Stop it!" I say, rolling my eyes.

The doorbell rings.

I jump up and go answer it.

Noah!

I drag him inside. "They're on a rampage," I whisper to him before leading him into the kitchen. "Save me."

"Hey, Noah," Mom says, pulling him into a big hug because Noah's been part of the family from the day we met in kindergarten. "Chai?"

"Hello, Mrs. Sangha," Noah says. "Hi, Meera Masi!"

"Beta, is that a rash?" Mom's fingertips hover inches away from Noah's cheek. The pink peeling skin looks too painful to touch.

"What happened?" Masi asks.

Subtle and tactful, that's my family. But you can barely see the sunburn anymore. Preet sent the tinted moisturizer Noah had asked for directly to his house so it would be waiting when he got home from vacation. She's the best sort-of adult ever in an emergency, and Noah is really good at blending makeup—in fact, he has the best collection.

He ducks his shaggy head a little. "Sunburn. It's bad, I know." His skin is so red it almost matches his hair.

"A little chandan and haldi will fix it," Mom says. She hands him a hot cup of chai. "Did Simi tell you about what she did yesterday, Noah? How she has the gift?"

Noah's eyebrows lift with surprise.

"There is no gift," I reiterate after swallowing a bite of omelet. "She already liked him. And he already liked her. Just moving things along that would have moved along on their own *anyhow*. Not. Rocket. Science."

Masi lifts my chin with her finger. "Puttar, how long have your mom and I been matching couples?"

"I don't know," I say, pushing her hand away. "Fifteen years?"

"Twenty," Masi corrects me. "But you saw something that we couldn't see yesterday. Why is that?"

"Unlike you, I find furniture boring."

"Even so, it takes perception to be a rishta scout," Masi says.

"It's not even close to a rishta!" I say. "If you're lucky, they might go out on a couple of dates is all."

She continues like I never even said anything.

"Not everyone would have picked up on it. You were the one that looked past the Singh Emporium T-shirt."

"Like a Singh Emporium T-shirt should automatically disqualify a guy!"

"I mean, you saw that he wasn't just a furniture salesman...."

"*Just?* That's so rude and snobby. He was nice about the accident," I huff.

"Nice and *well-educated*," Mom says. "I'm sure that matters to Preet, too."

Okay, maybe it does.

"And *you* kept her there long enough for them to connect. You set the stage, Simi. You made their paths collide."

"Pure dumb luck."

"There's no such thing as luck," Masi says with a laugh. "It's old instincts and new eyes. Instincts that go back through generations and fresh eyes that could see what we were too slow to see."

"And fresh eyes are what we need," Mom says. "We're getting too old, I think."

"If you just used that app Navdeep made for you, you wouldn't need me or anybody else," I say.

"An app?" Noah asks.

"Yeah, he spent a ton of time on it in his development class last year. He basically digitized Mom and Masi's process—pretty cool. Mom thinks it's impersonal, but Navdeep got an A."

"The old way is best. And you must—" Masi starts.

I leap up from the table and grab Noah's arm. "Time to go to school!"

"But I'm not done with my chai," he protests.

"Too bad." I pull him toward the door.

"We'll talk more about matchmaking later," Mom calls out.

"No, we won't," I reply as I slam the door behind me.

As we walk down the driveway, I tell Noah the whole story. "And now Mom and Masi think that I have the"—I make air quotes for emphasis—"'gift,' or something."

"You're a real matchmaker," Noah says. "That's so cool!"

"I'm not. And you're supposed to take my side!"

We make a left on Pine Street.

"Let me see the sketch you did of them," Noah says.

"Sure." I fish it out of my backpack and hand it to him.

"They really do look cute together," he says, staring at the image of Preet and Jolly. "Far better than That-Creep-Fake-Wannabe-Bollywood-Star!"

"They would've figured it out on their own, eventually."

"But they would've never met if it wasn't for you," Noah says.

"Complete. Accident!" I say. Though I do feel a *tiny* bit of pride in having seen the vibe between Preet and Jolly.

"Remember when you said Ms. Holt liked the new substitute teacher Mr. Wang when we were in fifth grade?"

"You mean Mrs. Wang now," I say, smiling at the memory. "Totally called that one."

"So maybe you're good at this stuff."

"Look, matchmaking is Mom and Masi's thing. Not mine. If out of all the things I could do and be in the world, I end up doing what my mom's mom's mom did...then it's like I'm practically abandoning my own talent—art. I've just gone along with tradition. With what everyone expects from me."

"But what if matching is what you're meant to do?"

"I'm not sure it's something anyone is meant to do. I mean, it had its place in Nanima's day. But now people have moved past that. It's so last century."

"If that were true, there wouldn't be all those dating websites and apps and stuff, and even shows like *The Bachelor* wouldn't be a thing."

"That's different!"

"I don't see how," Noah says. "Anyway, who started the matchmaking business?"

"My grandmother's grandmother's grandmother's...I don't even know how far back it goes. So many generations. They were all vichole."

"A witch-what?"

"Vichole. Vee-cho-leh." I smile at the thought of our family matriarchs as warm-hearted witches. That would be something I'd totally be up for. "It means 'middleman'— 'middlewoman,' really. Like a marriage negotiator."

"I would make an excellent matchmaker—middleman. I love making predictions about who's going to date whom. I could so be a love coach."

"You should join the Sangha clan, then."

"I would in a heartbeat. Adopt me! Your mom cooks way better food than mine."

We're at the end of the block, and Mayfield High looms in the distance.

I stop walking to take it in. Our school is huge. All redbrick and sprawling, with five floors built around a courtyard in the center, right off the cafeteria, that holds picnic tables where the upperclassmen eat on warm days. It doesn't look any different than last year, but the sight of it doesn't make us nervous like it did then. This year is our year.

"You ready?" I ask Noah.

"Ready," he says, squeezing my shoulder.

New year. New Noah and Simi.

chapter four

*N*oah and I join the crowd of kids streaming into the foyer. A few family friends call hello. "Hey, Arjun, Pooja, Arav," I say back, then steer Noah away. I see enough of them at gurdwara and family get-togethers.

"I need to meet new people," I whisper to Noah. "It's a fresh year, you know?"

"Sounds good to me," he says. He looks around and then blushes. What's up with that?

I turn to look and spot a new guy who basically stepped out of a magazine. Wavy black hair that falls onto his forehead, light brown skin, flip-flops, puka shells on his ankle, and a California vibe. Not really my type, but definitely Noah's.

"Who's that?" I say. "He's cute."

Noah shrugs. "I don't know." He turns away, but I can

see him tracking the new guy from the corner of his eye. "And I don't want to talk about it."

We usually talk about all the guys he thinks are cute, and he always disagrees with my picks, telling me I have bad taste. But I guess we're not discussing today. Not with this one. Or maybe just not right now. I change the subject.

"Okay. So did you figure out what Spirit Club is?"

"Nope. I know Amanda's president. Cami and Natasha are co-VPs, which is probably the only thing going for it. If they weren't such Amanda fangirls, they might be nice. I heard a bunch of freshmen joined. They don't know any better."

"Freshmen," I say. "Poor, innocent sheep."

We shuffle through the foyer.

Noah finds his locker at the start of the hall. "This is me."

"See you later." I head farther into the masses to find mine.

I push through the packed bodies headed in every direction. There are a lot of unfamiliar faces—freshmen, transfers, people who hit puberty over summer and morphed into unrecognizable beings. I catch a glimpse of a lanky brown guy loping up the steps two at a time. He's preppy—in an MIT sweatshirt, chinos, and lace-up canvas shoes.

Hmm. Freshman or transfer? Definitely Desi. Definitely cute. Actually, he looks a bit like the Indian prince in every Amar Chitra Katha comic book. That jaw, and that nose... he's a dead ringer. I'm smiling at the thought when he turns around and catches me staring.

His face lights up. He raises a hand in greeting.

Wait, do I know him?

My hand is already lifted in response, my face breaking into a goofy grin, when I realize that I don't know him at all—because he's waving at Marcus, who's standing behind me.

Wait, what's happening?

I shuffle back a step.

"Oof, watch where you're going!" a voice grumbles.

My feet tangle with a freshman girl I've never seen before. My backpack slips off and knocks into her and then the floor.

She glares.

I flush.

I've acted like a total idiot in full view of the cute new guy. Ugh! Today was supposed to be perfect!

"Sorry!" I tell the girl, grabbing my backpack. I turn, embarrassed, to see just how much he saw, but he's already disappeared up the stairs. I'm both relieved and disappointed.

What's wrong with me?

This is *not* how the first day of school is supposed to go. The new Simi isn't clumsy. She doesn't bump into people. The new Simi is perfect. At least, she's trying to be.

I hustle to my locker, where Marcus is still standing.

His pale white face holds a grin—he obviously saw me wave at a stranger and accidentally plow into a freshman. "That guy, MIT sweatshirt?" he says, putting his bag in the locker next to mine. "That's my friend Suraj. He just moved here."

Suraj. Of course that's his name. It means "sun" in Hindi and Punjabi, and he just scattered megawatts of sunshine all over the corridor through the simple act of smiling.

"We met at the East Super Conference for FTC," Marcus tells me.

"The what now?"

"The robotics competition. You know, the competition the Wallys won last year. Your brother's team? My team?"

"Oh, right. That!" The Wallys made state, East, nationals, and went all the way to the world competition. Navdeep bragged for weeks, and my parents were so proud and finally gave up on harassing him about being pre-med in college.

"The Wallys' robot beat Suraj's team—they were the reigning champs."

I shiver, my brain almost oozing out of my ears as Marcus pummels me with more tech words. Snoozefest. So boring. Sucks that Suraj turned out to be a geek, just like my nerdy brother. "So what's he doing in New Jersey?"

"Transferred. He's a sophomore like us, which is good because the Wallys can totally use him after Navdeep graduates."

"So he's from...?"

"Boston." Marcus smiles. "You like him?"

"No," I reply. How dare he ask me that? I hide the smile tickling my lips. Marcus walks off, whistling.

I spin the combination lock on the door of my locker and then, out of the corner of my eye, notice Amanda Taylor standing in front of a nearby locker.

My hand instinctively moves toward my hair like muscle memory, like trauma, like even each strand remembers. I catch myself and clench it at my side instead.

As usual, Amanda looks right through me, drumming her pink nails against her locker. The flower magnets decorating the door match her nails, which match her backpack and her socks. Let's just say Amanda is into pink in a big way.

"How could he not wave at me?" she says to Cami. She's already mid-meltdown. Not her first one this morning, I bet, because her pale white cheeks are already red and it's not from too much blush.

"He didn't see you. It's the first day of school and crazy busy," Cami assures her. She has long red hair, where Amanda's falls in rich brown waves down her back. Are those extensions? Those are definitely extensions.

They have the same fashion sense, though: pink, pink, pink.

"Of course you and Ethan will get back together," Natasha gushes. She's tall with black curls and rich dark brown skin. She could be the daughter of a movie star. She's a fan of pink, too. "You're, like, so destined. Your families are close. You're meant to be."

Ethan Pérez and Amanda Taylor? They dated for a nanosecond at the beginning of last year, mostly because their parents are friends and Ethan's too nice a guy to say no. He's been the star of Mayfield's soccer team since eighth grade, when they let him on early; he's popular because he's a killer athlete, and because he's kind to literally everyone.

Including me—which is why he and Amanda ended up breaking up.

Normally, I'd roll my eyes and move along. But today I snicker at Amanda's theatrics before I can stop myself.

"Did you just laugh at me?" she says, fixing her cold blue eyes on me.

Oops. That pep talk I gave myself this morning is going to get me into trouble.

"Me? Nuh-uh," I say, stuffing my notebooks and binders into my new locker.

"I definitely heard you laugh."

"Nope." I'm so not getting into a thing with her again. Not today. Not ever.

"What's your *problem*?" she asks, arms folded across her chest.

"Didn't you start a Spirit Club or something?" I say, faking interest to calm her wrath. "What's that about?"

Cami jumps into recruiting mode. "Oh, it's super fun!

We help student council—Amanda's running for president, please vote for her!—plan Spirit Week and run fund-raisers for parties and events all through the school year. You should join!"

"You can *apply*, Gummy," Amanda says, scanning me slowly, from my messy bun to my henna-decorated hands and ankles. "We have a lot of interest, but maybe you'll make the wait list."

I push my shoulders back and, since she brought up gum, I pop a piece in my mouth. Part of my strategy to own my past and stick it to Amanda.

"No thanks," I say, and blow a deliberately large bubble. Amanda narrows her eyes when it pops. I grin. "Doesn't really sound like my thing."

"Maybe you could help us design some posters, though?" Natasha asks. "We'll need flyers and things to get the word out. You're so good at art."

"Thank you," I say. If Natasha and Cami ditched Amanda, I might want to hang out with them. But one glare from Amanda kills that idea.

"No way," Amanda interrupts.

Natasha shrivels. It's ridiculous how Amanda can intimidate. She pushes her shoulders back and narrows her eyes, and everyone just does what she says. Her sister, a senior and star of the Mayfield softball team, has the same nasty attitude, and Navdeep hates being in class with her. And rumors swirl about her oldest sister, who graduated two years ago, and how she hazed people as volleyball team captain. It must be in the blood, but I don't think Amanda's even all that good at bullying; her insults aren't clever and her actions are mostly cliché, but the Taylor sisters have established a reputation, and Mayfield High students respect it.

"We have so many volunteers already," Amanda says. "We don't need you."

"Suit yourself." I shrug and go back to stuffing my school supplies into my locker.

Kiran Kaur squeezes past us like she's walking on eggshells, murmuring, "Excuse me."

"Sure," I say, and flatten myself against my locker so she can get past.

"Watch it, Sasquatch!" Amanda elbows Kiran and gets louder and louder. "Gotta trim that winter coat."

Heat races up my spine.

The ridiculous thing is there are at least ten kids standing nearby. But *no one* says anything. That's the Amanda Taylor effect. I've seen her get away with so much. *I've* let her get away with so much—specifically, the "Gummy" incident at the beginning of last year—and there's not a day since I haven't regretted it.

Kiran's usually super confident, at least when she's teaching at our gurdwara's Sunday school, but at Amanda's insult, she puts her head down and moves past without a word.

The old Simi wouldn't say a word, either.

The new Simi's got courage.

I take a deep breath and hook a finger onto my steel bracelet, buried in my stack of colorful glass bangles. It's a reminder that a Sikh stands up for the innocent. This isn't exactly how I planned on living my best life, yada yada, but here goes nothing.

I slam my locker and plant myself in front of Amanda.

"Really?" I can't believe how clear my voice sounds. "What did you say? You calling out people's body hair?"

Everyone in hearing range freezes. No one calls Amanda out on the things she says. Ever.

She pivots around, hair grazing her shoulders, surprise and annoyance written all over her face. "It was more like free advice." She counts on her perfect fingernails. "In fact, three pieces of advice. One, waxing; two, shaving; and three, Nair."

My face goes hot. "It's none of your business." The fact is, many Sikhs don't remove any hair for religious reasons, but I'm not about to tell Amanda that. It would be like I'm handing her a weapon to torment all of us.

"Uh...whatever," Amanda says, flicking a finger in my direction. "Disappear!"

"Oh, I'm not disappearing." I raise my chin slightly. I'm acting cool, though my heart is racing and my Sikh sherni hackles are standing up on the back of my neck. "But *you* should."

Cami and Natasha launch into excited whispers, and the almost-altercation dissolves as quickly as it started.

"Sparky alert!" Cami mutters, pretending to look at her phone.

"Sparky at ten o'clock."

I don't get it.

I look up and spot Ethan coming our way, surrounded by a group of juniors.

Sparky—God, they actually have a code word for him. How idiotic.

Amanda pivots away from me and snaps into sexy mode. She fluffs her hair and flashes her orthodontically perfect smile at Ethan, but his attention is on me.

"Hey, Simi."

I'm pretty sure Amanda's about to flip out. It drives her nuts when Ethan speaks to other people, other girls, *me*.

I give him a big grin, just to poke at Amanda. "Hey. Hope you had a good summer."

"Yeah, it was cool. Soccer practice, soccer camp, soccer games." He's tall and his face is freckly, the olive tone of it almost dusty, thanks to all the time he spends outside. He wears his hair long and in a ponytail, like some of the famous soccer players I've seen on TV. It looks nice against his varsity jacket.

He turns to nod at Amanda and her groupies.

"Hey, you," she says in a flirty voice, sidling up to him.

He shrugs her off—not in a mean way, but in an *I've got class* way. When he's swallowed up by the crowd, Amanda aims a poisonous glare at me, then flounces after him.

"Excuse you," she snaps, pushing past Noah, who's heading our way.

Noah looks confused, then worried. "Did something happen?" he asks me.

I roll my eyes toward Amanda. "She was rude to Kiran, and I called her out on it."

"You did not!"

My heart still hasn't slowed. Kiran gives me a grateful nod, but all my courage from moments ago dries up like a smudge of paint left out overnight, and now, I'm not sure I did the right thing challenging Amanda while everyone watched. I might've made Kiran a target. Or become one myself.

"Ethan came by before it got ugly. He said hello to me, and I swear, smoke actually shot out of Amanda's ears. Then she went chasing after him like a lovesick poodle."

"A pink poodle," Noah says. "With fangs." He fixes a concerned look at me. "I know we promised to stand out this year... but I wouldn't mess with her. She's vicious."

"Obviously," I say. "But her obsession with Ethan... He's completely wrong for her. Anyone can see that he's not interested. He deserves someone better, but no girl's brave enough to go out with him, because she'd become another of Amanda's targets."

Noah grabs my arm, eyes gleaming. "Simi! Ethan needs a matchmaker. Someone to find the perfect person for him. *We* could do that!"

chapter five

I'm already shaking my head. I might have been feeling brave this morning, but taking on Amanda like *this*? No way, no how.

Noah's beaming, like he just aced his final exams. "I mean, think about it, Simi!"

"Think about what? I don't even know what you're saying." I cross my arms and look at Noah. "You want to start matchmaking? At school?"

"Yes! And not just with Ethan. Half our school has no idea who they'd click with. Remember what you said about all the Desi kids?"

"That none of our parents ever dated? It's mostly true, at least for Mayfield. We only know about dating at all because of our friends or TV, or whatever."

"Bingo," Noah says. "And Desis are, like, a fifth of the

school. So let's help everyone out, huh? Set them up with the perfect match. What do you think?"

"Dating and marriage are like apples and oranges—two different things."

"They are not," Noah says. "You just have to see if people connect with each other."

"It's not that easy. And it's not my thing. It's Mom's. And Masi's. And Nanima's."

"You can do it your way." His eyes are big and brown and full of excitement. "You've got this in your blood, coming from generations of matchmakers. If anyone can help people like Ethan and Kiran find matches, it's you. And anyway, we agreed to take chances this year, right?"

I mean, yes, we promised each other we'd be our true selves, but that doesn't mean I don't mostly like my life. Art and Noah and school, my family. I'm not sure I'm ready to stir things up *too* much.

"Think about it," Noah goes on. "We could connect people. Change lives. The Shagun: High School Edition. Everyone will love it!"

"We could never get something like that approved."

"Who says we have to get it approved? We could just do it. Get the word out and sign students up. We could set it up online, and it'd be free. It sounds like Navdeep's already done a bunch of it for his development class. Bet we could get him to help."

I frown. "Okay, what have you done with my best friend who would never suggest anything so stooopid? And anyway, the app didn't work perfectly. There were glitches."

"So we'll help Navdeep fix it."

Oh, yeah, with all our tech wizardry or whatever. I just love all things tech.

The bell rings. "Let me think about it, okay?" I say. "We're gonna be late."

I check my schedule and push through the crowd; today I have art first period, which is the best way to start the day. The art room is my home away from home. My sanctuary. Last year, I took Intro to Art and Ceramics. This year I'm taking Honors Art Portfolio. They don't usually let sophomores enroll, but Ms. Furst, whom I had for Intro last year, recommended me. It's an all-year course where you can explore different media, have open-ended assignments, and work independently, plus complete a signature project, due at the end of this semester. My heart flutters at the thought of it.

I walk into the art room. It's massive. Floor-to-ceiling windows let in the morning light. There are different stations with easels, clay, watercolors, oil paints, and paper, and even a darkroom. It feels like magic to work in here, cocooned in all this natural light and the smell of paint, paper, and clay.

"Welcome, welcome, my young apprentices," Ms. Furst says from the doorway. Her grizzled gray hair is a mane around her pale white face. Her tunic hangs long and loose, the hem touching the floor, and she wears a glittery dragon pendant.

"Hi, Ms. Furst," we chorus.

"Find a place to work," she directs. "Your first assignment is to tell me all about your summer—through art. Choose your medium and get to work."

Everyone settles onto stools and workbenches and takes out sketchbooks. A hush falls over the room. I look down at my sketchbook and then up at the blank canvas in front of me. A shadow falls over it, blocking my light. I glance up, then grin.

"Hey, Aiden."

"Hey, Simi."

Aiden James stands next to my stool. He's taller and leaner than he was at the end of freshman year. His dark waves hit his shoulders now, and his pale hands still hold the trace of a summer tan, marked with those familiar spray paint speckles, reminding me of the scrawny little kid I met in first grade—though, back then, tempera paint streaked his hands. In elementary school, Aiden and I were the two creative kids who carried sketchbooks and hunted inspiration in the strangest places. He stuck with me, my art-class friend, even after he morphed into one of the cool kids.

My heart does a weird flip as he stands there watching me. "Wow, you must've gotten five inches taller over the summer," I say.

"Five and a half."

Well done, puberty.

"How was your summer?" he asks.

"Good. Pretty busy." Not really true, but he doesn't need to know that I spent the bulk of my time at home with Sweetie. And I checked out his social media all summer and watched with jealousy as he took art classes and worked in a museum. "How about you?"

"It was cool. I did that museum internship, and it turned out to be all right. You should do it next summer. Pretty sure the director will hook me up with a letter of recommendation when it comes time for college apps."

"Wow—so cool." I'm kind of envious—maybe I should have spent the summer interning, too—but Aiden's a great guy and a talented artist; he deserves any letters of recommendation he gets.

"Right?" He grins again, reaching over me to grab some cerulean paint. "Oils for me." He looks at my canvas. "What're you thinking?"

I shrug and stand. "Guess I better figure it out."

I do a lap around the room, running my hands over various art supplies, that familiar buzz working its way through my fingertips and into my system. I'm so lost in thought I knock over a can of brushes. Being klutzy is a side effect of getting excited. "Oops! Sorry, Ms. Furst."

"No apologies! It's okay to touch," she says, waving an arm.

Back at my station, I study the blank canvas. My summer, in art.

Nothing's coming to me.

My summer was a blur of suburban boredom: lounging in the yard with the dog, playing video games with Navdeep, watching Bollywood movies with my mom. Then it hits me: shattered vases. I reach for a charcoal pencil and start to sketch: first the swirls and twirls of the vase, then a rani and her raja, a royal pairing that looks an awful lot like Preet and Jolly.

Ms. Furst approaches me. "Henna," she says in a low voice, and points to my hands. "Did you do that yourself?"

"Yeah. Just playing around. Though my mom hates that I do it. Says mehendi—that's what we call henna—is special and only for important occasions." I pull my knee to my chest and brush off the last of the dark dried paste on my ankle. "What do you think?"

"I think I'd like you to do one for me," Ms. Furst says. "Whenever you have time."

"Absolutely." I smile at her. "I have some spare mehendi cones in my locker. I can bring them in next class."

Her eyebrows lift as if she just thought of something. "This might be an interesting medium for you to explore when you start thinking about your signature project."

I never thought of mehendi as a medium for art somehow. There's no reason why it can't be used that way, though. It could be really interesting to experiment with.

I start swirling my paints—a rusty red, rich like henna—in paisleys first, like I would with my mehendi. I grin at my handiwork, filling in the details. Soon the image morphs, and there are two figures, a queen and her king. A match made in mehendi.

At lunch, Amanda Taylor swans into the cafeteria with Cami and Natasha while I'm in the line. She's like the rani and raja in that sketch I drew in art class. Actually, scratch that. More like a lion on the hunt for its lunch. She must not find what—or who—she's looking for, because her eyes dim and she gets in line with her friends, a few people behind me.

The cashier up ahead must be new because she's cashing people out at a sloth-like pace. I try not to tap an impatient toe, but I'm starving.

There's a burst of giggles behind me, and then I hear my least favorite nickname: Gummy.

I try not to bristle as Amanda, Cami, and Natasha talk about me like we're back in middle school.

Three against one.

"You should've seen it," Amanda says, her voice getting louder and louder now. "It was everywhere—pink and sticky and *so* gross. All up in her hair."

The Gummy Incident hits me like a hot flash. I suddenly feel all feverish—my empty stomach combined with the lingering mortification that resurfaces whenever I'm reminded of the time Amanda Taylor stuck a mega wad of bubble gum in my ponytail.

"I'm surprised she didn't have to chop off her hair to get it all out," Amanda says with a laugh. "I mean, it was an accident, *of course*, and I probably shouldn't have been chewing that much gum, but honestly—I wasn't exactly sorry."

I peek behind me. Cami's laughing, but nervously. Her tense shoulders give her away. Natasha looks confused, like she's missing the joke, except *she's not*. Being a bully is never funny.

Amanda catches me looking and smirks. "Remember that day, Gummy?" she calls out. "How could you forget?"

I tuck a lock of hair behind my ear and turn to face her. "I sure do. Tell Natasha what happened next—you know, the part when Ethan found out what a monster you are and dumped you?"

The snotty smile vanishes from Amanda's face.

The memories come fast. She'd bumped into me in the locker room and put all the gum in my hair while we were changing for PE. But I didn't feel it because my braid used to be super long then. During our volleyball game, she and three other girls kept laughing at me. Amanda was in tears from all the giggles. Ethan stopped his basketball game on the other side of the gym to see what his then-girlfriend found so hilarious.

When she told him and he saw it, he looked absolutely horrified. He took me to the side and told me. It was all I could do to keep from crying. Amanda must've chewed half a dozen pieces, then worked the wad into the end of my ponytail when she "accidentally" crashed into me.

Ethan got a pass from his PE teacher and led me out of the gym. We went to his locker, where he pulled out his brown-bag lunch. Inside was a small container of peanut butter. He rubbed it into my hair, working the gum out, all the while telling me a story about how when he'd been at soccer camp a few years before, a couple of older guys had given him a hard time.

"They were probably jealous," I said. "Because you're so good."

He shrugged, humble. "Maybe. Doesn't really matter, though. There's never a good reason to be mean to other people."

"You should tell your girlfriend that," I said.

I was furious with Amanda, but I didn't feel so sad anymore. It helped to know that someone as popular as Ethan had once been bullied, too. Also, he'd gotten almost all the gum loose, and he was gentle about it. I wouldn't have to cut my hair, and I was grateful.

"She's not going to be my girlfriend after today," he said.

It was then that Amanda came jogging down the hall, still in her PE uniform. "Ethan!" she said, eyeing the peanut butter and the disgusting hunk of oily pink gum that sat on a napkin between Ethan and me. "You've been gone so long. I was worried."

Ethan wiped his hands on a spare napkin and squeezed my shoulder. "All good now?"

"Yep," I said, smiling.

He faced Amanda. "You and I need to talk."

And that was it—they broke up that day.

Amanda blames me, as if I forced her to stick gum in my hair just so her boyfriend would have an excuse to dump her. She's messed with me ever since, with that stupid nickname.

Now her eyes lock on Ethan, who's sitting out in the courtyard with a bunch of the soccer guys. She flips her hair and leaves the line to join him, Cami and Natasha trailing behind.

I shake my head. Poor Sparky—he can run, but he can't hide.

Thankful to be free of Amanda—and proud of myself for not letting her get the best of me—I buy my lunch and slide in next to Noah at our usual table, near the back corner of the cafeteria.

"Lots of new faces," I say, biting into my pizza. "Not all of them are freshmen, either."

"She's a transfer," Noah says, tilting his head toward the windows. He's gesturing at a tall Filipina girl who's stunning—all long, lean limbs and muscle. Her silky, dark hair is tied back in a ponytail. And while she may be new, she's already found her crew—the girls' soccer team.

"Does she play?"

"Oh, yeah," Noah says. "I heard she's really good, too. Like, college coaches are already scouting her."

"Wow," I say. "So the transfers are soccer girl, and that super-hot California guy, and…"

"And that guy." Noah points with his half-eaten slice of pizza.

Suraj—the kid I accidentally waved to this morning. Ugh, so embarrassing. "Yeah, I saw him earlier. He's from Boston. Marcus knows him from the First Tech competition. I wonder why he looks so ridiculously happy," I say.

It's weird. I mean, what's so exciting about school in New Jersey?

Noah raises an eyebrow at me.

"What?" I ask.

"He looks ridiculously *cute*."

"I guess," I admit. "He reminds me of the characters in the comic books that Nani got me from India. The Amar Chitra Kathas."

"Yeah, I remember," Noah says. "You're right. Not the mustache, or the crown, or long hair, sadly. I think he'd look hot in a dhoti…on a horse or something."

This makes me choke on my orange juice. I make the mistake of looking over at Suraj and end up laughing even more.

He waves, but this time I don't fall for it. I duck my head as heat climbs from my throat to my cheeks. Caught staring. Again.

Noah grins and waves, and the guy smiles back, right at us this time, before he slips out the cafeteria door. Who's supposed to be the matchmaker here, anyway?

"How was French?" I ask Noah.

"Not bad. How was art?" he asks.

"Great! Furst gave me a really cool idea of using mehendi for my signature art project. I mean, why not, right? Also, Aiden's in my class," I say, my cheeks warming. "He got tall over the summer. And is sort of cute!"

"Ooooh," Noah teases.

"Hey, it's not like that," I say. "I mean, we're art friends."

"You've always been the two art kids. And things change," Noah says in his best Mom imitation. "Be open to possibilities if you want to find a match! Especially if you want to find a match in the hot artist you've been googly-eyed for since elementary school."

I laugh, but I sneak a look around the lunchroom for Aiden anyway. I don't see him.

Noah swallows his laugh and freezes.

I tilt my head and try to read his expression. "What's wrong? What just happened?"

"Nothing."

"Hey, Noah!" a voice says from behind us.

I whip around to see who it is—California guy.

"Hey, Connor," Noah says, turning entirely red.

Connor smiles and keeps moving.

Meanwhile, my jaw has, like, hit the tabletop. "You know him? When did you guys meet?"

"This morning. In French," Noah whispers.

"Oooh! Tell me about him. Is he nice?"

"Yeah," Noah says. "I guess."

I can tell by his face he doesn't want to talk about Connor, so I let it go, taking another bite of pizza. Sunlight filters through my glass bangles and makes a rainbow on the wall.

"Simi, I love your bangles!" Jassi says, stopping by our table. She's super nice but belongs to a trio of girls who keep mostly to themselves. "I love your mehendi, too! I can do basic designs, but yours are unique."

I grin, flattered. "Thank you!"

"You're starting a trend, Simi," Noah says as Jassi hurries to her usual table.

"I'm just being me," I say. "Like we talked about."

"Which reminds me—" he begins, but I cut him off.

"Don't start!"

"Give matching a chance," he persists. "Think it through."

He's not going to let this go. When it comes to making a mark on our school—on the world—I've got my art. Noah wants more. It's not as if he's starving for popularity, but he does want people at Mayfield to like him, and I get that.

Everyone wants to be noticed. And I think he wants a boy-friend. If he thinks a matching app is the way to go, then what's the harm in playing with the idea? What's the harm in us doing something together? "Everyone deserves a love story" is what Nanima always told me.

"Okay," I say. "If you make a list of pros and cons, I'll consider it."

He grins. "Done."

chapter six

*M*om leaves me a note to come to her office after school. I gulp down the tea she left on the counter and grab a bag of salty, spicy namkeen—lip-smacking chickpea chips—to snack on as I make my way to the far side of the house.

Mom and Masi's business, Shagun Matchmaking, has its own wing. There's a separate entrance with its own parking spaces. Inside, there are two offices (one for Mom and one for Masi); a powder room; a little kitchenette complete with a mini-fridge, kettle, and sink; and a sitting area with lots of comfy couches and chairs. A matrimonial consultation sometimes involves the entire family, and you have to make everyone feel at home. There's also a large screen mounted on the wall that Mom and Masi can hook up to a laptop for video consultations. These days, there are nearly as many online consultations as in-person ones.

"Mom, I'm here," I say.

"Shhh!" Mom puts a finger to her lips and waves her phone in the air. She's wrapped in her wool shawl despite the warm September sun spilling into the room. She's definitely talking to someone on the auntie/beta network. These are not just your regular aunties-next-door, plugged into their network of family and friends, but also next-generation betas—mostly girls (and a few dudes) who have had good outcomes with Shagun and don't mind passing along info about eligible singles in their professional circles.

"Beta, how were we to know that he was interested in someone else?" she says into the phone.

Lately the beta leads have been outperforming the auntie leads, according to Mom. But that means there's a whole nother layer of nosy aunties-in-training to deal with when something goes wrong. "Even his parents didn't know. And parents these days are so out of touch with their kids. That poor girl! Yes, please see if anyone you know through the Young Jains Association might be a good potential match for her, okay? East Coast, West Coast, doesn't matter—the couple has to click," she says into the phone. "Thanks so much. Bye-bye!"

I flop down in a nearby chair. "You wanted me?"

"How was your first day of school?"

"Fine."

"Just fine? All that hoopla and shopping for just 'fine.'"

"It was busy. Still processing the details. And I have homework."

"Homework on the first day! Did you eat the namkeen and chai I left in the kitchen?"

"Yes, I still am." I hold up the bag of namkeen for her to see. "Can I go now?"

"Not so fast," she says. "I want to talk to you about working with me and Masi. You could start by sitting in on interviews and helping us file, no? If you're listening in on video consultations, you don't even have to be seen. Just listen and learn. You might be surprised...."

"Do I get paid?"

"Paid?" Mom's outraged. "You're helping your family."

"I'm being forced to do something I don't want to do," I point out.

Mom starts fussing in Punjabi.

"How about we offer you a stipend? A little money in addition to your allowance," Masi says, popping in from the file room. I didn't even realize she was here—or listening.

"Meera!" Mom says to her with a frown.

A stipend? The endless aisles of supplies at our local art store flash through my head.

"No, she's right," Masi says. "It's not like when we started back in Delhi. This is America. Time is money."

"Filing is hard work," I add with a smile. "And listening to consultations is boring." I wait for Mom's counterargument, but she doesn't say anything. "Wait, really?" I look to Mom for confirmation.

She shakes her head at first, then shrugs. "Theek hai, fine."

Wow. Not bad for my first salary negotiation. As far as listening and absorbing what they do—I've been doing that all my life, so getting paid for it is a bonus. And filing can't be worse than stocking retail shelves or working a cash register. Plus Nanima will be really psyched if I help out, and she's my most favorite person in the world. I can't wait for her and Nanoo to visit in October.

Masi winks at me; then the phone rings and she picks it up in her office.

"You'll be responsible for *all* of the filing." Mom waves a hand at the stack of folders on her desk. "I'll email you our consultation schedule," she adds. "Let's start with a couple of in-person meetings. You have to dress professionally, and you can get us some tea—but without spilling everywhere." Mom walks over to a glass cabinet filled with wedding invitations—souvenirs of their successes—and pulls out a book. "But before that, here's your first assignment."

The Shagun Matchmaking Guide. The thick red book is filled with three generations of matchmaking tips from all the vichole in our family. The cover is hand stitched and lined in red cloth, sort of like an old photo album.

"I'm out of copies of the guidelines." Mom unwinds the

book's string and opens it carefully. "I want you to copy this for me. Write it out and make it nice. You have the best handwriting in the family."

The book falls open to a well-worn page. The matchmaking guidelines are written in English, in Mom's handwriting, but it's a translation of the list on the adjacent page. That one is in Hindi, in Nanima's handwriting. It seems the script changes several times, from Punjabi to Hindi and now to English.

"Mom, can you read all these scripts?" Besides English, I can read only a few sentences of Spanish.

"Yes, but my Punjabi and Hindi are rusty after twenty years here," Mom says. "That's why Meera Masi and I have made notes, with Nanima's help. See here?" She points at penciled-in translations beneath the older notes.

The Shagun Matchmaking Guide, it says in large letters. *Top tips for an auspicious match.*

"Those are the bread-and-butter basics to ensure compatibility, but the real magic is in connecting people that have chemistry," she says. She closes the book and hands it to me. "You don't have to work on transcribing right away—homework first. Now come, let's get dinner ready."

I follow her and Masi into the kitchen. Noah's on his way over to study, but I have a few minutes to help out. I open the fridge and grab a whole cauliflower. Then I gather potatoes, onions, and garlic.

"Chop-chop," Masi says, taking the ingredients from me. "Do your homework at the table so you can taste my parathas before dinner. I just kneaded the atta."

"Parathas are my favorite."

"I know," she replies with a wink.

The doorbell rings.

"Noah's here," I say, and hurry to the foyer to let him in.

"Did you think more about my idea?" he asks before I can even get the door open.

"A little, and shhh." I pull him into the kitchen.

"Hi, Auntie! Hi, Masi!" he says.

"Hi, Noah dear," Mom says, then turns back to peeling and slicing potatoes.

We settle down at the table to work. I have math, English, and art homework. Way to start sophomore year.

Mom and Masi sound busy, too. "Did you pull the files for the Chaudhary boy?" Masi says, frowning over her onions as Mom shakes her head. "His consultation is at nine tomorrow."

"I thought you did that yesterday," Mom says. "That auntiji's expectations are ridiculous. She wants a doctor who cooks and cleans."

"Did you read the file? The boy needs the opposite! This is going to be a mess." Masi sighs as she rolls out dough for the parathas. "Maybe it's time to expand the computerization, choti. It might be worth trying to have people fill out the profiles themselves on the computer so we don't have to handwrite everything. Then we can note the responses that are different in the consultation."

"But the machines make everything so impersonal," Mom says. "It's hard to get good answers when people are inputting yes/no on a computer screen. And it's not our tradition."

Noah nudges me and makes a face.

"None of this is really traditional, is it? We're not in India anymore," Masi says as she flips over a paratha, slathering it with ghee. The buttery scent of the frying dough makes my mouth water.

"What made your mother become a matchmaker, Auntie?" Noah asks.

I kick him under the table. He just *had* to ask them more about matchmaking. He's obsessed.

"Ow," he mutters, and glares at me.

"Partition," Masi says, setting one of the hot parathas down in front of Noah and me to share. We rip it apart and shovel it down. "That's what made our grandmother finally get into the family business."

"Partition?" Noah asks through a mouthful of paratha. "What's that?"

"The division of undivided India into India and Pakistan in 1947. After the borders were drawn by the British—they really made a mess of things—families became refugees overnight." Little frown lines appear on Masi's face, and her eyes water. "And those were the lucky ones! So many people died in the riots. Millions!"

"The community networks collapsed," Mom explains. "Networks people depended on to arrange matches, to continue family lines, to find happiness. People didn't know who to trust to set up marriages for young people anymore."

"But in the refugee camps in New Delhi, people remembered that we were vichole," Masi adds. "People came to Nanima's mother for help. People trusted her. No one with bad habits, or a history of mistreating their daughters-in-law, ever came through her. Only good families and decent boys. It was like community service."

"What about Nanima? By then everything must have settled down, right? Why did she continue the business?" I ask, but the minute the words are out, I regret showing interest.

"There were a lot of demands on the girl's side then." Masi gives a shudder. "People wanted a dowry and gold and cars and *uff!*"

"What's a dowry?" Noah asks.

"Gifts and money the girl's family gives to the boy's family to accept their daughter," Masi says. "It's ridiculous and it's illegal."

"Don't get her started on how Nanima threatened greedy clients with the Dowry Prohibition Act of 1961." I roll my eyes, though I'm secretly proud of Nanima. "If you ask me, they should pay the girl's family."

"No, that just makes people marry their girls off to the

groom with the biggest price," Mom says. "Money should stay out of marriage; that's what I say. In any case, Nanima made sure there was never money involved in the matches she made." Mom's pride in Nanima warms her voice. "No greedy families ever found brides for their sons through her. She thought of it as her calling, once she got over her doubts."

I never knew Nanima had doubts about being a vicholi. I wonder what Noah thinks of it all. Here, things are totally different. You meet, fall in love, fall out of love, fall in love again, maybe get married. In India, *everyone* is involved— from grandmothers to neighborhood aunties to your dad's business partner's third cousin. And the stakes are high because divorce is usually not an option, though that's changing now.

"Nanima and her mother helped rebuild the community, in a way," Mom says. "Even today people thank Nanima for bringing their families together. That's the legacy of Shagun Matchmaking."

"All right, enough with the history lesson," I grumble, then feel a pang of regret at the hurt on Mom's face. I soften my tone. "Noah and I have to finish our homework."

"This is more interesting than French, honestly," Noah says. "Do you think things are changing in India now?"

Mom smiles at him. "Things are changing everywhere. People will always be looking for a good match, but now what they want is more complicated. Some people want to take their time to commit, not like before, when it was *chat mangni, pat vyah*."

"Like a really short engagement?" Noah guesses.

Mom nods. "Now sometimes we get a wedding card a year or two after we introduce a couple. As long as everyone is happy. We're just trying our best...but what happens after us, Simi..." Mom's voice trails off. "That's the question."

"Mom! I already said I'd help you."

Noah beams with pride. "Simi's going to make a great matchmaker."

I flash him the look of death. *Not now!* I mouth at him.

Sorry, he mouths back with an apologetic head tilt.

I'm so going to kill him later.

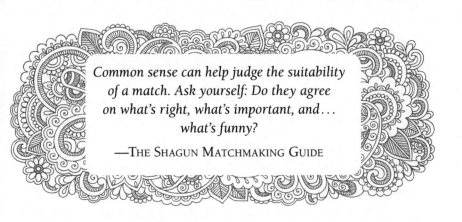

chapter seven

*U*p in my room, Noah and I print out our finished homework assignments. Then he hits me with his many reasons why we should become Mayfield High matchmakers: We have talent we can use for the greater good, matchmaking at school could help me decide if I want to be a matchmaker for real, fixing Navdeep's Shagun app will slash Mom and Masi's workload. And, most importantly, Noah says: "We want to matter."

"Okay," I say. "What about the cons?"

"Well, we might make some bad matches. We might get haters. And also, there's a chance we could get into trouble.

But the risk is totally worth it—I bet we'll become popular, Simi."

I consider, still wavering, because popularity? Eh. Haters? No thanks. "What if we go for it, but wait a bit before taking credit?" I say. "Just in case it's a disaster."

Noah rolls his eyes. "Wait? No! We should bask in the glory."

"Baby steps," I say. "Or I'm not doing it. In fact, I think we should sleep on it."

He's disappointed, but he lets it go with a grumbled "Fine."

Maybe he's right, though. Maybe we do need to do something big, something that'll leave a stamp on Mayfield, like matchmaking.

But if I had my way, my art would be enough.

The following day at lunch, I can't help but notice Suraj. He's at the table where the robotics team sits. The usual suspects are there—Marcus, Rebecca, Navdeep, and a few others.

Suraj grins when he catches me staring.

Again.

He's wearing an untucked plaid shirt over jeans with hipster glasses, giving off a preppy vibe. He waves. I turn away quickly.

"Hang on," Noah says after swallowing a fry. "I saw that. Do you suddenly know him?"

Noah's been sneaking looks at Connor, who's sitting a few tables down from ours.

"Not even a little bit," I say, focusing on my food.

"He looks like he knows you," Noah says.

"Nope."

"He keeps glancing over here."

"I've never even talked to him," I say, squirming. He's quizzing me like an old auntie trying to make a match at the gurdwara.

"Maybe he's into you. I swear, he's looked over here, like, a dozen times."

"Maybe he knows I'm Navdeep's sister." I shrug, because that could be a reasonable explanation, too. "Don't stare, or he'll think *you're* into him!"

"He's not my type," Noah says, his shoulders bunching up around his ears. He peeks down the row to where Connor's sitting and mumbles, "You should know better."

Oh, boy—Noah's definitely got a crush!

I give him a break until a few minutes later, when Connor grabs his backpack and leaves the lunchroom. Noah's shoulders relax a little, and I take my chance.

"You could talk to him, you know. You guys have class together—that's an easy opener. Ditch me for a lunch period and sit with him. Or ask him to join us."

"I have." Noah waves a hand, gesturing to the cafeteria at large. "But, you know, everyone sticks to their cliques around here. Soccer players in that corner, cheerleaders over there, robotics in the front, band geeks, mathletes, cross-country runners, theater nerds. I don't even know where Connor would fit in, but it doesn't really matter."

"Nanima said something like that once," I remember. I hear her voice, soft and lilting, in my head: *Perfect matches may pass each other by without ever noticing, like ships in the night. It is the matchmaker's place to create the moment when they truly see each other.*

"Wonder who we're missing out on," Noah says. There's something vulnerable in his voice that I haven't heard before. "Kind of depressing, when you think about it."

"Hey, you okay?" I ask, taking his hand.

He shrugs. "Have you thought about the matchmaking app? Like, seriously? Because I really think we should do it. Worst case, we'll get a certain reputation or whatever. Still better than being invisible."

"I like who I am," I say. Except maybe my clumsiness, but that's a charming flaw, right? "Or at least I'm trying to."

"So do I," Noah says. "But that doesn't mean we can't want more. And I seriously think we'd be doing this school a service. Think about it. Most of the people we know are single. But there has to be someone out there for everyone." His wistfulness makes me wonder if he's talking about himself. And Connor. "People are scared to branch out. We can help them take the first step."

I look around at all the groups in the lunchroom. Amanda and her sidekicks, who are currently pointing and laughing at a freshman with an unfortunate bowl hair-cut. Jassi, who was super sweet about my mehendi design yesterday but still scampered off to sit with her usual trio of friends. The robotics crew my brother rarely strays from.

Noah has a point. I remember Nanima's wise words about helping people truly see one another.

Noah and I could do that.

I take a deep breath and squeeze his hand. "Okay. Let's give matchmaking a try."

"Here are the guidelines I was telling you about." I open up *The Shagun Matchmaking Guide.* Its rich red cover and slightly yellowed pages seem to glow in the morning light. This might not be the ideal way to spend a sunny September Saturday, but at least we're in good company. Generations of vichole will guide us through this book.

"*Shagun Matchmaking Top Tips for an Auspicious Match,*" Noah reads.

"From what Navdeep told me," I say, "his app was built off these tips. According to Mom and Masi, the most important aspect of matchmaking is compatible values. What people think is right or wrong."

Noah tilts his chair back and steeples his fingers. "How are we going to figure out people's values?"

"Mom and Masi talk to clients about how they'd handle

different situations. I think we should use questions people can answer within the app."

Noah hops off his chair and writes this down on the whiteboard he's brought from his bedroom. We decided to work at his house today, and luckily his parents bought the "school project" excuse we used to take over the family room.

"But first of all, everyone has to fill in the basics: name, age, grade, gender identity, and sexual orientation," he says, scrawling the words on the board. "Then come the other questions. Like favorites... pizza or tacos?"

"Ice cream or cake?" I chime in.

"That's a good one." Noah writes lightning fast.

"Favorite color, maybe? We could have choices be red, blue, pink, yellow, green, orange, purple, and black."

"Beach or mountains. And favorite season," he adds.

"Now we have to do the values thing. It's kind of weird, but here's an example," I say. "Imagine that your midterm is tomorrow and your friend can't find his notes. He asks for pictures of your notes on group chat.... Would you take the time to send the pictures, even though you're busy studying, or be happy that you'll have a better grade than at least one person?"

"I mean, I'd totally share," Noah says, "but I don't know how many other people would take the time."

I smile. "It'll all come out in the quiz!"

"How about this one: You get asked to a party, but the

big game is tomorrow and your team is counting on you. Would you go to the party? Or stay in and rest like the coach asked?"

"That's great," I say, jotting down his suggestion.

Soon the board is covered with questions focusing on values. We move on to priorities.

"People value certain traits over others," I say. "Bravery, honesty, intelligence, talent, good looks. Like, do you think getting good grades is more important than a social life or getting a job to help out your family, and so on?"

"How do we check for priorities? Ask people to list theirs, or make up more questions?" Noah asks.

"Questions," I say. "Asking about a specific scenario is always better."

After covering priorities, we move on to aesthetics— what people think is beautiful, ugly, funny, or delicious.

"We should use memes to figure out what people think is funny," Noah says.

"Totally!"

"And artwork to figure out what people think is beautiful?"

"Yes—finally, something I can use my art for! And speaking of art, I think we should give everyone who completes the quiz a personal icon based on the personality traits that come through in their answers. Like, specific images for people who like athletics or academics or the arts...Let me draw some!"

I pull my sketchbook and a pencil from my bag, then draw an owl, a raven, and a fox on a blank page. I add a test tube next to the owl, numbers next to the raven, and a feather quill in the fox's paw.

"Cool," Noah says, peeking over my shoulder. "Science, math, and...literature? Academics, basically. I get it!"

He takes the sketchbook and pencil from me, then draws a seal next to a music note, a peacock dancing *en pointe* in ballet slippers, and a unicorn holding a paintbrush next to an easel.

"Oh, I love those!"

"We could add colors to the icons, too."

"Like for the values bit?" I say. "How about gold for sportsmanship and silver for academic achievers. Red for school spirit. Green for environmental awareness."

Noah tosses down the pencil. "I'm exhausted, Simi."

"This is just the beginning," I say. "We've got a long way to go."

"Then we need to refuel. Ice cream?"

"Klondike Bars, here we come," I say.

I'm grinning, but inside, I'm kind of worried. Noah and I are working hard and our combined ideas are good—we've got such a strong start!—but our planning will be for nothing if we can't persuade Navdeep to help us update the app he created.

We can't do this without him, and I'm not sure he'll help.

chapter eight

*N*oah and I spend all day brainstorming and writing
more quiz questions. My plan is to talk to Navdeep
about the app as soon as I get home.

Except he's out, and waiting around is making me nervous. I try white mehendi to kill time. I've mixed white
body paint with body adhesive—a formula I found online.
I'm trying the combo out on the back of my hand, with
Noah supervising via video chat. The white paisley I've
drawn looks sharp against my brown skin. I hold up my
hand to show Noah my progress.

"It looks better than the picture on the website," Noah
says.

It totally does.

The front door slams, and Navdeep's combat boots
stomp through the house.

"He's home!" I say to Noah. My heart leaps up into my

throat, like the sharp corner of a samosa going down the wrong way.

"Go talk to him," Noah shouts from my computer screen.

"I'll let him get a snack first," I say. "He's way nicer when there's something in his stomach." I listen for the clatter of dishes and spoons.

Sweetie dashes out my bedroom door to greet her favorite human. Traitor!

"Simi!" Navdeep yells. "What did you do to the dog?"

Oops. I put a sparkly bindi on her forehead for fun. And wrapped her up in a veil. She looks so cute dressed up.

"I better go," I say to Noah.

"Text me after you ask him," he says. "And good luck!"

I hang up and go to Navdeep's room.

"You said something?" I flash him my best little-sister smile and tiptoe inside. His floor is covered in metal bits and pieces. Or whatever they're called.

"Stop messing with the dog." He swivels away from the two blinking screens on his desk—like anyone needs a laptop and iPad on at the same time—and scowls at me. He looks tired and cranky and way too large for the little desk that he's had since fifth grade.

"Fine, fine." I unwind the dupatta I wrapped around Sweetie's face. "You just don't appreciate the artistry involved in styling dogs. Got to have a backup profession, right? In case the whole matchmaker thing doesn't work out. Happy?" I give him a cheesy grin.

"That's better." He ruffles Sweetie's fur. A smile breaks through his gloomy face. Ah, there's my big brother who might help Noah and me out. "Okay, go. I've got programming to do," he says. "And don't step on the robot parts!"

If this is what senior year does to you, I don't ever want to graduate. I think about just leaving and telling Noah that it's a no-go, but he'll be super disappointed. I secretly keep thinking this whole matchmaking app thing might be a way for him to explore getting a boyfriend. So I have to try. I want that for him. "Navdeep, I wanted to ask you something.... Noah and I have a cool idea, but we need your help to make it work."

"Okay ... ?" Navdeep stares at me suspiciously.

"We want to help you fix the app you created for Mom."

"She's not interested." Navdeep shrugs. "She'd rather do all the work on paper than try again. If I had more time, and some data to assess, the system would be amazing. I was so close."

"So let's do it without her."

"Can't," he says flatly. "I need actual beta users to fine-tune my algorithm. Where am I going to find them?"

"At school."

"School?" Navdeep runs a hand through his wavy hair, pulling it back into a low ponytail. He's growing it out to wear a pagri, like my dad. But he doesn't have quite enough yet to make it work. "Are you crazy?"

"No, I'm serious. Kids use all kinds of apps. Like, dating apps even."

"Not apps developed by *me*. I'm pretty sure this goes against some rule in the Student Code of Conduct. And even if it doesn't, what teenager would take the Shagun quiz anyhow? It's all about career paths and work-life balance and if your ideal car is a minivan or a sedan and if you want to travel the world or have two-point-five kids and a house with a white picket fence." Navdeep's already turning back to his screens. I have to close the deal.

"So we'll change the questions to make them Mayfield High specific. Situations that involve midterms, prom, sports, and clubs. Noah and I've been working on it. Look." I shove my iPad toward him, blocking his view of the computer screen.

He takes it reluctantly, but once he starts reading, he nods in approval. "Hmm, interesting... These are pretty good. But there's that whole thing about using personal data," he says. "We'd need consent, and we'd need to make sure only Mayfield High kids sign up, for safety." He starts clomping around the room in his dirty boots. Mom would be so annoyed.

"Now you're crushing robot parts," I warn.

"Shoot!" He sits down to pull off his boots. "You know, we can do what Mark Zuckerberg did at Harvard when he started Facebook. Back then, you had to have a Harvard email address to register. I could set it up so you'd need a Mayfield High email to register for the app. That will weed out all non-school people and limit it to one user per email address. But the real problem will be getting people to sign up."

"Noah and I were thinking we could make it fun—with, like, icons we could assign based on interests and personality traits." I swipe on the iPad screen. "Look at our sketches. We have four groups: Arts, Academics, Athletics, and All-Arounder. Each group has three icons. I've used colors, too . . . a rainbow unicorn, or a silver cat, or a purple owl. . . ."

"That's definitely a hook," Navdeep says. "People love personality quizzes. We could share the icons of their top five matches instead of names, if we're keeping them confidential. If we can get them to sign up."

"Leave that to me and Noah," I say. Navdeep doesn't even have social media accounts, but Noah and I do. It's sad when a techie is such a dinosaur. "Just set up the app so it can register people and let them take the quiz."

"You have all the questions?"

"I do!" I say. "I can email them to you now. How long will it take to set up?"

"Before the end of the weekend. I already have the forms and user interface. Email me the icons you want to use, and I'll upload them, too. Then I can publish the new version to the app stores, and it'll be ready to go."

I can't help it. I hug my brother. He swats me away like a fly. "Go already. If you want this done by tomorrow night, I've got work to do."

By Sunday night, everything's in place.

"What now?" Navdeep asks once the updated app is published to the app stores.

"We should post about it," Noah says from the video chat screen. "Like in group chats and on social media, right?"

"If we do that, people will know we created it," I say.

"But we want to make people love it! Take credit for all the happily ever afters!"

"I think we should wait and see if people even use it, and if the matches make sense. That way, if it bombs, we can trash it without having to own up to it."

"What about sending an anonymous tip to Mayfield High Secrets?" Navdeep says.

The Mayfield Secrets website is very popular. If we want everyone to know about the app, it's definitely the way to go.

I jot down a possible pitch:

MATCHED!
Looking for the perfect date, Mayfield High?

Don't call; don't swipe; just get Matched!

It's easy!

1. Fill in your profile.
2. Take a fun quiz.

3. Receive your personal icon.

4. Find your top five matches
in the most unlikely of places.

5. Want to meet your top matches IRL?
Message them via the app!
Or opt out at any time.

Download today!*

*Open only to current students
of Mayfield High

Noah nods with approval.

"It looks fine," Navdeep grunts after reading over my post.

I grin. That's high praise coming from my brother. He has two categories for everything—fine or horrible. We've escaped horrible.

"So post it to Mayfield High Secrets?" I pause with my hand dramatically held over my laptop. Once I press this button, there's no going back.

"Do it," Noah says. Navdeep nods.

My stomach flips as I click the enter key on my laptop. Maybe no one will use the app. Maybe no one will care. Maybe all our work was for nothing.

Or maybe Matched! will change everything.

chapter nine

"*U*nbelievable."

I stare sadly at my phone.

It's Monday morning, and Noah's come by so we can talk about what people are saying about the app as we walk to school. One major problem: The post about the app *still* isn't up.

"You think there's a chance the moderators won't post it?" Noah asks.

"I think they're timing it for maximum impact," Navdeep says, shoveling cereal into his mouth while staring at his phone. "Late weekend posts don't get a lot of views."

"Really?" I ask.

"Yeah." Navdeep looks at our upset faces with sympathy. "You guys seem stressed. Relax. I'll give you a ride to school, okay?"

Noah and I grab our backpacks without another word, though I'm glad we're going early so no one has to see us in my brother's busted car.

"Stop obsessing, all right?" Navdeep warns before rattling out of the drop-off loop and heading toward the senior parking lot.

It's just another mundane Monday. People walking to class. Chatting, laughing, checking out outfits, scrambling to finish homework—you know, doing regular stuff.

Until suddenly they're not.

The first person to break the news of the Matched! app is Marcus. He runs up to Noah and me, waving his phone. "Simi, Noah, did you see the post on Mayfield High Secrets?"

I freeze at the sight of our post on Marcus's screen, then try to unfreeze so I don't come across as weird.

"Um, no!" I say, trying to act casual. "What's it about?"

Jassi stops to listen to what Marcus is saying. Other people stop, too. Kiran, Rohan, Priya, Thomas, and Aiden, who looks over Jassi's shoulder, then meets my eyes with an intrigued smile.

Butterflies flit around in my stomach. Because of the app's launch, or because of Aiden?

"It's an app to find your love match in school," Priya says. She scrunches up her face distastefully, but I can tell she's interested. "Why would anyone bother with making a dating app for *our* school, of all places?"

"Hey, now," Aiden says. "Mayfield's all right, I guess. Why *not* launch an app here?"

I nod, like I haven't spent the last few days considering whether to launch this very app at Mayfield. I'm super excited that Aiden's interested, though. I hope he takes the quiz—if he does, maybe I will. Maybe some of our answers will align!

"I don't know...." Kiran says. "Is it a joke? It can't be real."

"Oh, it's real," Jassi says, a grin on her face. "I just downloaded it. The quiz looks fun!"

"Jassi!" Priya looks worried. "There could be like weirdos on it."

Aiden, Rohan, and Marcus laugh.

"Relax," Jassi says. "It's only for Mayfield High students. I tried to start an account with my personal email, but it wouldn't let me. And look at the questions on the quiz. They're all about Mayfield." She's all aglow, totally in her element. As I shoot Noah a pleased smile, she exclaims, "This is so much fun. Look at my icon!"

"Your what?" Priya says.

"My Match Icon." Jassi holds up her phone for everyone to see. The screen says *Quiz complete. Meet your customized Match Icon!*

A sky-blue peacock stares back at us—it's like watching a star being born. Noah and I exchange another celebratory grin.

We have our first user!

"A peacock is male," Marcus says. "They must mean peahen."

"He's beautiful, and he's mine!" Jassi says. "Like a Patronus, but cuter. You're just nitpicking because you don't have one. I think I'm going to call him Plume."

"Hey, what happened to the matching part?" Aiden asks.

"It says: *Please log in to see your top five matches in a week....*" Jassi squeals. "This is so exciting!"

By the time I'm on my way to the cafeteria for lunch, the buzz is solid.

Kiran stops me in the hall, grabbing my arm. "Simi, have you tried the Matched! app yet?" She flashes her phone at me. "My icon's a green owl."

I grin because it's perfect for Kiran, but then realize I'm about to give myself away.

"She's cute," I say.

"You should take the quiz. It's really fun!"

Noah waves at me from across the hall. "Uh, Kiran, I've gotta go," I say. "I promised Noah I'd help him with something before lunch."

"Okay, but sign up, Simi," Kiran says. "It's amazing!"

"In. Sane," Noah says, grabbing my arm and leading me into the lunchroom. We huddle in a corner to scroll through the app.

"There are a ton of people on here. Sure they're not creating duplicate profiles?"

"They can't. Navdeep only allows one account per email. I'm positive these are legit people—the blue peacock is Jassi, for sure. Rohan's the red dog, I'm guessing. And here's Eric, Bela, Marcus."

I wonder if Aiden signed up.

Noah and I keep watching the different profiles pop up in the app as students sign up and take the quiz during lunch. Most have avatars and random usernames.

Suddenly Principal Pinter walks into the cafeteria. A hush falls over the room. All cell phones vanish from view. We're not exactly supposed to have them out during school hours, and Principal Pinter has sky-high behavior expectations.

Hiding my phone under the table, I send a text to Navdeep.

Check the app stats. It's on fire!

Noah comes home from school with me so we can get an app update from Navdeep as soon as he walks through the door.

"Ah gayi, Simi?" my mom calls from the kitchen as we stomp upstairs. "I made pakore!"

"Yum!" Noah veers back downstairs.

Mom sets the crispy fritters on the table along with sticky, sweet-tart imli chutney—Noah's favorite—and a spicy coriander-and-mint chutney, which I love. We pile our plates high as she strains steaming chai into cups. I dump three spoonfuls of sugar into mine and Noah's as he chomps into his first pakora.

Navdeep's taking forever. And not answering my texts.

"Hey, I got the new foundations." Noah digs through his backpack and produces two tubes of makeup. "Alabaster and Barcelona. Want to try them out?" He's recently figured out that he can get free products by writing reviews and has been steadily building his stash of high-end makeup. He's really meticulous about his reviews, too, posting before and after pictures and everything. "I think you're Barcelona."

We head up to my room, and I sit on my bed so Noah can go to work. By the time he's done, my skin is flawless, my eyebrows are defined, my lips are glossy, and my shadow is smoky—and yet I look natural. I'm okay at doing makeup, but Noah is a freaking genius.

The door swings open and Navdeep walks in, munching an apple. "What happened to your face?" he asks.

"You're one to talk. I mean, look at *your* face!" His face has a few patches of stubble where he didn't shave right— Dad's always poking fun about his technique—but I decide that other things are more important than trading insults with my brother. "Spill, Navdeep. What's up with the app?"

He grins and opens the laptop he has under his arm. "You're not going to believe how many people downloaded it."

Noah and I hover over his laptop.

He points at the screen. "One hundred and twelve. And climbing."

"Really? That many people took the quiz?" I say, not really believing it.

"Now one hundred and sixteen. See for yourself." He taps the screen. "We have just over a thousand students at Mayfield High, so we have more than a ten percent adoption rate. That's pretty good for day one."

"That's pretty good for any day!" I say.

"Any problems yet?" Noah asks.

"Some people tried to create duplicate profiles. Some people kept changing their quiz answers. I've set it up so they can only edit their answers twice, just to stop people from goofing off and putting in silly answers. I'm sure some of them have, though."

"I know some kids have prank profiles on stuff like Tinder and MyLoL." Noah rolls his eyes. "We'll have to check to see if the answers are serious after you run the matches."

"That's why Mom and Masi talk to the clients directly," I say. "To make sure they're getting the right information. Sometimes families make stuff up about their kids just to make them sound better."

"We'll see," Navdeep says, and snaps his laptop shut. "Now if you'll excuse me, I have to write my Common App essay."

"Wait, can't you tell us—"

"No."

"But what about—"

"No."

Noah and I exchange frustrated eye rolls as he walks out the door.

chapter ten

J have a chance to see how Mom and Masi get their quiz answers firsthand, because I sit in on a late-afternoon client session after Noah leaves.

A young man is wedged between his parents on the couch in the Shagun office. He smiles nervously.

Mom and Masi have been chatting with the trio for the last hour. At least, it sounds like chatting, but really they've drawn the man and his parents into talking about their values and priorities. It's like watching two FBI agents gather facts from an unsuspecting informant.

"Enough gup-shup, right?" Masi says. "Shall we get to work?"

The parents and the young man put on their serious faces, thinking the actual interview is about to start. Clever, clever Masi.

"So you're a strict vegetarian?" Mom asks. "No eggs even?"

"Eggs are okay," the mother says. "No chicken, no pork, no fish, and"—she shudders—"definitely no beef."

"So ovo-lacto vegetarian," Masi says, writing on her notepad. Food is a very important part of matchmaking.

"We want him to settle down soon," the young man's mother says. "No waiting around till thirty, forty."

"It's not like he isn't outgoing," his father says. "He has many friends. And we always said that if you make a special friend, girlfriend, then fine. It's okay."

"But he's not finding a girlfriend on his own," the mother continues. Her son looks sheepish, as if he's let his parents down. He has a twinkle in his eye, though, like he's laughing at his own ridiculousness. I don't think he's ridiculous. From what I've seen, he's got a great attitude.

"So I said, fine, you can arrange something. Not arrange like in the old days," the young man says with a nervous laugh. "Just introduce. Get the ball rolling. You know!"

"Don't worry; it's very common not to be in a serious relationship at your age," Masi says in a reassuring tone. "It's just a matter of looking beyond your circle. We can help."

"But we want him to meet girls with a marriage-focused point of view," the mom says. "Girls that want to settle down, see? Not just go here and there and then say bye."

"No problem, ji," Mom says. "We have some very nice possibilities in mind. If you want to move to the next stage, then we can start the matching process and get you ten potential matches in two weeks, at the most. Okay?"

"Two weeks!" the mother says. "That is a long time!"

"All good things take time," Mom says.

After, Mom and Masi do a debriefing and discuss their first impressions of the young man and his parents. Most of the information they've collected is from the first, more informal part of their meeting. The soft data goes into a folder I'll probably have to file tomorrow. Lucky me.

Speaking of folders, there are hundreds sitting in mountains on the desk. *Uff*.

"How do you ever find anything in here?" I ask. "Some of these are so old."

"Yes, the old folders are labeled *Happily Ever After* because Shagun has made the match," Mom says, tapping the red-and-black label.

I hold up one of the files. "I know this person. She was matched so long ago, she has twins now."

"That should have been archived." Masi frowns at Mom. "We need to modernize, computerize, and I think Simi agrees with me."

"You can't match people through a machine," Mom says with a shrug.

"But Navdeep made a killer app for you," I say. "Maybe you should try it again."

"App-shaap!" Mom mocks. "It took too long to put in the data, and then it didn't work. Who has time for that?"

"I do, remember?" I say. "As your intern."

Mom and Masi ignore me. Mom holds up the paperwork about the young man who just left. "Finding a match for this boy is no problem. He's young, healthy, sweet-tempered. And he's going to be a doctor. I can think of three lovely girls off the top of my head without opening a single file."

"But we need ten!" Masi looks exhausted.

Sudden inspiration strikes. "I have an idea for a fourth match! You know Preet's professor—Miss Chatterjee? She came in and taught social science to my class in middle school once when Ms. Holt was out sick. She's a client, too, right?"

"Yes, but she's not in medicine," Mom says. "Do you think his family might accept a teacher?"

Masi consults her file. "She has a double major in American history and early childhood education," she says. "And she's starting a PhD in education administration at Rutgers, right near his hospital."

"He's going to be a doctor," Mom says. "She's an educator. Different professions, but both successful."

"It's perfect. MD, meet PhD," I say.

"Let me see." Mom's already pulled out her file. Somehow, she knew exactly where to look in the mountain of folders on the desk. "According to my notes from her visit, this could be a good fit."

chapter eleven

*I*t's Friday evening, and we're assembled in Navdeep's room for the first Matched! batch process. Navdeep and I are here IRL, but Noah is on chat, since he's stuck at home with a cold.

"Let's run some single matches first," Navdeep says. "Just as a test. Did you two take the quiz?"

"Not yet," Noah says.

"We designed it," I say. "We know the questions. Is it really fair to take the quiz?"

"Of course," Navdeep says. "You've had time to think about what your answers should be, so it'll be more accurate. I need good test data to see if the app is working properly. You're it."

I pull up the app screen. "Give us ten minutes."

"I'll go get something to eat," Navdeep says.

I fly through the quiz, then wonder what kind of match

I'll end up with. Hopefully someone who's cute and kind. Hopefully someone who likes art. Hopefully Aiden.

I wonder if he took the quiz yet.

As I select my answers, I also can't help thinking about how many matches Noah will get. The Gay-Straight Alliance at Mayfield is small, and Noah has never really been into the two other out sophomore guys that are in it. They've always just been his friends.

By the time I'm done, Navdeep's back with a bag of spicy Kurkure chips and a can of root beer. What a terrible mixture, honestly. He has such bad taste.

"Done?" I ask Noah.

"Yeah," he says. He looks nervous. "Submit on three. One. Two. Three!"

We hit the submit button simultaneously.

"I got a silver unicorn!" I say. "I love it!"

"Chill. You made it," Noah says.

"I still love it!" I say. "What did you get?"

Noah grins. "Purple basset hound."

I laugh, and he smiles. "I think it's working fine, Navdeep!"

"Hold on." Navdeep grins and cracks his knuckles. "It hasn't dealt with me yet. I'm about to submit my quiz."

"He's going to be a gray cat," I tell Noah.

"No, a pink rabbit," Noah shoots back.

"Wrong and wrong," Navdeep says. "I'm a blue fox."

"Fair," I say. "Would you say the app's doing what it should?"

"Reasonably," Navdeep says. "The real test is the matching process."

He starts the *Begin Matching* process by pushing a few buttons on his keyboard. We stare at the screen as the rainbow wheel goes round and round and round—hypnotic and frustrating at the same time.

"How long will it take?" Noah asks.

"Just give it a sec," Navdeep says, rolling his eyes.

I flash Noah a look and put Sweetie in Navdeep's lap to soften him up.

After a minute, he announces, "It's done."

"And?" I ask. "Do we have any matches?"

"Look on your app screens," Navdeep says. "You should have an update."

"Yes, I do," Noah says. "It says, *You've been Matched! Click to see your top matches.*"

"I have the same message!" I say. "Are these real matches or test data?"

"I ran it against the live data," Navdeep says. "They're legit. Just check and it'll show you the icons."

"I have five listed," Noah says. "The strongest match is a yellow peacock." His eyes light up. I know he's wondering who they are, just like me.

"How many did you get, Simi?" he asks. "What did you get?"

"*Your top five matches are,*" I read the screen. "A blue seal holding a music note. It says *Strong* next to that! Then there's an orange owl that says *Moderate*. The rest are *Weak*."

"Whoa! I wonder who the blue seal is."

"Lemme see." Navdeep clicks on his big computer display and scrolls down a screen full of data. "Yeah, doesn't surprise me. You want to know, Simi?"

"Sure," I say calmly enough, but my heart is pumping. I, Simi Sangha, have a strong match with someone?

"Any guesses before I look?" Navdeep says.

"Just say it!"

"Aiden James." Navdeep grins at me. "Woo-freaking-hoo."

On video chat, Noah nods like he's a freaking fortune-teller. "That is like actual magic, right there. You've done it, Navdeep. It's working."

My heart leaps like Aiden himself is in the room. We're a strong match—science thinks so!

But will Aiden? He's an artist but, like, an *edgy* artist. Also, he's hot. And popular. I bet he has a lot of options. And we've always been just art friends. Would he even see me in that way?

I'm going to have to think about this before setting up an in-person meeting.

"What about you, Noah? Want to know?" Navdeep asks.

Noah's cheeks flame. "You mind texting them to me?"

"I want to see them," I say. "You saw mine."

"Just want to see them by myself first, okay?"

It feels like a pinch.

Navdeep nods. "Give the dude some privacy, Simi."

"Hey, what did your matches look like?" I ask my brother.

He taps a key and his screen clears up. "Deleted," he says with a grin. "For good. The world will never know."

"Not. Fair." Double standard.

"Are we okay to run the match program on everyone else?"

"It's not going to notify them right away, is it?" I ask.

"Not until we've looked it over and made sure it's a good run," Navdeep says. "Just in case anything goes wrong. And they'll only see the icons of their top five matches, so it's basically anonymous anyhow."

"Go for it," I say, happy for the distraction from the fact that Noah won't share his matches with me. I avoid eye contact with him on the iPad.

Navdeep spins around in his evil-mastermind swivel chair, holding Sweetie, and faces his computer. "Process initiated," he announces. "Now we wait."

"For how long?" I ask.

"Ten minutes?" Navdeep guesses.

It's the longest ten minutes. I pace the room and pet Sweetie and steal some of Navdeep's Kurkure and get a soda. I pace some more, and Navdeep throws robot bits at me until I stop.

"Done," Navdeep says at last. "Everyone got their top five matches, unless there's not enough in a subcategory. The strength of the match is noted next to the icon."

"Show us a couple," I say.

"I'll print them out," Navdeep says. "I won't send out notifications until you've okayed the results. You want the actual names of the matches as well as the icons, right?"

"Yes, please," I say.

"Here it is," he says, grabbing a stack of paper from his printer. "And now you need to get out of my room 'cause I have to submit an AP Chem lab by midnight."

"Forget the lab," I say, scanning the report. "We have forty-two strong matches!"

"Yeah, yeah, yeah," Navdeep says, pointing at the door.

I march out holding Sweetie, the report, and my iPad with Noah's face on it, then settle on my bed. "So this shows a list of all the strong matches, according to Navdeep," I say, scanning the results. "You know what's weird?"

"What?" Noah says.

"I would not have guessed half of these. The app really mixed up the cliques. Do you think it's matching the right way?"

Noah looks worried. "These people picked the same answers on all the quizzes?"

"Not exactly the same. Remember: Navdeep said it

can sometimes be better to have complementary answers instead of identical...."

"Are they, though?"

"Yup..."

"Who are they?"

"They're all over the place....Athletes matching with band geeks. Debate-team stars with science-bowl whizzes. Short white people with tall brown people. And whoa..."

"What?"

"Kiran matched with Marcus. He's a great guy, but he's not Sikh. Her parents would never approve."

Noah goes quiet. He fixes a serious stare at me and tilts his head. "You matched with Aiden," he says.

"I did," I admit. "But her family is more traditional than mine, and they're super religious. At least, I think so. Forget Marcus."

"But they *matched*, right?"

"Right."

"So?" He looks offended that I'd think twice about introducing them. "Isn't that what matters most? Sometimes the people you least expect can be the most open-minded. And remember how we talked about people staying in their groups and not seeing what they actually have in common? What about that?"

I know Noah's right, but that won't stop all the aunties fussing about it—in their heads, everyone should stay in their own communities, with their own religions and cultures. "The auntie network will go on a rampage," I say as Noah rolls his eyes. "But you're right. The world won't end if Kiran and Marcus get frozen yogurt and watch a movie together."

"Exactly," Noah says.

"You know who got the strongest ninety-six-point-five percent soul mate match?"

"That has to be a couple that's already going out," Noah says. "Matt Phelan and Jessica Dowd?" He looks suddenly horrified. "Wait—it isn't Amanda, is it?"

"Worse," I say. "It's Ethan."

"No!" Noah buries his face in his hands.

"Yes. And he matched with Teá."

"Teá Dimaandal...? The girl who just transferred and is, like, the new star of the girls' soccer team?"

"The one and only. Amanda's going to *freak out*."

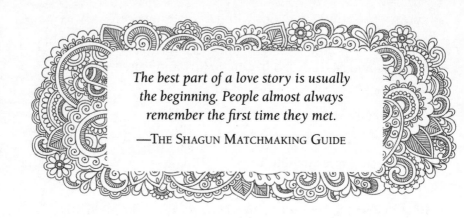

The best part of a love story is usually the beginning. People almost always remember the first time they met.

—The Shagun Matchmaking Guide

chapter twelve

*N*oah and I are at peak stress levels Monday morning. The matches are made. But that feels like the easy part. Soon we'll have to share them.

Thankfully, first period is uneventful. I have PE second period, so I'll be outdoors, burning up the energy I would have otherwise dedicated to overthinking Matched!

The morning sun is hot on my shoulders, and it feels good to get fresh air. Running a mile is not my favorite activity, but it has its perks. No phones, for one.

I still can't believe Aiden is one of my matches. I wonder what he'll think when he finds out. Thinking about him makes me grin—that slow grin, the way he can talk about art for hours. The way the blue seal is a perfect fit—playful, sweet, and smart.

Will he guess the silver unicorn is me?

I'm so in my head, I don't notice when a tall boy starts running alongside me. Then he pulls ahead slightly, faces me, and starts running backward. What the...?

It's Suraj. And he's smiling at me.

Suddenly, I can't breathe. Which is a problem when you're doing an oxygen-intensive activity like running. Or living. My feet stumble and he catches me. Old clumsy Simi is trying to make a comeback.

"Hey, I'm Suraj," he says.

I know, I think. I've seen him in second-period gym a few times before.

"Simran," I say. "Simi."

He's barely broken a sweat, so it's obvious he's sort of athletic. Maybe not a complete robotics nerd like my brother. He isn't wearing his glasses. I guess you don't wear glasses if you're running? I have no freaking idea. His hair flops onto his forehead with each step. It's kind of cute.

"You're fast," he says.

"You call this fast? Running sucks. I only like to do it when my dog, Sweetie, is chasing me." True. All this is true. I'm not babbling. Not at all.

"Ha. That's funny," he says.

"So...Suraj," I say. "To match your sunny disposition?"

"Is that supposed to be a joke?"

I cringe. Ugh! I'm so not funny. Next time I try to reboot my personality and my life, I'll work on humor.

He laughs, though. Slow at first, then a full chuckle.

He grins. "Where's your friend today?"

"Noah?" I wipe my face with my wristband. "He has a bad sunburn and can't be outdoors for more than ten minutes. They let him run the mile on a treadmill."

"You guys are tight?"

"Friends since kindergarten," I say. "Practically brother and sister."

"Your actual brother is president of the robotics club, right?"

"That's Navdeep. King of the nerds."

Suraj grins. "Hey, I'm a nerd. You're not into robotics?"

"Not even if you paid me!"

Up ahead someone—I think it's Bela Sharma—stumbles and collapses. She hates running even more than I do, but she's never fallen before.

"Oh my God, look!" I say.

Some runners check on her.

Suraj stops, and I smack straight into him.

"Ooof!" He absorbs the impact and steadies me, both hands on my shoulders, with my arms wrapped around his waist. We're breathing hard and still holding on to each other. Kids run past us on both sides. One whistles. My stomach does a flip-flop. Embarrassment tangles with excitement.

"Oops!" I detangle myself from Suraj, my face burning. *Why am I such a klutz?* This isn't the New Me.

"No problem. You okay?"

"Yup, fine!" I say, jogging in place. *Can this please be over?*

Maybe he can see what I'm thinking, because he launches into an apology.

"I'm sorry. . . . I didn't mean to . . . My fault totally . . ."

"It's okay," I huff out.

He decides to cut his losses and run. Literally.

"Nice chatting with you, Simi!" he calls over his shoulder.

He vanishes into a herd made up mostly of the track team.

I'm left trying to catch my breath, watching Bela limp off the track.

I push through the gym doors, looking for Noah, dying to tell him about what just happened. I round the corner, cutting under the gymnasium seats, even though we're not supposed to.

I spot Aiden running on an elliptical machine. He gives me a nod and a crooked grin. After my run-in with Suraj,

I'm all out of energy. I wish I could just run straight past him without saying hello, but our high matched score flashes in my head, and he keeps smiling at me like he wants me to stop and say something.

I was able to avoid him in art first period, too amped up about the fact that he and I are such a strong match.

So I attempt to lean against the empty machine next to his and say hello, but I'm still sweaty from my run and I nearly slide to the ground. I stand up—*real smooth, Simi*—and give him a flirty smile. "How'd you get out of running on the track?"

"Sweet-talked Mr. Tate," he says shamelessly. "It's hot out there!"

"Yeah, no kidding," I say, gesturing to my damp hairline.

Aiden grins. "I like your hair like that—the curls are cute."

Umm. Holy crap. I'm melting—but in the best way. Did he just say that?

"Next time, I'll try to get Tate to let you hang out on the ellipticals with me," he says. "If you want."

"Yeah, sure."

He points at the mehendi design on my ankle. "Where'd you learn how to do that?"

"Nanima—my grandmother. She taught me when I was little, when she was visiting from India. I've been obsessed ever since."

"I like it—it's kind of like tagging, but instead of spray paint, you use henna."

"Yeah," I say, grinning. "I've never thought of it like that, but you're right. I can show you how to do it sometime, if you want. You know, after school or whatever."

I can't believe that last sentence just fell out of my mouth.

Did I just ask Aiden, my crush, to hang out after school? Is this a date? What's happening? Who am I right now?

Is he *nodding and saying yes*?

"That'd be cool," he says, blotting his forehead with a gym towel. It's so unfair that boys can pull off the whole winded-and-sweaty PE aesthetic. Just when I think this conversation can't get any more surreal, he adds, "Hey, what about that app, though? Have you taken the quiz?"

"I . . . have. What about you?"

"Oh, yeah. Can't wait to see who I'm matched with."

"Same. Any guesses?"

He gives me the world's most charming smile. "Not so much guesses as wishes."

Okay. I can't be sure—because this all feels way too good to be true—but I *think* he's hinting that he'd be okay with me as a match. Maybe. I'm so not good at this decoding-boy-behavior thing.

I feel like I'm filled with actual helium.

Aiden punches a few elliptical buttons, and the machine slows so he can cool down.

I wave and head toward the treadmills, where Noah has just finished. He's standing awkwardly, wiping sweat from his brow as he watches someone across the gym.

My pulse slows its Aiden-induced sprint as I crane to see who has him all pink under his tinted moisturizer.

Connor from California.

He's walking through the gym like a god. Jet-black hair, light brown skin, sleeves rolled up to show the tattoos that mark his arms—wow. I wonder if they're all real. He hesitates when he passes Noah. Like he might say something.

Noah glances over his shoulder and catches my eye.

I raise an eyebrow. *Say hi! He's right there!*

Noah steps forward.

"Hi, Connor," he says, and it sounds like the squeak a mouse makes when it's stepped on.

Uff. I do a mental face-palm for the both of us. But at least it's a start.

Connor takes out his earbuds and smiles. "Hey, Noah. See you in chemistry later." He heads to the changing rooms.

Noah flushes.

"Um, that was smooth," I say, handing him a water bottle. "You have chemistry with Connor, too? Get it…chemistry?"

"He's my lab partner," Noah says, not laughing at my joke.

"He really is cute."

Noah looks away. "So?"

"So what do you think? Is he one of your matches?"

"I don't want to talk about this right now."

"Why?" I push. "You still haven't told me your matches."

"I will when I'm ready, okay? Like not everyone is out, and I don't think it's cool for me to out them to you. Even if we're the ones behind this whole thing."

His words burn. "But we're going to be matching other LGBTQIA+ couples. I've already seen some in the results."

"Just stop pushing me, okay?" He looks away.

"But...okay..." I try not to cry. I'm so not a crier, but he and I never fight. We might fuss or bicker, but never like this.

He takes my hand. "Saw you talking to Aiden."

I bite my bottom lip to keep it from quivering. He's impossible to stay upset with. I should stop wishing that he'd just tell me. I should respect what he said and give him space. But it all makes me feel like there's a wedge between us now. A secret.

Noah smiles. "Definitely a win."

"Also, I talked to Suraj. I was running the mile outside and he caught up—he may have been on his second lap, come to think of it—and started talking to me."

"What did he say?"

"Not much, because right after, we...collided."

"Collided? How?"

"My fault. As usual. But anyway, it was awkward and he apologized and ran off."

"Next time, try not to be such a klutz?"

"I've been a klutz all my life," I say glumly. "Too late now, especially because I'm so distracted."

Noah laughs. "Uh-oh. Watch out, Mayfield! Things are about to get broken."

The shenanigans start at lunch.

Rohan jumps up on a bench and announces his icon. "I am a red dog," he says with a flourish. He eyes Priya. "What's your icon, Priya?"

She frowns. "Not saying. And anyway, why do you want to know?"

"Because when I get my matches, I want to know if one could be you," Rohan says.

"We won't get matches till the end of the week."

From halfway across the cafeteria, Rohan rounds on me, calling out, "Is that true, Simi?"

I nearly choke on my sandwich. "Why're you asking *me*?"

"Because you're the matchmaker!"

I shoot Noah a surprised look before asking Rohan, "Who told you that?"

"Oh, come on! Your family runs a matchmaking company. You guys found my cousin a husband even though she's like forty. All the aunties love you guys. So any idiot can do the math. What I don't get is why you wouldn't take credit."

I fold my arms. "A matchmaker should be inconspicuous. It's not her job to insert herself in the matches she creates."

Rohan's face lights up. "So it *is* you!"

Thanks to Rohan, everyone in the cafeteria is staring at me, their phones and friends forgotten, their expressions awed and a little anxious. My heart beats against my ribs; in all my life, I've never had all these eyes on me.

Beside me, Noah's beaming—all but affirming Rohan's claim.

Well. We're not wallflowers anymore.

RIP, anonymity.

chapter thirteen

elcome, welcome, Sat Sri Akal!" Dad has put on his best turban and brushed out his neat salt-and-pepper beard for the dinner Mom's hosting for Jolly and his family.

Masi's place is still being painted and most of the furniture has yet to be delivered (though Jolly's working on it!), so we get to host the Singhs, the Sanghas, and the Bhullars. Mom and Masi took the day off to cook and clean the house. Spicy wafts of cumin, cardamom, and cinnamon scent the air, warm and inviting. Sweetie has even been to the groomer and come back all fluffy, wearing a pink bow.

There are more people than I expected, since Jolly's youngest masi just moved to New Jersey and brought her family, too. Preet has been going on about how the masi's son, Jolly's cousin, is "wicked smart," which is not a term I've ever heard her use before.

Everyone settles into the living room for introductions. Jolly's all smiles. He's wearing a white kurta with jeans and a black leather waistcoat, which manages to look both respectfully Desi and a bit edgy. Preet is in full kudi Punjabi mode with a chiffon salwar kameez in a delicate lilac-and-silver pattern. They've been seeing each other since that day in the furniture store and look relaxed and comfortable. "There's someone I'd like you and Navdeep to meet," Jolly says to my brother and me. "This is my cousin Suraj."

It takes me a second to realize that the person he's introducing is *the* Suraj. Suraj Singh. From school. He's wearing his trademark hipster glasses and a blue kurta over jeans. My smile freezes on my face, but he doesn't look surprised.

"We've met," Suraj says to Jolly.

"I thought you might have run into each other at school," Preet says.

"Yeah, literally," I say, keeping a straight face even when Suraj chokes down a snort of laughter.

Navdeep nods at Suraj. "Why didn't you mention Jolly?"

"I had no idea," Suraj says.

Seriously. Smallest world ever.

"Dude, is that your FTC team coach?" Navdeep asks, pointing at Jolly's masi.

"Yeah, Mom's the engineer in the family," Suraj says. "She loves helping out with FTC."

"I've seen her before, but I didn't realize you were related," Navdeep says. "My cousin Geet—Preet's sister—is our coach."

"No way," Suraj says. "Is she here? We should introduce them before they clash."

"Too late," I say, pointing across the room to where Geet, who looks sleek in a red sheath dress, is talking with Suraj's mom. Given that my father is a physician who needs help setting up the Wi-Fi, and Mom is a matchmaker, it's a good thing a tech brainiac like Geet was around to help Navdeep and coach the robotics team.

Seriously, though, where was *I* when they were handing out the Science Goddess genes to Punjabi women?

Navdeep and Suraj fist-bump. "Here's to being on the same team," Navdeep says. "Let me get you a drink. Mango lassi okay?"

Suraj nods and turns to me when my brother leaves. He's looking at me and my stomach gets all squishy and weird. I adjust the pretty sky-blue salwar kameez Nanima brought me from India and I wonder if he can see the wrinkles.

"So, you're Jolly's 'wicked smart' cousin," I say, using air quotes.

"In the flesh," he says. "And you're Preet's artsy cousin."

I do a silly little curtsy while he runs a hand self-consciously over his head. Looks like he's still getting used to the sensation of short hair. "New haircut?"

"Kinda, yeah. Still feels weird, not wearing a turban."

"Did people give you a hard time at school or something?" Some kids get bullied because of their turbans.

"Oh no. The long hair was just annoying, no offense. All the washing, combing, and tying...It was too much effort. For me, that is."

"And your parents let you cut it?"

"Sure," he says, glancing over at them. His dad has a turban, like my dad's. "They're pretty laid-back. They explained why it's important to them, then left it up to me."

His parents sound cool. "Your father's a doctor?"

"Yeah," he says. "Yours, too, I heard."

"Yeah. He's very disappointed that Navdeep is a total techie."

"Same!" Suraj says, and laughs. "At least I haven't disappointed my mom. Yet!"

"How do you like Mayfield?"

"I mean, I miss my friends, but other than that I really like it. I don't have to wear a uniform, for one thing. And it's huge compared to my old school. There were only sixty kids in my grade, and they were all boys. Here it's so diverse. And there are clubs I didn't know existed, like Intersectional Feminism."

"Are you thinking about joining Inter-Fem?" It's funny to see him all excited about things that seem completely normal to me.

"Would they let me? I mean, I think it'd be interesting to get a female point of view. I don't have any sisters, and I went to an all-boys' school. I probably need some help talking to girls."

"You don't want to join Inter-Fem," Navdeep cuts in, handing Suraj a mango lassi. "Amy and Sophia can be seriously scary."

"Stop with the stereotypes, Navdeep," I say.

"You should join, Simi," Navdeep says. "You've got time, since Art Club went under."

"There was an Art Club?" Suraj asks.

"You like art?" I ask. "*And* tech?"

Suraj smiles. "Can't a guy be into both? I like stuff that combine art and engineering—like product design or architecture. I did some pretty big sculptural pieces last year at camp. They were metal, and I got to use a blowtorch. But I didn't have room for art with all the APs I'm taking this year, and anyway, I've fulfilled Mayfield's art requirements already."

"You should think about applying to Cornell," Navdeep says. "Great architecture program. And that big dragon thing they make every year? It's cool."

"It's definitely on my list," Suraj says.

Mom calls the crowd for dinner, and we all file into the dining room. I smile in surprise when Suraj automatically pulls back a chair for me.

"Thanks," I say, sitting down a little too fast and almost sliding off. Ugh!

"Smooth," Navdeep mutters.

I stick my tongue out at him, angling my face away so no one else sees. Suraj is kind of interesting. A techie who is also into art.

Mom and Masi's food is delicious—saag paneer, chicken tikka, kali daal, and rogan josh—and Dad keeps everyone happy with drinks ranging from lassi and lemonade to Patiala pegs of his favorite single malt whiskey. As we finish eating, he raises his glass in a toast.

"To new beginnings, and all the young people in the room. And especially to Simi, the reason behind our new friendship, and Shagun's latest junior matchmaker."

I fumble my glass, spilling some mango lassi on the white tablecloth.

After the cheers die down, Suraj leans toward me.

"You're a matchmaker?"

"I help out with Mom and Masi's business," I say, leaving it at that.

"Your family business is matchmaking?"

I flush. Some people think matchmaking is backward—I mean, even I used to. "Yeah," I say. "It goes back generations."

"That's cool. Does that mean you guys really are behind the matchmaking app everyone's talking about at school?"

Over Suraj's shoulder, I notice Masi straining to eavesdrop on our conversation. He grimaces in pain at my well-aimed kick. I make an apologetic face but also narrow my eyes at him, probably confusing the heck out of the guy. Navdeep flashes a quick thumbs-down in Suraj's direction, too.

He takes the hint and drops it, thankfully.

It seems Mom caught a bit of the conversation, though. "Those matching apps don't work," she says. "Much better to talk to people face-to-face to get a sense of who they are before matching them. How can a program do that?"

"Ekdum right," Jolly's masi says. She can probably get a program to do anything, come to think of it, but she's polite enough not to say so.

Suraj waits until after dinner's cleaned up to pull Navdeep and me aside to ask for an explanation. I guess we owe him one.

"I thought your mom and masi would be into the idea of a matchmaking app," Suraj says. "You didn't tell them about it?"

"Mom doesn't believe in matching programs," I say. "You heard her. And I'm sorry about kicking you. Are you okay?"

Suraj grins ruefully. "It's fine. You know, I did wonder who at Mayfield would have the matchmaking know-how *and* the programming expertise to pull off an app like that."

Navdeep and I exchange a guilty look.

Suraj grins knowingly. "So what made you guys do it?"

"I wanted to fine-tune the app so I can prove to our mom that it works," Navdeep says.

I don't say anything. When Noah and I first started

this, it was a little more for him than for me and part of our let's-be-new-people-this-year plan. But now it feels like it's becoming something else.

He nods. "That's a whole lot of coding," Suraj says. "The user interface is so clever. The icons are pure genius."

"Noah helped with those, too. You've taken the quiz?" I ask.

"Not yet. But now that I know you guys are definitely behind it, I might give it a shot."

He and Navdeep fist-bump again. I roll my eyes and go off in search of more mango lassi. Suraj's icon will be in Academics for sure.

I wonder who his matches will be.

I wonder if I should run the search again, just to see if he shows up in mine.

chapter fourteen

*T*he next day, I have economics first period, and class begins with morning announcements, broadcasted through the school via the SMART board in each classroom. After the opening jingle, the usual hosts appear onscreen. "Hello, Mayfield High! Marcus Matson here."

"And I'm Amanda Taylor!"

"Today we want to talk about what's really going down at Mayfield High," Marcus says, then swings his gaze toward Amanda.

She flashes a dazzling smile. "The Matched! dating app!"

My stomach bottoms out.

"If you haven't tried it, what are you waiting for?" she says like a bubble about to pop.

Marcus takes over. "The Matched! app is a fun quiz geared specifically toward Mayfield students. It's meant to reveal your values, personality, and interests and guide you in finding possible romantic matches."

"We took the quiz," Marcus says, "and are ready to share our personal Matched! icons, or as people have started calling them: MIs."

My first-period teacher, Ms. Holland, who's usually super enthusiastic, looks bored to tears. But my classmates stare at the SMART board, riveted, as Amanda and Marcus pull T-shirts from beneath the desk in front of them and put them on.

"My MI is a purple peacock," Amanda says.

"And mine is a white raven!" Marcus says. No surprise there.

"So, Marcus, I've heard the best is yet to come as far as Matched! is concerned."

He nods. "The next phase of the app is promised to release on Friday. That's when we'll find out who our top matches are."

Several heads swivel around to look at me; my classmates are grinning like we've all been best buddies for ages. Rohan's cafeteria spectacle has clearly made the rounds.

"We can't wait!" Amanda says, her voice even more grating than usual.

"Have you taken the quiz and claimed your MI?" Marcus asks, shooting the camera his best newscaster smile. "Keep us posted!"

My phone buzzes with a text. I sneak a glance at its screen.

This is brilliant!

No—this is nuts.

I don't have a chance to reply before Noah has sent another text.

Our adoption rate's gonna skyrocket. Not to mention our social standing.

Ms. Holland's trying to call the class to order, but everyone's talking excitedly, pulling out their phones despite school policy. The Matched! app stares back at me from at least a dozen screens as Ms. Holland claps her hands and tries again to get everyone's attention. I think she's about to start throwing phones into the trash.

Noah and I might be making strides toward Mayfield fame, but I'm starting to worry we'll end up in trouble before we have a chance to enjoy it.

On Friday, right after school, everyone who took the Matched! quiz receives a message containing the MIs of their top five matches. Just after, Navdeep becomes nervous about the next phase of the project: introducing couples.

"I'm not going to leave them hanging after all this work," I say, stomping my foot on the floor of his bedroom. Noah came home from school with me so we could double-team my brother into seeing things our way. "They have to meet! There's no other way to make sure the matches actually work."

"Who cares if they work?" Navdeep says. "There's enough data to show Mom that the process is valid. We have what we need—proof that the app can match people."

"But that's not all that's important," Noah says.

"Yeah, we have to know that the app can match people *well*," I stress to Navdeep. "That's what Mom needs to see. She doesn't trust technology. And she won't until we can show her that couples have met, gone out, and connected. We need feedback."

"You guys are asking for trouble," Navdeep says. "We're already pushing it matching Mayfield students anonymously. If Pinter finds out we're setting up actual students, presumably on school grounds, she'll be livid."

Secretly, I'm worried about Principal Pinter, too—not to mention the possibility of some vague policy about dating apps buried in the school's Code of Conduct. But I've also become invested in the app. Noah has, too. He says, "We're not doing anything illegal. It's all for fun!"

I nod. "No one made kids sign up. If they exchange personal information, it'll be because they've chosen to."

Navdeep looks unconvinced. "I don't want any disciplinary actions on my record before applying to colleges."

"I totally get that," I say. "We'll make sure everything is all good before we start intros. Walk us through what we should do?"

He sighs, then starts clicking rapidly on his keyboard. "First, you get the okay from both parties about setting up an intro. That's the most important thing, from a legal standpoint. Then you set a specific time and place to meet."

"The library!" Noah and I say it together. We laugh and high-five each other.

"The library?" Navdeep asks. "Isn't that too public a place?"

"I think a public place might be good for first meetings. People will probably feel more comfortable without the pressure of, like, a private meeting. Also, there are like secret nooks there."

"True," Noah says. "So, okay. Matches show up in the library. Then what happens?"

"Their app will be in intro mode," Navdeep says. "Which means that if they get within fifteen feet of each other, the app will open a chat channel for them. Both have to click okay for the channel to stay open. If one or both say no, the channel closes. That's the end of the intro."

"If one of them says yes and the other person says no, don't you think that would hurt?" Noah asks.

"We need to set the expectation that there *is* a risk of rejection," Navdeep says.

I nod. "No risk, no reward."

"So who are the people who have strong matches?" Noah asks.

I look at the most recent stats printout Navdeep's given me. "Kiran Kaur and Marcus Matson. Rebecca Chen and Hasina Bagayoko. Also Teá and Ethan. They're nearly identical on the values and priorities quizzes. They loved the same memes and had nine out of ten things on their Hate List that were the same. They had the same personal hero—some soccer player I've never heard of. It wasn't even an option on the multiple-choice quiz. They both wrote her in."

"Teá's new, so this might be a great way for her to get to know some new people," Noah says.

"She's not going to make many new friends when Amanda finds out she's been matched with Ethan," I say. "Some students will shun her because Amanda says to, and who even knows what Amanda will do to her. But she seems tough. Mom always says it's better to see if someone could be your match despite the obstacles."

Navdeep smiles. "I think she was quoting *The Shagun Matchmaking Guide*."

"You should bring the guide to school on Monday for good luck," Noah says.

I imagine the big red book at our school. There's never been anything so rare and beautiful in our library, for sure. Maybe it will bring us luck, along with good fortune to everyone we've matched.

I smile. "I will."

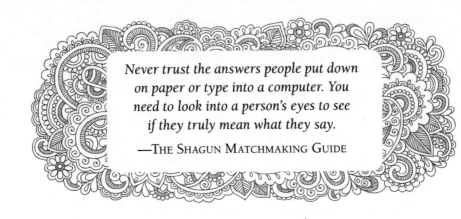

Never trust the answers people put down on paper or type into a computer. You need to look into a person's eyes to see if they truly mean what they say.

—THE SHAGUN MATCHMAKING GUIDE

chapter fifteen

I've brought *The Shagun Matchmaking Guide* to school as a good luck charm for introduction day. Mom's practically got it memorized and doesn't look at it very often, so I'm hoping she won't miss it.

"Where's Navdeep?" Noah asks as we head into the library. It's still early; our potential matches won't be here for another ten minutes.

"Cramming for a quiz he has second period. He's swamped with school stuff. From now on, we'll probably be running the app mostly by ourselves."

"He's bailing after the epic launch we had?"

"I know, I know." I'm a little bummed about my brother bailing on us for a while, but excitement's still zipping through me. "He was interested in the tech part.... What we're doing now—the human stuff—is making him nervous."

"The human stuff? We're setting up potential soul mates, Simi!"

I scoff. "Soul mates in high school? Yeah, right."

"Oh, come on. Where's your faith in the vichole techniques of your ancestors?"

"I have faith. But I also like proof." I think on the techniques of my foremothers and attempt to channel the Science Goddess genes of the badass Sikh ladies I know instead, like Geet and Suraj's mom. "Let's get some of these people together and see how well the app's really working."

The way Navdeep described the app's intro mode unfolding sounds pretty straightforward. I think. I hope. Don't let this blow up in our faces. And he promised he'd be around "virtually" to troubleshoot in case there's a snag and people need technical help. But Noah and I are the boots on the ground.

"I'm glad you brought this, Simi," Noah says as I place *The Shagun Matchmaking Guide* on the table between us. "Can I touch it?"

I laugh. "Go ahead! Read something from it."

"Isn't most of it in Punjabi or Hindi?" he asks.

"Yes, but there's English, too. Mom's been working on translations of the most important stories and instructions."

"Like this." Noah points to a page he has open. "It's the definition of *vichole*."

He reads aloud: *"Vichole means 'middlemen' in Punjabi. Anyone that sets up a deal, brokers an agreement, or brings two parties together for any purpose is a vichola. There are vichole for business deals, property disputes, and the buying and selling of cattle. All good vichole should have a reputation for honesty, be able to resolve differences, and have knowledge of the field they are in. There are also vichole for marriages. But vichole who set up marriage matches need special skills. They need to be observers of human nature, planners of lifetime alliances, and students of love. Some are so well respected that they are paid highly for their skill and knowledge. This type of vichola, or vicholi, since they are almost always women, is becoming rare."*

"Our family matchmakers were exclusively vicholi," I say.

"I love it." He keeps reading. *"There may be a day when no one in our family has the gift. However, if one of our children does have the predisposition to be a matchmaker, let them not waste it. There is great need in the world for those who can help love and happiness take root and lay a firm foundation for families that last."*

I squash the pang of guilt that surfaces. I'm still not interested in being an actual matchmaker, even though Mom and Masi think I have the gift....Nanima would be disappointed.

"I wish your nanima would adopt me," Noah says,

reading my mind. "That way I can stop the Shagun tradition from dying out, since you're too stubborn to carry it on."

"Or, now that we've launched the app, maybe people can make their own matches and potential matchmakers can pursue jobs they might like better," I reply. "Like being an artist."

"Do you hear that?" Noah says, closing the guide. "I think there's someone coming."

I check my silver wristwatch—a gift from Nanima's last visit from India. My heart thumps hard as I grab the matchmaking guide and slide it into my bag. Then I pull out a novel so I can pretend I'm occupied. Noah makes as if he's busy on his computer. The door to the library opens and closes a few times as some of our first matches walk in. I try to be subtle about watching while Rebecca and Hasina turn into the Data Processing and Computer Science aisle, Jason and Liz take over Dictionaries and Encyclopedias, and Rohan and Priya head to the Science Fiction and Fantasy section.

"I wonder how Hasina and Rebecca will react when they see each other," Noah says.

"We'll find out. Navdeep said he'll give us the status of all ten matches via email. If they opened the chat channel or if one or both bailed." My phone vibrates. "Here's something from him now!"

"What does he say?"

"All the matches are currently on open chat channels," I say after reading the message. "Wow!"

"That's great!" Noah stands and cranes his neck to look over the bookshelves. "Better than expected."

"Sit." I grab his hand and pull him down.

"I'm dying to see what they're up to," he says.

"We don't want them to feel like they're in a fishbowl or whatever."

Not a full minute later, movement at the front of the library catches my attention. "Noah, look over there!"

Hasina and Rebecca are walking out of the library. They're not holding hands or anything, just walking, but *walking together.*

Noah and I grin at each other as we grab our bags and head out of the library.

Matched! is working!

I'm on my way to first-period economics when Aiden stops me in the hall.

"If it isn't Simi, matchmaker extraordinaire," he says.

"Guilty," I say.

"I can't believe you didn't tell me!"

"Yeah, I was kind of hoping to keep a low profile for a while. Rohan and his big fat mouth ruined that!"

"I say own it. You guys created something cool."

"Thanks," I say, gazing up at him. And if this was the emoji version of my life, my eyes would be flashing with hearts.

"This means you have all the inside info, right? I bet there's a list of matches right in your backpack."

"No way! I'd never bring it to school."

"But you can spill about who's on it," Aiden says. "To trusted friends only, of course. Like, if you *really* wanted to, you could tell me who my matches are?"

Me! I think. *I'm your match!*

"Uh, I could, but, like, that wouldn't be fair," I say, even though the secret tickles the tip of my tongue and I want to tell him so badly that it's me. But Noah would kill me. "You're going to have to wait and see."

"Build up the anticipation," he says, smiling. "I get it."

A twinge of fear twists a knot in my stomach. I hope he isn't disappointed. But he's flirting with me, right? Like this is what flirting is... I think?

The warning bell blares through the crowded hallway.

"I've gotta go," Aiden says. "See you later."

Well. Not a bad start to the day. Not a bad start at all.

When I get to economics, Amanda's in class—unusual, because she's usually doing the morning announcements. I can feel her ice-blue eyes boring into the back of my head as I take my seat, slinking down into my chair.

The SMART board flickers to life. "Good morning, Red Hawks! This is Natasha Qureshi and Marcus Matson with your morning announcements!" Apparently Natasha's taken over for Amanda, which isn't terrible news. I find her way nicer to listen to, but I'm curious why Amanda would bail on the broadcast.

"We have some more news to report about a certain popular app that's gone viral in the halls of Mayfield High."

Oh no. This can't be good. I sit up in my chair, laser-focused on the broadcast.

"Rumors have already been swirling, but we can confirm with certainty that the app developers are Mayfield's own Navdeep Sangha, Simran Sangha, and Noah Siegal."

I'm redder than Noah's hair. I want to legit be a ghost. Right here and right now. Poof! Be gone! RIP! Everyone turns to look at me.

Natasha goes on: "When asked about the app, Ms. Pinter said this is the first she has heard of it, and that she will request that Mr. Wall of the technology department review the app, then make a recommendation to the school-leadership board."

School leadership? *Oh no.* Ms. Pinter doesn't have patience for students stepping out of line, especially when what they're doing is creating distractions on campus.

Are we about to end up in major trouble?

Marcus starts talking. "So long as the app doesn't violate the Code of Conduct, Ms. Pinter says, she won't take issue with it, but she does ask that no students use the app during school hours and says she'll be in touch with the app's creators

regarding a review meeting. As a satisfied user of Matched!,"
he continues, grinning, "I hope the review goes splendidly,
and I'd like to be the first to offer Simi, Noah, and Navdeep a
huge congratulations for coming up with such a cool app. This
is Marcus and Natasha, signing off."

The room bursts into applause.

My face is on fire, but I attempt a gracious smile, giving
my classmates a little wave—until I notice Ms. Holland looking at me with disapproving eyes and her signature scowl.

She's not the only one in the room who doesn't seem
impressed by the news—Amanda's practically green. Maybe
it's envy. Maybe she's sick and about to vomit. Maybe she's
traded in pink for this new color. Now I understand why she
wasn't on today's broadcast. She'd come to school makeup-
free and pink-free before she'd sit in front of the whole student body singing the praises of something I helped create.

All day, people stop me in the halls and approach me in
class. My phone won't quit buzzing. And at lunch, Noah
and I end up in the midst of a swarm.

"How did you guys think of it?"

"It's freaking kickass!"

"I mean, it's great that it's free and all, but I'd pay money
for it!"

"Did you draw the icons?"

"Who helped you with the quiz questions?"

"Navdeep is legit going to be the next Steve Jobs or something."

Jassi comes by with praise for Matched!, then asks if I have my mehendi cones with me in the cafeteria. "Seriously, Simi, you're so talented. I'd love one of your tattoos. Maybe you can do them for matched couples? Part of the service."

I wolf down what's left of my lunch, then spend a while creating an intricate design on her wrist, chatting with her and Priya about designing the app. Beside me, Noah finishes his lunch, adding his part of the story here and there, jokingly taking full credit for the idea. Which is mostly true. Without him, I'd never be doing this.

When I finish Jassi's mehendi, she blows softly on the design, then holds out her arm to admire her decorated wrist. "It's so pretty!" she says, giving me a one-armed hug. "Really, Simi, you're so good."

"Thanks," I say. "Make sure you scrub it off with oil, not water. That way the color will get darker."

"I will." She smiles, thanks me one more time, and then she and Priya prance off to join their friends.

I look after her, feeling fulfilled. Maybe I will make an impression with my art—even if it's not in the exact way I thought I would.

The day continues in a blur. It seems everyone wants to congratulate Noah, Navdeep, and me on Matched! While I'm glad it's a hit, all the attention is making my head spin. Also, my teachers have been super annoyed with the distractions, and I'm starting to worry someone's going to report the disruption to Principal Pinter. And then, to Mom.

But now that the news is out, we have to go full speed ahead, with or without Navdeep's help. Which means Noah and I have a lot of work to do.

chapter sixteen

*I*t feels weird to go from high school dating drama to the seriousness of a real-life Shagun consultation—one that might end in an actual wedding. But I'm excited, too. Because this one was my idea.

Mom ushers Maya Chatterjee into her office. "It's nice of you to come see us on such short notice."

Maya Chatterjee has come by herself, without any family in tow. She's average height and has a warm tan toasting her already brown skin, and an even warmer smile. She's wearing jeans and a silk sweater set. She looks just like she did back when she was a substitute teacher for my seventh-grade class.

"Simran," she says. "You're all grown up!"

"Hi, Miss Chatterjee," I say.

"Please, call me Maya."

"Simi is interning with us," Mom says. "She's going to

be sitting in on our session today. Are you all right with that, Maya?"

"That's totally fine," Maya says. "Are you interested in joining the family practice, Simi?"

"She has the aptitude for it," Masi says.

"That's fantastic." Maya laughs. "People like me need all the help we can get."

"Rubbish," Mom tells her.

Turns out, Maya's pretty talkative. It's been a while since she started the process at Shagun and Mom is only now ready with her matches, but she's not upset about the delay.

"I'd rather wait a while and get matches that might actually work," Maya says. "I'm so tired of the online-dating scene. And between teaching, grading, and working on my thesis, I don't have time for a social life. But I would like to have a family one day, so this is a step in the right direction, right?"

"Right," Mom agrees, and then she gets down to business. "I'd like to go over some details, just to make sure we have the right information. You left the dietary restrictions section blank?"

Maya shrugs. "Because I don't have any."

Mom gulps. "You eat . . . beef?"

"Uh-huh."

I grin at the shock on Mom's face.

"Wahe Guru," Masi says under her breath. "Uh-oh! The guy and his family are vegetarians. Could mean trouble."

"I didn't while I lived at home with my parents, so don't

blame them," Maya says. "It's best to be honest about stuff like this, right?"

"True, true." Meera Masi nods in sympathy. "It's best to be honest about everything at the start than find out later. And you can always give up meat, no?"

Maya is nothing if not forthright. "Not likely. Okay, maybe I can give up red meat because that's healthier anyhow, but not seafood. I love fish!"

Mom makes a note, then asks, "How old did you say you were, beta?"

"Twenty-nine." Maya notices the quiet glance Mom and Masi exchange. "Am I beyond hope, then?"

"Not at all," Masi says. Maya is the same age as the young man we met with, not younger like the other matches Mom pulled out.

"We had discussed backgrounds," Masi says. "And you had said it's okay if the boy is not Bengali. You're open to other states. Is that right?" She means other states in India, as in Gujarat, not California or Minnesota.

"Right," Maya says. "Our family isn't at all orthodox. As long as we can visit pandals for Durga Puja once a year, I'm happy."

"Good, good. Let's look at some of the profiles we've selected," Mom says. "We have a ladies-first policy, as you know, so none of these gentlemen have your information yet. Please read through the profiles and let us know if you'd like to meet any of them. Then we can move the process along."

Maya opens the folder. The first profile belongs to the Indian doctor who came in last week. Mom made it my job to pull the files on all the guys, so I was careful to put him on top. Not that the other profiles Mom and Masi pulled are terrible, but I ship Chatterjee-Khanna.

"Great! I'll have a read and get back to you," she says, blushing a little. "It's okay to call if I have questions, right?"

"Absolutely, beta," Mom says, putting an arm around her. "We are here for you!"

The next day, when I get to art class, Aiden's waiting in my workspace.

"Hey, Simi," he says. "I heard we're blending paints today."

"Oh, are we?" I say. "What are you working on?"

He pulls the tarp off his easel. Underneath are the bare bones of a sketch, the start of a painting. "It'll be a portrait of my grandmother," he says. "I never met her, because she died when I was a baby, but I've been working off this old photo." He picks an old black-and-white picture up off the table, holding it out so I can inspect it.

"Wow. I bet it'll be beautiful."

"Yeah." He's quiet for a second, staring at the sketch. "I just hope I can do her justice."

"Will this be your signature project?"

"Nah. This one's just for me, you know? I've got something large-scale in mind for the big project. Something

I'm gonna do with spray paint." He pulls out the paint bin and starts sorting. "I heard you're doing something cool for yours. Seems like Furst is excited."

I nod. "I'm excited, too. But it's a lot—something I've never tried before." I pull out some of the mehendi cones I brought from home and gesture to the design on my ankle. "I mean, I've done mehendi before, obviously. But this—"

"Is going to be good." He grins, handing me a few tubes—brown and russet and burgundy and wine, all the right tones. Our hands touch as I take the tubes from him. I swear I feel a spark, the tingle everyone always talks about. He grins again, and though I manage to smile back, I suddenly feel bashful.

I've daydreamed about Aiden-induced tingles for so many years. It's weird, in a good way, being within arm's reach of something I've wanted since middle school.

We both turn to our easels, ready to work.

I wonder if he has any idea how strong a match we are.

"I feel like everyone is watching us," Noah says as we walk into the cafeteria.

He's right—our remote corner of the cafeteria is more crowded than usual. I'm so thrown by the influx of people, I nearly slip off the bench as I slide over to my place. "Sure you don't miss blending in?" I ask, recovering with passable grace.

"No way," he says, then pauses to fist-bump Rohan and Jordan before taking his usual seat. I've always like known people and been friendly, but like people want to know me now and hang out.

"Hey, Simi! Hey, Noah!" Sophia says, pushing through the crowd with Amy, Rebecca, and a few other Inter-Fem Club girls in tow.

"Congratulations on the app," Amy says.

"Thanks," Noah and I say in unison.

Sophia smiles. "I saw the henna design you did for Jassi—it's beautiful. Do you have your cones with you today, by chance?"

"I do." I pull one out of my bag to show her.

"We'd love to get #NOM henna tattoos to help us stay mindful of the issues surrounding the school mascot," Amy says seriously. The Inter-Fem Club, as well as a few other groups, recently pushed to have our school's mascot changed from the Red Men to the Red Hawks, a campaign I'm happy worked.

"Some people refuse to embrace the fact that we're now the Mayfield Red Hawks," Rebecca adds.

"Yeah," Noah says. "But #NOM? I don't get it."

"Stands for 'not our mascot,' right?" I say to the girls.

"Yep," Rebecca says.

I smile, pulling a few more cones from my backpack. "I like it. Where do you want the tattoos?"

They agree on their wrists, and I get started, snagging

bites of my lunch between tattoos. I add swirls and flour-ishes to the letters so they look pretty as well as powerful. As I finish the last, Suraj stops by our table. The Inter-Fem girls know him, too, and call out hellos before heading for their usual spot in the cafeteria.

"Did you end up joining their club?" I ask.

"I went to a meeting, but they meet the same time as the Poetry Club," Suraj explains. "I'm going to be involved, but unofficially."

"Cool," I say, wondering what kind of poetry he writes. "You want a #NOM tattoo?" I'm only kidding, but he imme-diately pulls up his sleeve and bares his forearm.

"Really?" I'm taken aback, not gonna lie, because he hasn't been at school very long, but I like that he's in sup-port of the mascot change and totally cool with rocking a mehendi design. "Okay, then!"

My hands shake a little as I start to swirl the mehendi over his arm—what's up with me? I take a breath and steady them, focusing on the conversation Noah's having with a few people who've joined us at our table to keep my nerves in check. I manage most of the tattoo before the cone runs dry. "Sorry, I'm out of mehendi."

"No, you're not," Noah butts in, handing me a fresh cone. He gives me a conspiratorial wink and a pointed poke with his elbow.

"Oh, sorry! Noah, this is Suraj. Suraj, my best friend, Noah." They do that head-nod thing guys do to each other.

144

I go back to the design on Suraj's arm, finding that if I hold my breath, my hands don't shake as much. I manage to do a decent job getting the letters onto Suraj's arm, which I'm now noticing is muscled. "All done."

"Thanks, Simi," he says before heading to his regular table.

Noah leans back in his chair.

"Hey, Simi?" he asks with a teasing smile. "You sure Aiden's the right match for you? I think you have like a thing with Suraj."

I think he might be right—there *is* something between Suraj and me. But what about the tingles I felt this morning with Aiden in art class?

If only matching myself was as easy as matching others.

I roll my eyes, because Noah *so* doesn't know what I want. I mean, I barely know what I want. His attention shifts to the far side of the cafeteria, and I'm happy to be done with this topic of conversation. I follow his gaze to Teá, who's standing in the hot-lunch line. She's wearing gym shorts, a basic T-shirt, and sneakers. But she makes it look good. Amanda's a few people behind her, and while Teá's vibe is effortless, Amanda works for it. Her hair looks like she just stepped out of a salon; her bangs are always flawless.

"Weird!" I say to Noah, because when Amanda notices me looking, she turns and gives me a casual wave. "Is she actually talking with us now?"

"Because of the app," Noah says, waving back with a

dubious expression. "She wants to be a part of anything and everything that's deemed cool. But that may not last long if we introduce Ethan and Teá. Think we should?"

"Definitely," I say. "Matched! isn't about Amanda. It's about bringing people together."

"I hope they're a good fit."

"Well, at the very least, they can talk about soccer. The rest is chemistry. Nothing we can do about that."

Noah crumples the paper his sandwich was wrapped in and tosses it into a nearby trash bin. "We'll have to see how it—"

"Oh, oh!" I clutch at his hand. "Teá's looking at Ethan." She peers out from behind her water bottle, taking another sip. He catches her, smiles, then turns back to the lunch line. "She doesn't even know he's her match, but she still checked him out."

"News flash!" Noah says, rolling his eyes. "The whole cafeteria has checked Ethan out at one point or another."

"Aha!" I turn his chin five degrees to the left. Ethan's looking at Teá now.

They are *so* a match.

I lift my bottle of juice and tap it against the carton of milk Noah's holding. "Cheers to successful matches!"

chapter seventeen

*T*wo weeks and twenty very smooth introductions
later, we've run into our first rejection.

Unfortunately, it's the pair we were most excited about,
too: Ethan and Teá.

Teá is the one doing the rejecting. She has corralled
Noah and me into the library to let us know her worries.
What's crazy is that she doesn't even know who her match
is yet.

Cold feet, I think.

"I honestly don't know why I even filled out that quiz,"
Teá says, moving her hands as she talks. She's a ball of
energy.

"So many people say that," Noah says, using his most
soothing voice. "But you took it. That's cool. Why not see it
through?"

She pulls the hair tie from her ponytail, and her glossy

hair falls around her face—she's gorgeous. Lots of freckles on her light brown nose. She shoves her seat back and bounces up. "I just—I'm not sure it's a good idea. I'm sorry I wasted your time."

"No, no." I wave her back into the chair, thinking maybe we should get her comfortable talking to us before we bring up her actual match. "How are you liking Mayfield, by the way?"

"It's great," she says. "We moved here for the soccer program. The Nunezes are legendary coaches. At my old school there weren't many kids playing at my level. . . . Oh, that sounds like I'm bragging!" She flushes in embarrassment.

"No, no, it makes sense," I say. "I bet the Nunezes are thrilled to have you." Noah clears his throat, and I keep going. "Let's talk about your match. Why are you worried about talking to him?"

Teá looks doubtful. "Is there really a match? Or does the app make everyone think they've got a chance?"

Noah and I exchange a smile. "There's definitely a match," he says.

"And not just any match," I add. "We're really psyched about it because it's almost perfect—the highest percentage of compatibility we've had so far, right, Noah?"

"It's really impressive!" he says, beaming at Teá.

"I wonder who it could be. I've been spending all my time with the girls' soccer team, so I haven't really met a lot of people," she says.

I pull out my match sheet and start reading. "This is some of the information entered by your match," I tell her. "Favorite athletes: Wambach, Pelé, Hamm, Messi, Ronaldo—in that order. Favorite song: Shakira's 'Waka Waka (This Time for Africa).' Favorite movie, *Victory*."

Teá's eyes are wide. "That's…almost exactly what I entered!"

I fold my arms and give her my *I told you so* look. "I've got more, but do you see what we mean?"

"I'm starting to. But I'm surprised. I didn't think there could be anyone who I could have so much in common with."

"There is." I look at my watch and realize our next class will start in a few minutes. "So the question is: Would you like to meet him?"

Teá runs her hand through her hair. "It just feels so… awkward!"

"Maybe for a few minutes," Noah says. "But no risk, no reward."

Teá sits up straight, throwing her shoulders back. "Okay," she says. "I'll meet him."

Today's the day. Introductions twenty-one to thirty, including Teá and Ethan, Kiran and Marcus, and Aiden and (ahem!) me.

Noah is at our table by the window in the library, in

charge of any frantic last-minute texts from our couples. I stop by to say good morning and to leave *The Shagun Matchmaking Guide* with him—I've started bringing it every Match Day, for luck.

I leave my backpack at the table, too, and head to the art section of the library in search of *Graffiti Art Styles* by Unknown Urban Artists. I'm curious because Aiden is into urban street art in a big way. I've never tried anything like it, never even held a can of spray paint, but he's amazing at this stuff.

I pull the book from the shelf and flip through it. I'm early, but worried that Aiden isn't here yet. I'm admiring the glossy photographs of colorful street art when my phone beeps. I pull it from my pocket. The app is set to intro mode, and the alert on it tells me that Blue Seal (aka Aiden) is in the area. I try not to fidget. Or throw up. I focus on my feet and the little sun tattoo I've hennaed onto the top of my left foot.

It's silly to be nervous—Aiden and I are already friends. Just friends. But it doesn't keep me from getting all sweaty and feeling like I'm about to knock down a whole shelf or something. My feet even feel like they're about to get all tangled up and I'll trip over my own shadow.

When I look up, he's standing in front of me with a smile on his face, his backpack slung over one shoulder. He points a finger at me and raises a questioning eyebrow. I tap the *Say hi!* button on the app, and my MI, a silver

unicorn, turns into an actual picture of me with the word
Hi! on it. Aiden laughs. His blue seal turns into a picture of
him. *Chat channel initiated*, the app says. I put it on silent
so we can talk IRL—far less awkward.

Aiden laughs. "Simi!"

I smile. "Surprised?"

"Silver unicorn," he says. "Suits you. And no, not completely surprised. I told you—I was kind of hoping my
match would be a certain someone." He clears his throat
and looks down at the floor, then shyly back at me. "In case
that someone was you. But you knew we were a match,
right?"

"Right," I admit. "I was nervous, though. I didn't
want to tell you and have you end up disappointed. That
would've..."

"Sucked," he finishes for me.

"Big-time," I say.

He takes a step toward me, his bashfulness evaporat-
ing. "For the record, I'm *not* disappointed. If I'd known we
were matched, though, I wouldn't have waited to tell you. I
guess you had to think about it, huh?"

I laugh. "Not *too* much."

"I'll take it," he says, grinning. "So what's next?"

"Most of our matches spend a couple of days chatting.
Then decide if they want to go out."

"We know each other. So maybe we could skip a step?"

Noise on the other side of the library catches my attention, and I'm suddenly too distracted to respond to Aiden.

A horde of soccer types are flooding through the library doors. Ethan was supposed to come alone, but apparently, he decided to bring his friends. Teá is never going to feel comfortable talking to him if they have an audience.

"Sorry, Aiden. I think another match is about to crash and burn. Noah might need help. Can we talk later?"

"Yeah, of course," Aiden says. "Do you want to come over after school tomorrow and help me with a graffiti art project?"

I imagine spray-painting a bridge or a wall or something and wonder if hanging out with Aiden is worth getting in trouble for. "Is it, um, legal?"

He laughs. "It's on plywood panels set up in my backyard. No vandalism involved."

"In that case, yes!"

"I'll see you around four? Oh, and wear something you don't mind getting paint on!"

"Will do," I say.

I have my first date!

"It's an invasion," Noah says when I reach him.

The entire Mayfield boys' soccer team is milling around the library, disrupting the quiet. "What part of 'come alone' didn't he get?"

It'll be a miracle if Teá doesn't bolt.

"Where's Teá?" I ask.

"In the American History section," Noah says. "I guess she doesn't realize these guys are here because of her match."

He points to Ethan, who's taking baby steps toward the section where Teá's waiting, per the instructions emailed via the app.

"This is ridiculous. If we don't get rid of them, she'll take off." I text a message to Ethan quickly, in all caps:

> SEND YOUR FRIENDS AWAY! NOW!

Noah takes my phone from me and adds:

> OR THE INTRO IS OFF!

Ethan checks his phone, freezes, and then turns around to wave wildly at his teammates. There's muffled laughter, but they start moving toward the library exit. He turns around, looking relieved, and rakes his hair back with one hand. He heads toward the history section.

From my vantage point next to Noah, I can see that Teá looks flustered.

Ethan clicks on his phone, waits a second, and then raises his hand in a hesitant hello. Teá's lips tug up in a shy smile.

TRRRRRRILLLLLLLLLL! A whistle shrieks, and there

are cackles from Ethan's teammates, who are spying from the windowed library door. Teá looks horrified. She turns around and walks away from Ethan, leaving one of the most popular guys at Mayfield High in a position he's never been in before. Rejected.

Face. Palm.

Noah and I descend on Ethan. "Well done," Noah says. "That had to be the worst way you could possibly have handled this."

Ethan's frowning. "I'm sorry—I know! Once the guys got wind of why I was headed for the library, they wouldn't leave me alone. Did I blow my shot?"

"Maybe," I tell him. I'm extra grouchy, seeing as how his team's stunt interrupted *my* introduction, too. "And after all the convincing Teá needed to give this a chance."

A grin lights up Ethan's face. "So that's how you say her name? Tay-yah," he says, trying it out. "I've seen her play. She's the best."

"She transferred to Mayfield because the girls' soccer team is so good." I lean back and look at him. "She's serious about it."

"She reminds me of Tiffany Roberts," Ethan says. "When she played for the 1999 national team. She's a college coach now. Recruited my sister to UCF."

"Wait. Is that Tiffany Roberts Sahaydak? Teá listed her as one of her inspirations, because she's Filipino American and a national soccer star. A connection that wasn't even on your quiz!"

Ethan gives me a crooked smile. It's easy to see why girls like him. He's adorable even when he's embarrassed and wearing mud-crusted soccer sneakers.

"You know," Noah says. "You and Teá were the strongest match we've had so far."

"Whoa!" Ethan says. "With the bizarre answers I put in?"

"It doesn't work unless the answers are genuine," I say. "Don't tell me your soccer buddies put in answers for you."

"They did," Ethan says.

"What?" I yell, earning a glare from the librarian. "You're supposed to fill in your own quiz!"

"The answers were all mine." Ethan grips his hands together nervously. "Kevin, Brad, and the other guys—they asked me questions without telling me what it was for and filled the quiz out for me. Said they wanted to see if there was anyone weird enough to like the real me."

"Well, there is," Noah says. "Except Teá isn't weird—she's cool."

Ethan sucks in a breath, then releases it slowly. "How's there anyone who likes soccer movies from the eighties in Mayfield that isn't my dad or my uncle Mark? Much less someone as pretty as Teá."

"Relax, we've checked," I say. "Her answers are legit.

You guys were a nearly perfect match on the values and priorities section. And the memes and the free-form section, too."

"Really?"

"Yeah. Like, she said that her best friend is her rescue dog from Buddy Dog—a yellow dog with a curly tail."

Ethan's eyebrows shoot up in surprise. "I love Buddy Dog—we adopted my dog, Noel, from them. It's wild that she has a dog from the same shelter."

"Would you like to try another intro with her?" I ask gently.

"What's the point?" Ethan asks. "The look on her face when she saw me..." He glances at his phone, and his face drops. "Yup, the app says the introduction has been declined." He squints at us from under his hair. "I totally messed this up."

"We could try to talk to her," Noah says. "I'm not sure she declined because of you personally. I think your stupid friends scared her."

"I don't want to bother her again. And anyway, this whole thing makes me nervous. I'm not an expert on"—he makes air quotes with his fingers—"'dating.'"

Figures. Ethan, who's compassionate and kind and admired by almost everyone at school, is nervous about talking to a girl. He must have the beginnings of a crush on Teá; otherwise why would he care?

"I have some ideas," I say. "Maybe it'll go better if you

guys run into each other doing something you both like. Like at a soccer game, or the animal shelter…"

"Too bad Woofstock got called off," Noah says. "Would've been perfect."

"What's Woofstock?" I ask.

"The annual fund-raiser for the Buddy Dog shelter," Ethan says. "It's a charity soccer game between the Buddy Dog volunteers and the guys' team from Rutgers. But Rutgers had a game rescheduled because of weather, and they can't play."

Noah nods. "Sucks!"

"You know about this?" It's not the type of thing that he's usually into.

"Yeah. We adopted Winston from Buddy Dog. I'm still on their mailing list." He grabs my arm. "Wait!" I know that look in his eyes. A plan is taking shape.

"Is the fund-raiser just a game? Or was other stuff supposed to go on?"

"In the past, there's been an adoptable-dog showcase at halftime," Ethan says. "Food stalls. Face painting. But none of that works without the game. It's the main event."

Noah grins. "I have an idea. But I'll need your help convincing Pinter and the Nunezes."

"What're you thinking?" I ask.

"That the Mayfield soccer teams could play. People could buy tickets to watch a boys versus girls charity match. The proceeds would benefit Buddy Dog, obviously.

And after those dudes"—he points to the door behind which Ethan's teammates are still making silly sounds— "screwed up your introduction, it shouldn't be hard to convince them to volunteer to play. That'll give you and Teá a chance to talk. No pressure. Plus you'll help raise money for an organization you both care about."

I'm grinning. "You're brilliant, Noah," I say. "We'll make it happen!"

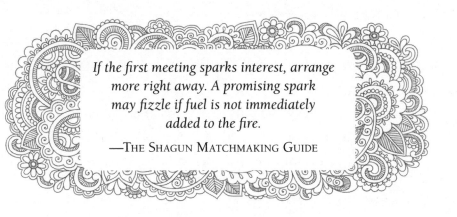

chapter eighteen

I look over my torn jeans and faded middle school T-shirt that says WILSON WILDCATS for the tenth time. Aiden did say to dress in something I didn't mind getting paint on, but I still want to look cute. I send Noah a selfie with a question mark. He sends me back a thumbs-up emoji.

"Mom, I'm biking to Aiden's to work on an art project," I yell on my way to the door.

"Wait, who's Aiden?" Mom asks, coming out of her office.

"Aiden James," I say. "Remember when you volunteered in the lunchroom in elementary school? He's the white boy with the curly hair that had to sit at the nut-free table because he has an allergy. Plays the clarinet."

"Oh, yes," Mom says. "What's he like now?"

"Older, taller," I say. "Still into art. He's in my class with Ms. Furst."

"I didn't know you did projects together," Mom says.

"We don't, normally. This is…something new."

"But I thought everything in your portfolio had to be made by you?"

Honestly, what's with the interrogation?

"It does. Aiden offered to show me how to use an art technique I've never tried, and I might teach him a thing or two about mehendi. I'll be back by six, okay?"

"Text me if you're running late," Mom says before ducking back into her office.

Aiden's waiting for me in his driveway.

I'm glad I didn't dress up, because his T-shirt is covered in paint and his jeans have holes, too. He has a bandanna holding some of his long curls back, which makes him look a bit like a pirate. My heart does a little flip at the sight of him. "You ready to tag some boards?" he asks.

"Sure." I hit the kickstand and leave my bike in the driveway.

Aiden leads the way into the backyard, where a large

brown dog with a gray muzzle jumps up to greet us with a howl of joy.

"Down, Rex," Aiden says. "Sorry about that."

"No worries," I say. "He probably smells Sweetie, my dog. Hey, won't he knock over your boards or get paint on himself?"

"Oh, no, he'll go back to sleep after he's done saying hi."

Sure enough, Rex goes to his sunny spot in the grass and curls up while Aiden shows me some huge boards covered with street art in various stages of completeness. They look really complicated. I'm super impressed.

"Do you just throw those pieces together, or do you plan them out?" I ask.

"A bit of both." He hands me his sketchbook. "I usually try and do a sketch first."

"These are great!" I flip through the pages, each covered with miniature graffiti art made with markers in every color imaginable.

Aiden points at one of the plywood boards. "I'm working on finishing this one. Want to help?"

"I don't want to mess up your work," I say.

"You definitely won't." Aiden hands me a spray can of green paint. "Before you start, you need protection. Scarf, hat, gloves…"

"You're not wearing gloves," I point out.

He hands me a set of rubber gloves and a mask. So much for looking cute. "I'm used to it. Ready?"

He shows me the basics of tagging, and soon we're working alongside each other. I try some of my mehendi motifs on the plywood board Aiden uses for practice, giving him a few pointers as I go. I'm used to working in miniature, but I love the feeling of letting loose and creating them on a huge scale, reaching high and wide with paisleys, peacocks, vines, and lotuses.

Aiden seems to be as blown away by my work as I am by his. "That looks fantastic," he says.

"Yours, too," I say. "Though to be honest, I have no idea what that spells out."

He laughs. "It's wildstyle. You're not supposed to be able to read the letters."

"I love the shadows and shading. And the colors!"

"Want to add some of your motifs around my letters?"

I hesitate. "Isn't that your good board?"

"Nah. I'll roll paint over the whole thing and start again tomorrow. This is just practice."

"Okay," I say, excited by the idea. I get to work, swirling paint over the huge board, a lot like I swirl henna over ankles and palms. When I've had my fill, I say, "Thanks for letting me waste your paint."

Aiden smiles. "You can waste my paint anytime."

"In that case." I shake a can of paint and point it at him. "Maybe I will."

"Ooooh no." He shakes his head.

"Ooooh yes," I say. But instead of spraying him with

paint, I grab my bottle of water and squirt him with it. The stream catches him on the chest and face, soaking his curls.

"Hey, that feels good," he says. "You should try it... with a hose." He dashes toward the porch, grabs the garden hose, and cranks it on.

"No!" I run across the grass laughing while Aiden chases me with the hose. Using my water bottle, I retaliate as best I can. Even Rex jumps up to join in the fun. A few minutes later, we're all soaking wet and gasping for breath.

"I think the app was right," Aiden says as we sit on the lawn, letting the sun warm us up. He leans close, picking a blade of grass from my hair, and for a second, I think he might kiss me. But Rex jumps between us, licking Aiden's face, then mine, until we're rolling in the grass, laughing again.

It's the best afternoon I've had in forever.

"How was it?" Noah asks the following day. We're at the mall, checking out a new makeup line he's been researching before we're due to meet up with Teá. Every so often, he turns to look at me like I've grown horns. Like he expects me to be different. I want to tell him that I'll spill about Aiden if he tells me who he matched with but I don't. I know I could force Navdeep to tell me, but even the thought sends a hot wave of guilt through me.

"So. Much. Fun!" I say. "We tagged but, like, legally. I think paint is going to live under my fingernails forever, even though I had two showers after. And get this—he invited me to go to 'Burban with him on Friday."

"Oh, yeah," Noah says. "I've heard he and the popular kids go there a lot."

"He told me it's his friends' tradition: pigging out on sweets every Friday night. You know, as a way to start the weekend."

I don't mention that I'm nervous about it. Not because I'll be hanging out with Aiden—I know now that he and I have fun together—but because his friends aren't exactly *my* friends. They're on another level, socially, is the truth of it. I like hanging out at 'Burban, our local coffee and dessert café, but with Noah. I'm not sure where I'll fit in with Aiden and his group.

"Whoa," Noah says. "Two dates in less than a week, and one with his friends? You're moving up in the world, Simi. I'm kind of jealous."

I roll my eyes.

"You have your matches. How's it going with that?"

He flinches. "Fine."

"What does fine mean?"

"Like fineeee. I'm figuring out who I like the most."

"So, you're like chatting?"

"Yeah."

"When did you start?"

"Questions much?"

I bite my bottom lip. He'd usually gush about it all and tell me everything he liked about each guy. He's all about the details.

"Just want to keep it to myself. I've been on other apps before and—"

"You what? You have?" My eyes feel like they're going to fall right out of my face.

"Yeah, just to chat. There are so few out kids at our school."

"But…"

He then starts rambling about this and that, and pulling out more makeup for me to try.

Aren't best friends supposed to share everything?

"Tell me more about the project you two worked on yesterday."

"It was street art, on a big board. Aiden's a genius with a can of spray paint. It was weird trying to supersize mehendi designs," I say, playing with a bright purple eye shadow. "But in a good way. A creative stretch."

Noah hands me a rosy gold shadow instead. It's gorgeous. "Did you like enormous mehendi better than regular mehendi?"

"I don't think so," I say, rubbing some on my hand to check out the effect. "There's something special about the way traditional mehendi is so organic. You know?"

"Get that one, for sure. And yeah, I think I do," Noah

says. "The stain looks different on each person's skin. Just like makeup."

"Exactly. You don't get that with the white henna I tried, either. It's just paint and it looks exactly the same every time. . . . The mehendi always turns out unique. Something to do with pH. The problem with using it as an art medium is that it fades, so it's temporary. I think whatever I come up with for my signature project has to be permanent."

"You could take pictures of your mehendi designs," Noah says as we head toward the checkout. "The photograph could count as your project, right?"

"But I'm an artist, not a photographer," I say, trying to take frustration out of my voice.

Noah shrugs. "You'll figure it out, Simi."

"I hope so. I'm running out of time for my signature project."

"But you've been busy with the app. Speaking of which—Tea's in half an hour, right?"

"Yeah. Let's hope we can convince her to go along with the Woofstock charity soccer match. Your idea was great!"

"I think she'll do it for the dogs," Noah says as the cashier rings up our purchases—the eye shadow for me, and a whole basket of stuff for him.

"And we can tell her Ethan's helping us organize it because he loves dogs, too," I say. "That might help push her toward giving him another chance."

"Worth a shot," Noah says.

"So you bailed," I say, pushing a mocha toward Teá.

We decided to meet at the coffee shop in Teá's neighborhood because Noah suggested she might be more comfortable. I think he was right.

"Yeah, I'm sorry—it all happened so fast. I've seen that boy on the soccer field. What's his name?"

"Ethan Pérez," Noah says, and I can't help chuckling.

"What?" Teá asks.

"Nothing," I say. "It's just that everyone at Mayfield knows Ethan's name."

"I'm mostly trying to remember my teachers' names," Teá says, sounding apologetic. "I can't keep track of every kid."

"Sure, that's understandable," Noah says. "You just got here."

"So Ethan," Teá says after a sip of her mocha. "Doesn't he have a girlfriend? I've seen him with that brunette girl and her friends."

"Amanda Taylor," I say. "They went out last year. And yes, she still hangs around him, but they're definitely not a thing. Ethan's not interested, and he's made that pretty clear."

"Maybe, but if they have history, I don't know.... She doesn't seem like someone to be messed with. And besides…"

"What?" I ask.

"I'm not really the type to date the hottest guy in school, especially when there's already someone in the picture. It's just not me. I have so much to deal with right now. School, practice, matches, tests, homework. I don't have time for drama. I may not have known Ethan's name, but I know he is popular. We're too different."

I reach out to squeeze her hand, like I've seen Mom do with her clients. "There's nothing wrong with Ethan being popular and you being new. The fact that you have different friends shouldn't stop you from hanging out. If you'd have been here last year, I bet you'd be popular like him. You're both like the best soccer players in the whole school." I pause and smile. I finish with, "Really, Teá. Ethan's a great guy."

"I believe you," Teá says.

"What if we could figure out a way for you and Ethan to hang out that's a little more normal?" Noah asks. "Somewhere without the pressure?"

"Yeah," I say. "Would you be cool with that?"

Teá smiles shyly. She's considering, and I'm excited. If Noah and I can see her and Ethan's match through even after their rough start, we'll be able to consider our app—and ourselves—successful.

"Okay," Teá says. "I'm open to getting to know Ethan."

The next day at school, I'm flying high. Not only did Teá agree to try again with Ethan, but this morning, Ethan,

Noah, and I met with Principal Pinter and convinced her that Mayfield High's involvement in Woofstock is a fantastic idea. She was supportive of our community helping a local organization, especially one that has a connection with so many families in our student body. She okayed the charity soccer tournament, and right after, Ethan got the soccer teams and their coaches, Mr. and Mrs. Nunez, on board.

Everything's falling into place!

"We made the school paper again," Noah tells me when I join him for lunch in the cafeteria, this time at a table near the gym exit. As soon as we were outed as Matched!'s creators, people began swarming our old table, some wanting to know the ins and outs of the app, but most wanting the lowdown on who their top matches are. We've taken to moving to a new table each day, the only chance we have to talk in private, at least until we're spotted. He waves the *Mayfield Mirror* in my face. "It's an actual review!"

"Are you serious?" I set my tray down, then spend a minute gently turning down a few classmates who've come requesting mehendi designs. Once they're gone, I say to Noah, "Will you read what it says?"

"*Hot and Trending*," he says in a mock newscaster voice. "*The Matched! app is full of awesome! When the post announcing the app first appeared on the Mayfield Secrets page, people were intrigued.*" Noah looks at me and grins, then continues. "*But now the app has become a sensation. Created* by Mayfield's own Simran and Navdeep Sangha and Noah Siegal, it's Match.com meets Harry Potter."

"Go on!" I say, enjoying every line.

"*Most of Mayfield's students have been analyzed by the app—like a twenty-first-century sorting hat—and discovered their unique Match Icon, an indicator of each user's personality. Match Icons are appearing all over school. Are you an owl, a hawk, or a seal? And who's your perfect match? Mayfield High students say they're having a blast connecting with others.*"

"It's a glowing review!"

"Wait, there's more," Noah says. "*There was a rumor that the app might have been a beta test by a famous software company, or a well-funded startup, but our investigation confirms that it's a Mayfield High student-run program that's full of awesome!*"

"Full of awesome!" I beam at Noah.

"You read the rest," he says, and I take the sheet of newsprint from him.

"*But what's next from the Matched! app? Rumor has it that the app's creators—the Sangha sibs and Noah—have been hard at work pairing users up in the school library.*"

I stop reading—oops. Principal Pinter's not going to like this. She made it clear that she didn't want students using the app during school hours, and now the fact that Noah and I are setting couples up on school grounds has been published in the paper.

This could mean trouble.

Noah looks worried. "I think we need to talk to Ankit about this. He's editor in chief, and we have to get ahead of the news—especially with Woofstock coming up."

"But he's all about breaking stories." I pause to wave at Jassi and Priya, who are passing by, watching Noah and me with curious expressions. I lower my voice, not wanting to add fuel to the gossip fire. "I'm not sure he'll cooperate."

"Word is that Maya Ramachandran and Ankit like each other because of Matched!," Noah says. "I'd say he owes us."

He's right. Ankit owes us. "I'll talk to him. Maybe we can promise him a Woofstock exclusive."

The *Mayfield Mirror* must be having its best circulation day in history. Seems like everyone in the cafeteria has a copy. I page through the one I snagged from Noah. "What else is in here?" I ask. "It can't just be the Matched! review selling out the paper."

He flips back a page and points: *Student Council Proposes a Student Dress Code Review.* "They're suggesting all visible tattoos be banned, including temporary tattoos."

I roll my eyes. "That's got to be Amanda's doing." She was recently elected class president, and she's been suggesting the most ridiculous policy changes.

"Do you think mehendi will count?" Noah asks.

"I think it annoys her that people ask me for tattoos now. Between mehendi and Matched!, I think she's decided I'm getting too much attention. She doesn't like it when others snatch the limelight away from her—especially me. But a tattoo ban will never fly. The Inter-Fem Club alone will flatten it."

Speaking of the Inter-Fems—they're walking toward our table.

"Did you see the thing in the paper about tattoos?" Amy demands.

"We're requesting a meeting with Pinter," Sophia says. "The cheerleaders don't like the idea, either, so they're coming along. I mean, what's wrong with temporary tattoos? Or permanent tattoos. Doesn't that new kid from California have a bunch?"

"Connor has one tattoo," Noah clarifies. "A little pug. He only got it to remember his dog when she passed away. The rest are temp."

"How do you know that?" I ask Noah, eyeing him.

He brushes away my question like it's a nagging fly, and says, "It's not fair."

"Who is Amanda to make the rules for the rest of us?" Sophia yells. "This is a free country and a free school. Who's with me?"

"We are!" Noah and I shout along with everyone else in earshot.

chapter nineteen

"imi, it's beautiful," Noah says a while later.

I stare at the black sheet of construction paper in front of me on the kitchen table. It's covered in a floral design I made with white henna I had left over. It's not bad, but it's kinda one-dimensional, not like traditional mehendi.

I shrug. "It's too flat and"—I curl my hands into fists—"artificial looking. It's just paint, you know?"

Navdeep wanders into the kitchen. He's been studying, but now he's rooting through the fridge for a snack. "What's she going on about?"

"She likes organic henna better," Noah explains. "Right, Simi?"

"Definitely. But I can spray white henna with a sealant, and it becomes permanent. The organic henna bleeds and blots on paper or canvas, and I can't spray the dried paste on, either. . . . It'll just look gross."

"You should talk to Suraj," Navdeep says. "He's researching mehendi for an AP Chem project. I'll text you his number."

"I can't call him!" That would be so awkward.

"Fine, I'll tell him to call you," Navdeep says, tapping out a text.

"Don't you dare!" I warn.

"Too late," Navdeep says. "You'll thank me later. That guy has become the king of henna."

"What does that even mean?" I ask Noah after Navdeep leaves with an apple and a box of crackers.

"You're about to find out," Noah says.

"Do you think Suraj knows that I hung out at Aiden's house?" I ask. "And that we're going to 'Burban tomorrow?"

Noah laughs. "I guess you'll find out about that, too. You know I think he's way hotter than Aiden, right?"

"Aiden's *fine*!" I say.

"But Suraj is practically perfect."

"That's the problem," I point out. "You know, that's exactly what my mom would think. Suraj is perfect for the same reasons that a career as a matchmaker is perfect. It's exactly what everyone expects."

"Hey, don't hold that against him," Noah says.

My phone rings, startling me.

Noah leaps out of his chair, hopping up and down, biting his fist so he doesn't give himself away. I compose myself and answer. No big deal, right?

"Hey, Suraj."

"Hey, Simi. Navdeep says you need help with henna?"

Noah grins. I frown.

"I'm trying to use it for an art project, but not on skin or hair. I want to do something more permanent on a traditional art surface, like paper or canvas. Navdeep said you've looked into henna for a chemistry project and you might have some info."

"Yeah! It's really interesting. Paper didn't work for me, either, unless it was really dense. Have you tried wood?"

Wood—huh. "I haven't."

"For my experiment, I used balsa wood. Tried different ingredients to see what produces a stronger dye stain. Acid base works best with the lawsone stain."

"Um...what?"

"Lawsone? The hennotannic acid is also known as lawsone."

"Okay, you've lost me now."

"Maybe we should meet up. It'll be easier to explain. Do you want to come over?"

"Sure."

"Wait, what?" Noah says when I hang up.

"He wants to meet up," I say. My phone buzzes with a text from Suraj—his address. My heart is doing this weird flip-flop thing.

Noah gathers my materials and pushes me toward the door. "We better get going."

175

I stop short and shake my head. "*I* better get going. And *you* better get going, too. You know—to *your* house."

He grins. "It was worth a shot."

Suraj's home is huge. Like four thousand square feet for three whole people? That's really extra. We have two kids, a dog, and a home business, and our house is still smaller than this. Suraj is in sweatpants and a hoodie—not so preppy today. His eyes sparkle through hipster glasses he doesn't wear at school as he takes my jacket. We settle on the backyard deck, where the afternoon sun casts a warm glow.

Suraj's mom is excited to have me over. I can tell because she keeps popping outside with snacks and smiles.

"You want pakore?"

"You need more mango lassis?"

"You probably should turn the lights on out there."

He sighs every time, and I laugh.

She hovers almost as much as my mom.

Suraj is taking his mehendi project seriously. He has a bunch of wood pieces taped to a poster board. "Okay, so here are some samples of henna pastes I tried. This one is henna powder with water and oil. This one also has lemon juice. And this final one has black tea instead of lemon juice."

"Interesting," I say. "I usually have black tea, lemon juice, and oil."

"All three?" Suraj is genuinely interested. "I'll have to try a batch of that against my control." He points to the pieces of wood taped to his poster board. "The ingredients for each version are listed along with the length of time the paste stayed on the wood, plus other information, like the pH of the mixture, et cetera."

"This is amazing," I say. "Does it matter what surface you put it on?"

"Yeah, so it reacts with the protein on skin and the keratin in hair and sinks to the lower level of the dermis and hair follicle to give them the distinctive red color." He holds out his arm, where there is still a faint mark from the #NOM tattoo I did for him. "Thanks for this, by the way. That's how I got the idea for the project."

"You're welcome." I'm flattered that my little henna tattoo launched his experiment. "Will the stain on wood fade like it fades on skin?"

"It should be around forever," Suraj says. "Doesn't bleed, either, like on paper."

"This is perfect," I say. "I never would have thought of wood on my own. I want to play with different layers of mehendi so I can have tones and shades."

"You know what's fun?" Suraj asks. "Smearing some of the mehendi over the wood. It's like finger painting and it feels squishy.... Want to try?"

"OMG, yes!" I snap on the blue latex gloves he hands me and pick up a handful of henna. It's a good thing we're on the deck, so I can't stain anything fancy. I hum to myself as I stroke some henna onto the wood. Then I grab a henna cone and do a detailed drawing in the center of the board. It's a picture of Sweetie in all her fuzzy glory. I step back to take a better look at the picture and look up to catch Suraj just sitting there, staring at me.

"You like?" I ask.

"Oh, yeah," he says, still watching me.

I'm flustered. I'm not used to someone as *handsome* as Suraj looking at me this way.

"Hmm," I say, stripping off the gloves. "I should get going."

I kneel and start to pick up the materials we've scattered over the deck. He bends down to help and our hands touch. Surprised, I move to stand, and smack my head into his. Ouch! My skull is throbbing, and Suraj has a hand to his nose—did I break his face?!

"Oh my gosh! Are you okay?"

He pinches the bridge of his nose: still straight, no blood. He smiles. "I'm fine. But I've got to say, you're kind of hardheaded, Simi."

I giggle. "Not the first time I've heard that."

"Are *you* okay?"

I rub the back of my head. No bump, and the ache's already faded. "Totally. I'm a known klutz. Also, I like to thank people for helping me by physically assailing them when it's time to clean up."

He laughs. "I can't wait to see your latest mehendi designs. Promise to show me?"

I grin. "Definitely."

I'm halfway through a pre-calc homework problem when I get a message on Matched! chat from Aiden.

> Any progress on your art project?

>> Not really. Didn't like the way the white henna turned out. But I have another idea. Have a ton of math to do first, though.

> Too bad! I'm looking forward to 'Burban tomorrow night.

>> Me too! But hey, I've got to get back to homework...sorry.

> No worries. G'night!

>> G'night!

I'm just getting back into my pre-calc rhythm when my phone buzzes again. Jeez—at this rate, I'll be working all night. But when I see who's texted, my annoyance evaporates. It's Suraj.

Hey! Have you talked to Preet and Jolly?

Yeah. They have no news...yet.

No news is good news, right?

I think so. I won't be surprised if we're celebrating their engagement soon!

No better people no news could have happened to.

Agree. Thanks again for the help today, and sorry, again, about head-butting you.

I'm seriously fine! And you're welcome. Night, Simi.

G'night, Suraj.

I toss my phone into the air, giddy.

A good-night text from one guy, let alone *two*.

chapter twenty

*I*t's 'Burban Friday.

I'm a little nervous, and a lot excited.

Because I know my family incredibly well and have spent a lifetime enduring nosiness from my well-intentioned parents and my pain-in-the-neck brother, I tell Aiden I'll meet him at the café. I go to Noah's first to get his outfit approval, and so he can make up my face in his subtly gorgeous way. He doesn't disappoint, declaring me "colorful and chic, ready for a night out."

I thank him by bouncing out of his desk chair and giving him a big hug. He laughs, but when I pull away, I'm surprised to see that his expression isn't as cheerful as it was when I arrived.

"What's up?" I ask, joining him as he sinks down to sit on the floor.

He reaches up to the desk to gather a fistful of makeup

brushes and runs his hand gently over their soft bristles. "It's nothing," he says finally.

"Oh, come on. You look bummed. Did I do something?"

He lifts his chin to meet my gaze. "No—I don't know. Not on purpose, I guess."

I frown, puzzled—he was nothing but smiles while he was performing his makeup wizardry. "Noah, if you're mad, I want to know why. I want to fix it."

"I'm not mad. It's stupid. Go on your date. Woo your art boy. Have fun."

I'm pretty sure he means it, but his voice sounds flat, and his eyes have lost their shine.

"Nothing you're feeling is stupid. And there's no way I'm going to have any fun if I'm worried about you." I give him my best puppy-dog eyes, hoping he'll tell me what's up.

He does. "I meant what I said, Simi. I'm not mad. I guess I'm…disappointed. Or jealous? It's weird, you know? Everyone gets to have someone to love except me." He drags a hand over his face, giving a self-deprecating laugh. "I sound pathetic, don't I?"

"No, of course not." How would I feel if he was suddenly with someone that could be something—something real? Jealous. That's how.

But Noah doesn't look jealous. He looks…sad.

"You could never be pathetic," I tell him sincerely. "And I get it. When your dream boy comes along"—*Connor*, I hope but don't say—"and you're busy swooning over him all the time, I bet I'll feel a lot like how you're feeling now."

He squeezes my hand. "I'm happy for you, though, too—that's the strange part. I'm like a pinball, zipping back and forth. I need, like, a hot bath, or a nap, something to help me chill out."

"What you need is a milkshake," I say. "How about I bring you one on my way home?"

He smiles. "Thanks, Simi."

I slip my hand from his so I can use it to frame my face, giving him my best top-model pout. "And thank *you* for working your magic."

Aiden meets me at 'Burban's entrance, looking extra cute in a gray T-shirt and jeans. He's pulled his curls away from his face, securing them with a loosely tied band. There's almost no paint residue on his hands. I hide a smile—he got all spiffed up for me.

"You look nice, Simi," he says, offering me his hand. "I like when you wear your hair down like that."

"Thanks," I say, slipping my fingers between his. Prickles of excitement dance up my arm. I'm holding hands with Aiden James, at 'Burban, on Friday night. I haven't stumbled or dropped anything. I haven't said anything jumbled or silly. I've manifested into the New Simi, the Simi I hoped to become when the school year started.

I try to pinpoint the moment I changed—the catalyst that pushed me into embodying her.

It was the app.

Matched! made me known at school, just as Noah had said it would. Matched! gave me a different outlet for sharing my art—the mehendi tattoos I've given new friends at lunch. Matched! put me on Aiden's radar as a romantic possibility.

It *matched* us.

I look up at him as we walk through the café, to where a group of Mayfield students are gathered around a big table. It's sort of surreal, being here with him, but amazing, too.

We take a seat; I wave hello to the group, which includes Rohan, Thomas, Natasha, and Cami, who are all smiling in a welcoming-enough way. Amanda, on the other hand, is launching ice daggers with her tapered gaze. I shrug her snub off as Aiden asks me what I want—frozen hot chocolate, please!—and try not to see the fact that he's a part of Amanda Taylor's friend group as a strike against him. It's not like they hang out all the time at school or anything.

"So," he says, giving me his full attention, despite the tableful of people. "Talk to me about the signature project you're going to turn in to Furst. How far along are you?"

"Uh, the brainstorming phase—barely. I'm having a hard time getting inspired."

"No way! Simi, when I think about you, I think art. I never would have imagined that you weren't overflowing with ideas."

"Not this time. I mean, I have ideas, sort of. I know I want to do something mehendi related—that much is decided—but I haven't figured out how to execute it. Or what my subject will be. What about you? Please don't tell me you've already finished!"

"Almost," he says as the waitress serves our drinks: my frozen hot chocolate and his strawberry shake. He thanks her and goes on, "Just a little bit of polishing left to do. I'm going to bring it in for Furst on Monday morning."

Whoa, already? He must've done some serious work between my visit and now.

"I bet she'll love it," I say, thinking about how much catching up I have to do and wondering who else in our class is already ready to turn their signature piece in.

Aiden takes a long drink of his shake, then says, "Hopefully."

He pivots in his seat to face Rohan and Thomas. The three of them become quickly occupied. They're animated, and they're loud. They're not leaving me out, exactly, but there's hardly room enough in the conversation for the three of them, let alone me butting in with my opinion.

So I sit quietly by Aiden's side, sipping my frozen hot chocolate, absorbing bits of the chatter that hovers around me. I feel out of place, just like I worried I would.

Someone taps my shoulder.

Amanda Taylor—just as I was thinking I couldn't feel more uncomfortable.

"Simi," she says, sitting primly on the empty chair next to mine. "Congratulations on the Matched! app. It's become a sensation."

"Thanks, Amanda," I say with false politeness.

There. Now hopefully she will move along.

"I wanted to let you know that I haven't received my matches yet."

"I know. We're releasing them in batches, just to be sure everything's going smoothly."

"Well. Since we're hanging out tonight, maybe you could tell me who I've been matched with. Save a step, you know?"

It's so hard not to roll my eyes. She's pretending we're friends to get information out of me? I don't think so. "Sorry, Amanda. That's not how it works."

She clenches her jaw. "Why? Because you enjoy the power that comes with being all-knowing?"

"Hardly. Because everyone else has to wait. And so do you."

Her face relaxes as she morphs from Mean Amanda to Manipulative Amanda. Her voice is saccharine when she says, "But Ethan *is* one of my matches, right? I mean, he must be! There's no harm in sharing at least that, is there?"

"I really can't. That wouldn't be fair to others who are also waiting."

Her eyes narrow—oh, boy.

"This is your problem, Simi. You meddled. You stuck

yourself between Ethan and me last year, and now…what? You're going to try to keep us apart with your silly app?"

"Matched! is about bringing people together, not keeping them apart." I nod toward Cami and Natasha, who are chatting on the other side of the table. "I bet your friends are missing you—though I can't imagine why."

Anger flashes in her eyes and, for a moment, I wonder if she'd stoop so low as to hit me. But then Aiden turns around, looping his arm around my shoulders. "All good, Simi?" he says, his gaze jumping between Amanda and me.

"All good," I say, swinging my attention back to her. "Right, Amanda?"

She swallows and stands, retracting her claws, probably. "Right," she says, before slinking off to her groupies, who gather her into their fold, murmuring all sorts of reassurances.

Amanda doesn't come near me during what's left of my time at 'Burban, and Aiden turns out to be a good date. He's super attentive, minus the ten minutes he spent yakking about music with his buddies. We talk a lot about art—of course, since that's our greatest shared interest—and then he offers to walk me home, not minding when I tell him I need to swing by Noah's with a chocolate shake.

When we arrive at my house after the quick detour, I stop on the sidewalk, just in case my parents or brother happen to be scoping out the front porch.

"Thanks for inviting me tonight," I say, gazing up at Aiden. His eyes are extra enticing in the moonlight; I feel like I could sink into them.

"Thanks for coming," he says, his voice low and kind of raspy. "That app of yours is onto something—I have a lot of fun with you, Simi."

"Same," I say, smiling.

My heart rate kicks up as he ducks his head and moves closer.

This is it—he's going to kiss me!

I want him to. I have for so long. But I've never been so nervous in my life.

At the last moment, though, just as my eyes are falling closed, he veers toward my cheek, laying the softest kiss there. It's innocent and sweet, but all the same, shivers fan out over my arms.

Am I cold, or are my goose bumps Aiden-induced?

If only actual dating was as instinctive as matching.

"That was—tonight was, um...really nice," I say, trying my best not to stammer. I take a careful step back; it would be the worst time to trip ever. "Thanks again, Aiden."

His grin lights up the night. "See you Monday at school?"

The shivers were Aiden-induced—they *must* have been.

"Definitely," I promise.

I skip toward the house, thinking, *Matched! for the win!*

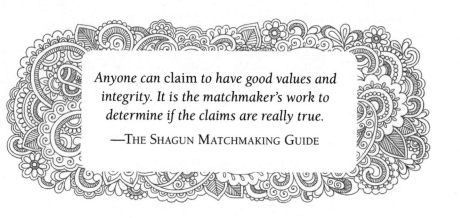

Anyone can claim *to have good values and integrity. It is the matchmaker's work to determine if the claims are really true.*

—THE SHAGUN MATCHMAKING GUIDE

chapter twenty-one

"What is that thing?" Noah asks. We're walking to school on Monday when Aiden drives by in a pickup truck with a big object in the back, covered in a drop cloth splattered with paint. He throws up a wave as he passes.

"I think it's his signature project," I tell Noah.

"It's huge. Have you seen it?"

"I saw a concept sketch and an early version the day I went over."

"You two going to hang out again anytime soon?" Noah asks.

"I hope so. Friday night was great, but I've been feeling kind of guilty about not telling my mom. I mean, I told her when I went to Aiden's to hang out, and I told her that I went to 'Burban, but not that either was sort of a date."

"So next time tell her."

I give him a dubious look; I'm not exactly sure where things stand between Aiden and me. I'm pretty sure he likes me and I like him, too. He paid for my frozen hot chocolate, and then there was the goodbye kiss out on the sidewalk, but if I'm being completely honest, I've been thinking about Suraj an awful lot since I went to his house to talk mehendi.

"We'll see," I tell Noah noncommittally.

"Class, I want to share Aiden James's signature project with you," Ms. Furst says. She has it propped up on one side of the art room, leaning against the wall. "I know you've all been working on your own projects, but it's nice to share early and often. Keeps everyone inspired and competitive. Gather around!"

"Where's Aiden?" I ask. He isn't in the room.

"He said he'd be late because of band practice," Ms. Furst says. "But he gave me the okay to share. Without further ado..." She pulls the drop cloth with a dramatic flourish. "Ta-da!"

There's a gasp from everyone in the room. The board

is larger than life and glowing with neon colors and dark-edged letters in wildstyle—it's the same design Aiden showed me at his house. But the reason I gasp is because the board has all of my henna-inspired motifs—the motifs I drew—clustered around the letters. It's stunning, the way the swirls of mehendi mix and mingle with the bold characters from Aiden's graffiti style. A standout work of art.

"Impressive, right?" Ms. Furst smiles proudly at us. She glances at the classroom door. "Aiden! You're just in time!"

Aiden walks in. His face looks a little warm, like he rushed to get here.

"I was just saying that this piece is very impressive! I particularly like the art surrounding the letters. That's not your normal style. I'm so glad you're pushing yourself."

My face is getting a little warm now, too. I look at Aiden, fully expecting that he'll mention my role in the piece.

"Thank you" is all he says.

My heart drops. Is he really not going to say anything? I catch his eye. He gives a wink in response to my raised eyebrows. My face is flaming now.

What am I supposed to do?

Ms. Furst goes on, showering Aiden's project with compliments. With every second I wait, the moment to speak up, to say something in defense of my work, diminishes.

"All right," she finally says, clapping to signal the start of class. "Let's get to it!"

Everyone scatters to their workstations, and the room

goes quiet with concentration. But I can't focus, because my stomach is all twisty. I should have said something. Anything. A Simi who doesn't speak up when it's important is not the Simi I want to be. But Aiden can't have meant anything by what he's done. Maybe he doesn't realize that it's wrong to take sole credit for the piece when I played a part in its creation.

I'll talk to him later.

But... I can't stop thinking about it. I keep expecting him to come by my workstation with an apology. Or an explanation. *Something.*

He doesn't. The minutes tick by.

He works.

My classmates work.

I keep trying to catch Aiden's eye, but he's studiously focused on his piece, avoiding my gaze. If I don't say something, though, I'll burst. So I walk to the supply cabinet next to his workspace, hovering and rummaging through the paints, giving him the opportunity. To do something. Say something. Fix it.

"Aiden," I whisper-shout, and he looks up, like he's been in a daze, and grins. He gives me a thumbs-up, like we're on the same team and just won or something. But we're not on the same team. Not if he's claiming my work as his own. "Are you gonna tell her?"

"Tell her? Who? What?" He feigns confusion so well.

Like he's had a lot of practice playing dumb. His eyes are crinkling now, the way that usually makes me melt. But right now, all I feel is fire. "It looks great, doesn't it?"

"Yes. Because you and *I* made it together. It's my work just as much as it's yours."

He shrugs. "I don't know, Simi. It became my work the minute it hit my canvas. What do they call it? Found media?"

"They call it bullshit. Are you gonna tell her or am I?"

He shrugs again, like it doesn't affect him either way. "Do what you have to do. I thought you'd be proud to share a canvas with me."

"Proud?" I'm so stunned I'm speechless. But if I don't do something now, he'll get away with it. And from the smirk on his face, I think he's kind of counting on that.

I stew. After painting together, laughing together, in his yard…After 'Burban and the kiss…*I have a lot of fun with you,* he said. And yeah, I have fun with him, too—at least, I did.

Now I feel used.

I feel *betrayed.*

I can't take it anymore—I approach Ms. Furst's desk. "The henna motifs on that piece are my work," I say, my words coming out soft, rushed, and awkward.

She looks up from her computer. "Do you mean that you showed him how to do the technique?"

"No," I whisper. "That's not what I mean."

She frowns. "Are you telling me that you did some of the work on Aiden's piece, Simi?"

She doesn't have what you would call an inside voice. *Everyone* hears her.

I nod.

She turns to Aiden. "Is that right, Aiden?"

He gives me a reproachful look, but I boldly hold his gaze. If anyone should be ashamed, it's him.

"Well," Ms. Furst says, taking Aiden's silence as confirmation. "It's beautiful work, but it can't be on your signature project, Aiden, because it wasn't completed by you alone. And in the future, please tell me when a piece is a collaboration. Am I clear on that, everyone?"

"Yes, Ms. Furst," the class choruses.

"And well done, Simi," Ms. Furst says. "Your mehendi brings something special to the piece."

"Thank you, Ms. Furst."

I walk back to my work space.

I'm glad I said something, but I don't feel better.

And Aiden doesn't quit shooting me looks of reprimand—like *I'm* the one who did something wrong.

I don't draw or paint anything for what's left of the period.

"What a jerk!" I say, spooning a big helping of choco-lava ice cream into my mouth. Noah and I decided to stop at 'Burban on the way home. It's therapeutic—the ice cream, and the newer, better memories I'm making within the walls of this café.

"What a loser!" Noah says. "That whole edgy urban vibe? It's an act. All of it. He was teeing off at the golf club in a pastel whale shirt last weekend. Marcus told me."

"His parents probably made him," I say. "Anyway, I didn't like him just because he's an artist. I thought he was cute. And talented. And, you know, a *nice* guy."

"He definitely isn't that," Noah says.

"I feel like such a moron."

"You shouldn't," Noah says. "If anyone should feel bad about themselves, it's him."

"You're right," I say, drawing my shoulders back. "He totally tried to steal my work. And I almost let him get away with it. Imagine being so very mediocre and so very entitled. I can't believe I liked him." My cheeks are all hot again, and I can feel the tears building. But I won't cry about this. About that ass.

"You know who's so not a white male entitled jerk?" I raise a brow at Noah, who's grinning. "Suraj."

"True."

"And Suraj is nice."

"He definitely is," I say. I can't help but smile. "He also gets excited about things like the chemistry of mehendi."

"Whatever. It's cool to be yourself," Noah reminds me. "It's cool to take ownership of your interests and your talents. You did that in art today, Simi."

"Thanks," I say, beyond thankful for my best friend. "RIP, my first match, huh?"

"Good riddance," Noah says. "On to better possibilities!"

At home, I log in to Matched! as an admin and delete my profiles—both my admin and my personal matching ones. It's not that I don't believe in the app—I totally do. I'm just not sure it's right for me. After, I sit in the kitchen with Mom and a plate of hot onion pakore.

"Hey, Mom? When I went over to Aiden's last week..."

She eyes me curiously. "Yes?"

"It was sort of a date."

I stop chewing my pakora. Mom stops sipping her chai. It's so quiet I can hear Sweetie yap out little barks in her sleep as she lies on her blanket by the sofa.

"How was it a date?"

"He asked me over not as a friend."

"But you just painted, right?"

"Right. But then we went to 'Burban on Friday night."

"And...?"

"We had dessert. It was no big deal, actually. I just wanted you to know."

She raises her cup of chai, inhaling its steam. "Okay. Will you go out again?"

"No."

"Why not?"

"I didn't like something he did in school."

Her hands grip her chai cup a little too tightly, I notice.

"Oh? What was that?"

"He took credit for some of the painting I did on his signature art project. So I told the teacher that it was my work."

"Good. You did the right thing."

"Yeah."

"It must have been hard."

"It was."

She smiles. Pride shines in her eyes. "Your cup is empty. You want some more chai?"

"I'd love some."

chapter twenty-two

Simi and Noah,

I know lots of people have had good matches, but it turns out all five of my top matches are weak. It makes no sense! I'm perfect for Ethan Pérez. We've dated before and we're meant to be. Why haven't we been matched yet? There must be something wrong with your system. Let me know when to expect my intro.

Thanks.

Amanda Taylor

Simi and Noah,

I'm disappointed that I haven't heard back from you. What kind of service is this? I should have been the first person to have strong matches and I don't even have one.

This is completely unacceptable!

Amanda Taylor

Simi and Noah,

Is there a way to strengthen a match? I can pay any fees for my choice of match: Ethan Pérez. This could be a good chance to make money for your company. Please respond ASAP!

Amanda Taylor

Simi and Noah,

I demand to know why I still don't have any strong matches or introductions, and why no one is responding to my complaints! Honestly, does anyone even check these messages?

Amanda Taylor

Simi and Noah,

I've found out from friends of friends that Ethan has taken the quiz!

The app should have matched us right away. Why are other people getting matched when popular people like me are not? Is this a sick joke?

Amanda Taylor

I guess it doesn't matter if I want to quit the app. Because apparently it won't quit me. And now Amanda's stalking it. And us. I can't make Noah deal with this solo.

"She's spamming the app!" Noah says. "It's ridiculous."

"Amanda is ridiculous," I say. "Why's she trying to force what isn't there? She's changed her quiz answers twice, and none of them have come close to even a weak match with Ethan. Navdeep should ban her from the app."

"What about when she finds out about Ethan and Teá? If things go well between them at Woofstock, that'll happen sooner than later," Noah says.

"Then she'll finally have to learn that sometimes you don't get everything you want."

Most matches are going off without a hitch. But there are a few problem ones.

Kiran and Marcus are a problem match. They've been talking virtually, but getting together IRL has been a no-go so far. Kiran doesn't want to go out in public with Marcus.

Because what if someone Desi saw them?

"I'm *not* telling my mom about this," Kiran squeaks. Noah and I are visiting her at her house, trying to get a read on why she's being so secretive about Marcus. "Not yet, anyway."

"Why'd you take the quiz anyway?" I can't help asking.

"Are you kidding me?" She grins. "Total peer pressure. How could I not?" She looks down at her hands. "And I wanted to. I'm curious. I want to be like every other fifteen-year-old out there. Hang out, have crushes, maybe get kissed."

I get it. I do. But if my mom was as old school as Kiran's, I don't know if I'd be brave enough to do it.

I raise an eyebrow. "Makes sense. Okay, well, here's your chance." If it works out. "Why don't you go out and see if you guys hit it off in person? Then you can figure out next steps if you need to."

We convince Jassi, who has her driver's license, to give Kiran, Noah, and me a ride to the mall. Marcus will meet us there. Noah and I will stick around at Kiran's request, in case she runs into someone who knows her parents. "You guys can be our lookouts," she says.

At the mall, Noah and I sit in the food court and keep an eye out for anyone Kiran might know while she and Marcus grab drinks and snacks at the juice bar a few stores down.

I don't see anyone from Kiran's and my combined circle of friends and family who will be a problem, but it's not long before I spot Suraj. "Hey, Simi!"

Noah pokes me with his elbow. He's grinning, but there's something uncertain about his expression, too. I thought he liked Suraj?

"Suraj, hey," I say, still keeping an eye out for Desis who might interrupt Kiran and Marcus.

"Would you like a bubble tea?" he says. He glances around. "I mean—unless you're meeting someone?"

"I'm not," I say, giving him my full attention. Hopefully Noah will pick up the surveillance slack.

"Oh, because I heard about you and Aiden." Suraj rakes a hand through his hair. "Not that it's any of my business."

"It's fine. Aiden and I are...friends. Maybe not even that anymore."

Suraj's lips twitch. "Oh, yeah? Sorry about that."

"Don't be," I say, shaking my head.

His small smile becomes a big grin. "So if you're not meeting anyone, what are you guys up to?"

"Kiran and Marcus," Noah says. "They were matched through the app."

"Wow. I don't know Kiran, but she seems cool."

"She is," I say. "But her parents are old-school, so she doesn't want them to know about Marcus because he's not Desi, so..."

"You guys are on lookout duty," Suraj says. "Got it. So you're probably *really* in need of a bubble tea, then."

I smile. "Lychee, please. With boba."

"Noah?"

"I'm good. Thanks, though."

As Suraj walks away, my phone buzzes with a text from Kiran. She's sent a cute picture of Marcus and her, both holding plastic cups full of fancy gourmet juice.

It's not long before Suraj returns with two teas. He hands me one. "I've got to run—I'm meeting my mom at the movie theater—but how's the surveillance going?"

"Good," I say. "And thank you—I owe you money for this tea."

"We can square later," he says. "I'll leave you to it."

I smile at his retreating back. He's cuter than Aiden. He's got an interest in mehendi—a scientific interest, but that's still cool. And he bought me my favorite boba. So what if he's "expected." I'm starting to think maybe that's not such a bad thing after all.

He turns around and catches me looking—making me spill a dribble of tea.

Same old Simi.

He laughs good-naturedly, then waves before turning back. My heart does a happy dance.

It doesn't miss Aiden at all.

"Hey," Noah says, touching my arm. "There's something I've been meaning to tell you—it has to do with Suraj."

"Uh-oh. Should I be worried?"

He hesitates. "Maybe? This morning, I took a look at the latest stats printout, and he took the quiz. He's got a match. A strong match."

"Oh," I say.

"It's Jassi. Jassi's his strong match."

Jassi? No way.

"Does she know?"

"No," Noah says. "I wanted to tell you first. You okay?"

"Yeah, totally. Jassi's great."

He nods. "She is. But so are you . . . Simi."

There's a hollow feeling in the pit of my stomach. Even the heartwarming sight of Kiran and Marcus walking toward us, hand in hand, doesn't make it go away.

"Jassi texted," Kiran says. "She's waiting by Nordstrom. Should we go?"

"Yep!" I say brightly. Jassi doesn't know about her match yet, so I won't have to talk to her about it during the ride home.

At least there's that silver lining.

"You like Suraj," Noah says after we get back to my house from the mall. "You've been acting bummed since I mentioned the Jassi match. He's cool; just admit you're into him."

I bury my face in Sweetie's fur and mumble, "Okay, fine. I like him. I didn't really give him a fair chance at first. Then we were busy with all these other matches, and I was caught up in the excitement of going out with Aiden, when really, I should have tried to get to know Suraj better. Too late now, though, right?"

"It's never too late," Noah says. "We don't have to introduce him and Jassi. We can ignore their match."

"But a strong match is a strong match, and we should stand by our app. Plus, we're doing this to figure out if the Shagun method works and if we can automate it. We need to study our top matches. And what if they're right for each other and we get in their way? I mean, I like Jassi. If her match with Suraj brings them both happiness, they deserve it."

"Fine," Noah says reluctantly. "You're a good person, you know that, Simi? I'll go along with this for the app—not because I think Jassi deserves happiness any more than you do."

A car horn beeps outside my window.

"Got to go; Mom's here," he says, standing. "Do me a favor, though. Don't send out the new intro invites tomorrow. Take a day or two to be sure this is what you really want."

Wise advice, maybe, but a real matchmaker would never get in the way of a true connection. I don't even have to look at the book to know that.

The next morning at school, on my way to a meeting Ms. Furst asked me to attend, I run into Suraj. He's looking even cuter than usual in a gray sweater that makes his eyes appear more deeply brown. I duck into the art room to avoid talking to him because the Jassi match has really thrown me, but he follows me.

"Hey," he says. "How was the bubble tea?"

"It was great. Thanks again." Ms. Furst hasn't arrived yet, so I move to my work space and start taking out my materials.

"You look busy," Suraj says. He lowers his voice, mock stern. "Why are you always so busy?"

I can't help but smile. "Why *aren't* you?"

"Oh, I am. But I've got time for you."

My cheeks flood with heat. "Nice of you."

"Glad you appreciate it," he says. "So I got asked to meet"—he makes a dramatic flourish in the air—"a match!"

I cross my arms. Can't he be a little less excited about this whole thing?

"You wouldn't happen to know anything about it, would you?" he asks.

"I would," I say. "Obviously."

"And...?" He leans in a little and smiles conspiratorially. Little shock waves go off in my nerve endings and I step back. It's hard to be businesslike when my face is so hot.

"And you should go to the library to meet her."

He presses his lips together and gives me an exasperated look. There's a smile in his eyes, though, which makes my stomach flutter. "You could drop a little hint."

Ms. Furst walks into the room, spots Suraj, the non–art

student, and raises her eyebrows. I've never been gladder to see her grizzled gray hair.

He raises his hands in concession and hustles out of the room, leaving me flustered.

"Everything okay, Simi?" Ms. Furst asks.

"Um...yeah," I say. I take a deep breath to get my mind right for our meeting. We take seats at the front of the room, Ms. Furst behind her desk, me in a chair pulled up to it.

"Thanks again for the lovely mehendi bracelet," she says, holding up her hand to show off the dragon bracelet I did for her the other day. It's clearly visible, though the bright orange has faded to a soft peach. "I've had so many compliments on it."

"I'm glad you like it."

"So I wanted to discuss what happened with Aiden's project," Ms. Furst says. "I have to say I was disappointed. I thought he had more artistic integrity."

"I wasn't trying to get him into trouble," I say, and I can't quite look at her. "I thought we were just hanging out. That he liked me. And that it was a cool collaboration. Or whatever. I guess he thought something else. Or wanted something else. But I couldn't let him take credit for my work."

"No, you were right to tell me," Ms. Furst says. "And I must say that I loved how your motifs turned out in that medium. They're so unexpected, supersized like that. Have you thought about using something in that scale for your project?"

"No," I say. "First of all, spray paint is Aiden's medium. I did love using it, and maybe I'll try it again sometime, but right now I want to do something personal to me. And I love working on miniature pieces with traditional henna. But I think I'm going to try it on wood. I just haven't decided on a subject yet."

"That, Simi, is up to you," Ms. Furst says. "My advice is to choose a subject you have a deep feeling for. Use a medium you have mastery in. Allow yourself to experiment and fail. Only something good can come out of that process. Right?"

"Right," I say with a nod.

But I still have no idea what that subject is going to be.

"How did it go?" I ask Noah during our walk home from school. I'm curious about this morning's intro between Suraj and Jassi.

"It was interesting," he says. "Suraj was definitely surprised."

"He wasn't weird about it to Jassi, was he?"

"No, he was a gentleman."

"He didn't decline?" I ask, undeniably envious of Jassi.

"He didn't decline," Noah says.

"Well, I hope they're a good match."

He shrugs. "They have a lot in common and they have

208

a similar sense of humor. Definitely a possibility for something there."

"Good," I say tersely. "The app's doing its job."

Noah raises an eyebrow, looking ready to challenge my response. But then his expression changes. He grabs my hand and drags me across the street.

"What are you doing?" Then I see Connor coming down the sidewalk on his bike. Most people our grade drive to school or walk, but he makes riding a bike seem cool. He sails past, looking like a Greek god. He doesn't seem to notice us in the crowd.

"What?" I say. "It's just Connor. Why didn't you say hi?"

"I don't know," Noah mutters. "I'm waiting for some signal from him or something, but he's not giving up anything."

Dear God, we are both such a hot mess right now. Suraj and I may be a lost cause, but maybe I could try to save Noah and Connor. The problem is, Noah can be so painfully shy and sensitive; sometimes it hurts to watch. I put an arm around him. "There may never be a signal. You might have to just take the leap."

"I don't know, Simi. I don't think I'm there yet."

"It's okay," I relent. "There's no rush."

Some matchmakers we are. Both of us miserable about crushes we can't or won't do anything about.

"There's so much stuff going on right now," Noah mumbles. "Woofstock. Your grandparents visiting. And we're in the midst of ensuring the most spectacular matchmaking coup in Mayfield history—under Amanda's nose, at that. That's all the drama I can handle at the moment."

He isn't wrong. We do have a lot on our plate.

"Okay, but don't think you can get away with avoiding Connor forever."

chapter twenty-three

"Choorian," Nanima says, handing me a little cardboard box. I remove the sparkling glass bangles from their layers of carefully wrapped newspaper.

It's eight on Saturday morning, but we've all been up for hours—since my grandparents' flight from India arrived at Newark at five a.m. I'm low-key exhausted, but I'm on my second cup of my dad's spicy chai—strong and milky—so I should be wide awake any minute.

"They're beautiful!" Holding my arm up, I admire the stack of bangles on my wrist. I definitely don't have this shade of purple. "Thanks, Nanima!" I curl up next to her and give her a hug. She's the same sweet-faced, gray-haired grandmother I've always known—she always smells like sandalwood and roses in full bloom, and she doesn't seem to be aging at all. This visit, she's brought me dozens of sets of bangles, in every color of the rainbow—which is good, because I've outgrown all my old ones.

The last set is real silver, a simple, classic design that will go with everything.

"And here's your remote-controlled car, Navdeep," Nanima says, looking slightly worried. "I hope it's okay?"

Navdeep usually sends Nanima a shopping list well before they leave India. He's found a place in Delhi that stocks cheap stuff for his robots and other contraptions.

"Yesssss!" Navdeep grins, revving the wheels furiously. "No one sells this frequency here! It'll be perfect for our new project—after I make some adjustments!"

"*Uff*, stop that racket." Mom pops her head into the family room, trying to get Navdeep to chill, but it's no use. The rest of the day he's racing the car all over the house, driving everyone, especially poor Sweetie, absolutely nuts. At least this means he's taking a break from writing essays for his early-action college apps, which is all he's done lately. The stress cloud he's wrapped in is so thick you can cut it with a knife.

No one has been in the kitchen today except to make chai. Masi brought over a home-cooked brunch and so did some of our neighbors—it's Desi potluck day. We can just relax and hang out with Nanima and Nanoo.

Except they're jet-lagged and ready to sleep at noon.

"Just push through the next several hours," I tell Nanima. "If you stay awake till the evening, you'll sleep through the night and be over it tomorrow!"

"I'm fine," Nanima says. "He's the problem."

Nanoo's head has slid sideways in his armchair. He's gently snoring.

"Nanoo." I shake his arm. "Wake up!"

He wakes up with a start and gives me a sheepish smile. "Keep talking; that'll keep me awake." His long white hair and beard make him look like Dumbledore. He's always had the wise-wizard thing down.

"No, you talk, Nanoo," I say. "And I'll listen."

"What should I talk about?"

I settle in on the sofa. "Tell me about how you met."

Nanima laughs—I've heard the story so many times—but it only gets better. So she drapes her arm and shawl around me and pulls me close.

"Nanoo was in college with my brother, and they became friends," Nanima starts. "Then one day he came over to visit, and that's when it all started."

"I didn't live far away, so I rode down on my cycle," Nanoo says. "It was faster than walking. But when I got close to my friend's house, I saw him walking down the lane with the prettiest girl I'd ever seen."

"Nanima!" I chorus with Geet and Preet, who sit on the floor in front of the sofa, their arms and elbows resting on Nanima's knees, since there's no room left on the couch.

"Yes, and I stopped looking at where I was going and rode straight into a ditch!"

Nanima laughs. "He looked like a scarecrow when we fished him out of the nullah. Luckily it was full of rainwater—not anything worse."

"Both me and my cycle were soaked and dented when we got ourselves out," Nanoo says. "I was so embarrassed."

"Then what happened?" Preet asks.

"Bhai-sahib went to get him a change of clothes, and my mother went to make hot chai," Nanima says. "She told me to get the angeethi started so he could warm himself. I felt so self-conscious starting the fire with this big, damp fellow staring at me. He was sitting there in a T-shirt, towel, and topknot, not saying a word."

"Why didn't you say something to Nanima?" Geet asks.

"I was tongue-tied," Nanoo says. "Your nani was so pretty, and the smoke from the angeethi was going in her eyes, even though she kept waving it away. It made her face all red."

"It wasn't just the smoke," Nanima says.

"I helped fan the coals to get the fire going. By the time the chai and clothes came, the flame was blazing," Nanoo says, and then adds with a twinkle in his eyes, "In more ways than one!"

"Then he started cycling down every day," Nanima says. "And bringing books for my brother, and newspapers for my father, and homemade atte-ki-pinni from his grandmother for my mother. She had quite a sweet tooth."

"Wait, what about you guys being from different religions?" I asked. "I mean, it had to be a big deal that you weren't Sikh, right, Nanima?"

"Nothing is a big deal unless you decide to make it so," Nanoo says. "We just lit a lamp for both Wahe Guru and Mata Rani in our home after we got married and called ourselves doubly blessed. It's been that way at our house ever since."

I've seen Nanima's little mandir, which has pictures of the Sikh gurus and Nanima's favorite devi—Sherawali Mata, the one that rides a tiger. Nanima and Nanoo go on pilgrimage to both the Sikh Golden Temple in Amritsar and the hilltop shrine of Nanima's Mata Rani. One day I'll go with them.

"That's such a beautiful story," Preet says dreamily. She's dreamy a lot these days.

"But I hear that there is another beautiful story happening in the family now," Nanima says. "Who is going to tell us about the new one?"

"Jolly!" I say, because he suddenly appears. Talk about timing.

He's dressed up for the occasion, in pressed pants and a button-down, even though the rest of us are still in pajamas.

"Very nice to meet you, Nanima, Nanaji," Jolly says, looking adorably nervous. "Hope it's okay to visit today. You must be so tired."

"No, no, young man." Even Nanoo's eyebrows are smiling.

215

"You're the most interesting thing to have happened since we were here last. How are you?"

"Thank you, sir," Jolly says, going pink behind his clipped beard. "My mother sends some atte-ki-pinni. She was told Nani likes it." He goes even redder as everyone laughs. "What did I say?"

"Nothing, beta," Mom says. "There was a story Nanima was just telling us that also had atte-ki-pinni in a starring role."

"Was it a good story?" Jolly glances shyly at Preet.

"The best!" Preet says.

After brunch, I give Nanima and Nanoo a drawing I've been working on all day, lying on the floor with my sketchbook even while listening to them and everyone else catch up.

I went with Ms. Furst's advice: *Choose a subject you have a deep feeling for.*

It's good, I think, but I'm nervous about whether my grandparents will like it. What I've drawn is such a personal memory for them that it might have been completely different from how I imagined it.

It's them when they first met—I based it on the black-and-white pictures I've seen of their wedding. They're sitting by an angeethi, looking into each other's eyes, and woodsmoke from the glowing coals is curling prettily around them.

"This is so beautiful," Nanima says. She sounds all choked up.

"Just how I remember it," Nanoo says. "What talent. You're going to be a great artist."

"She is going to be a great matchmaker." Preet's right hand is tucked into Jolly's.

Nanima cups my chin with her wrinkled hand, looking at me fondly. "So I've heard. I'm so glad there will be someone to carry on our family's sanskars and traditions. Simi, I can see it in your eyes. You must embrace your gift, for it is rare. Like me, you are a stubborn girl. But in time you will learn just how special it is."

I nod solemnly, trying to let Nani's words sink in. No disrespect, but I'm so not there with matchmaking yet. I need to see for myself that it's right for me.

"Preet and I have an announcement," Jolly says. He looks shy and proud at the same time. "We've spoken to both our parents. And with their blessings, we've decided to get engaged."

The family explodes into cries of badhaiyaan, back-slapping, and hugs. After I stop jumping from excitement, Geet hands me a pinni—it's traditional to "sweeten the mouth" after getting good news.

I bite into the atte-ki-pinni—sugared wheat flour browned in buttery ghee and pressed into fist-sized balls with raisins and cardamom—and think that the taste of it will always remind me of happy endings. Both old and new.

chapter twenty-four

*I*t's only October," Nanima says as she zips up her wool coat. "And still so cold." The crisp fall air—ideal Woofstock weather—isn't warm enough for her. She wears a muffler and mittens. Both Nanoo and Nanima have their internal thermostat set to Delhi temperatures and need to layer up at anything below seventy-five degrees.

There are stalls for food and fun, including my henna stall. I'm supposed to do tattoos during the first half of the game to raise money for Buddy Dog. But it's hard to focus—there are people and pups everywhere. And the crowd gathered on the bleachers and the sidelines of the soccer field is already totally taking sides. At least half the school must be here, along with assorted adults and kids from the community. I even spot Amanda presiding over a section that seats what I suppose is the whole Taylor clan—all brunette, olive-skinned, and fit.

"Look at that dog." Nanima points at an Afghan hound. "I've never seen a dog like that before."

The Afghan isn't the only exotic breed in attendance; there are dogs of every shape, size, and age at Woofstock.

I hand Nanima the designer coffee I bought her at the 'Burban stall. "Try this. It's called the Puppychino, in honor of today." She takes a sip of the whipped confection and smiles.

I spot Jassi, Kiran, Rebecca, Marcus, Connor, and lots of others from school. Random people I've never talked to keep saying hello.

Noah walks over. We got here early this morning to set up for the event, but he ran home to shower and change after the heavy lifting was done. He hugs me and then leans in to whisper in my ear. "Look over there. To the right. That's Ethan's mom." Noah points toward the Taylor clan.

"The one chatting with Amanda's mom?"

"Uh-huh." He lowers his voice. "They're in the same church group, and all their older kids were or are teammates in one sport or another. Amanda's dad's company sponsors some of them, including Ethan's club soccer team."

This would be a good thing if Amanda and Ethan were still together, or in any way compatible. But I'm starting to get why Amanda's so into Ethan. Her older sisters are serious athletes, and it looks like her mom and dad could knock out a marathon without breaking a sweat—they're

219

both wearing fancy running shoes, and Mrs. Taylor is hopping out of her seat with excitement, like a cheerleader ready for the big game. Amanda probably thinks that if she can't excel at a sport, she'd better date someone who does, especially when that someone has already earned her parents' stamp of approval.

Noah nudges me toward the soccer field, where the teams are gathering. "Look."

Ethan stands on the edge of the gathered crowd, looking more awkward than I've ever seen him. He's kneeling in the dirt, focused on his dog, but I catch him sneaking a peek at Teá, who's got her own dog on a leash and is laughing with some of her teammates. The minute she turns around, he goes back to playing with his dog.

Okay. These two need an intervention.

"I'll be right back, Nanima and Nanoo," I say, grabbing Noah by the hand and heading to center field. We stop where Ethan is kneeling near his dog, Noel, a white pup with black patches wearing a Red Hawk bandanna. Teá's dog runs over to us, and she follows.

"Let me see: yellow dog, curly tail..." I scratch the dog under her chin. "You must be Neva!" She tilts her head in ecstasy and starts to paddle her back leg. "Hey, Teá!"

"Hi, Simi! Thank you so much for setting this up!"

Ethan stands with a shy smile. "This is my friend Ethan, remember?" I say, and grin. "I hear you two have a lot in common."

Neva sniffs Noel, tail wagging furiously, and Noel flops on his back in a state of blissful submission. Teá and Ethan laugh.

"Hey," Ethan says. He's scuffing the grass with his soccer cleat, but his eyes don't leave Teá's.

"I saw you play in the game against Branch Brook last week," Teá says. "That save—you were amazing."

"Thanks," Ethan says. "Your team is incredible. Today's game should be fun."

"Nanima packed some samosas, Noah," I say, devising a smooth exit. "Want to go try?"

"Sure, I'm starving." As we walk away, he says, "Well done."

We're headed back to where Navdeep has set up folding chairs for my grandparents when Connor appears. "Hey, Simran. Hey, Noah! I heard you guys helped plan this."

"It was all Noah's idea," I say.

Noah can't wipe the grin off his face. "But it was a total team effort."

"It's cool to see all the rescue dogs," Connor says. "We're in the market for a new puppy. Lost my old dog in California. That's half the reason I didn't mind moving. It just didn't feel like home without Penny." He shows us the little pug tattooed on his biceps. "That's her."

"Adorable," I say.

"They've got some watermelon-strawberry ices over by the girls' team," Connor says. "You guys want?"

I shake my head, but Noah beams. "Yeah, I'll come with," he says, and they're off. I grin as I watch them walk away, then join Nanima at our seats. A cooler sits on the ground, and Nani unpacks some snacks for us. Sweetie sits in the shade by Nanima's side with her tongue wagging.

I watch Rebecca and Hasina, sitting in the bleachers, their heads close together as they laugh. They're holding hands. I can't believe we made that happen, me and Noah.

A whistle blows and all eyes are on the field.

The teams trot out and shake hands. Ethan and Teá exchange grins when it's their turn, and then the game is on.

When the game starts, I go over to my henna stall. Not much of a stall—it's just a folding table with a box of henna cones, a sign, and a jar for donations. There are a couple of chairs, one for me and one for whoever is getting a tattoo. Noah tied a few balloons to a stone and put them on the table for greater visibility. They look colorful and festive bobbing in the breeze.

"I'll be doing small designs," I say to the line that's forming. "And one hand only. Just so I can get to everyone."

"I'd like a raven."

"Oh, I want a Lab."

"Hawk, please."

"Kitty for me."

"What kind of mehendi are these kids getting, beta?"

Meera Masi asks. She and Mom have come to the field to support Buddy Dog, and me. "I don't understand about the kutta-billis. What's wrong with a classic flower design?"

"It's a fund-raiser for an animal shelter, Masi; what do you expect?" Though I've got a hunch that the animals are more about the app and its personality MIs than about the pups. I still haven't told Masi and Mom and Nanima about Matched!, but I'm starting to get excited about what they'll think of it!

Masi takes off to find our family while I wrap up another tattoo. As another girl hurries off, shouting her thanks, a shadow falls over me. Amanda Taylor, who's apparently next in line, standing with Cami and Natasha. "Hmm," she says. "That looks messy, and it smells weird."

I mentally count to ten.

"I don't have time to do any more anyhow," I say with a casual smile.

"Please, Simi?" Cami asks. She looks apologetically at Amanda. Why is she asking for permission? It's so dumb.

"Maybe I can fit you in," I say. Not to make trouble or anything. "Sit down."

Cami happily takes a seat, but Amanda hovers over her. "What if you get that stinky stuff on your clothes? What if you hate the design? What if Simi screws it up? She probably will."

Cami looks suddenly unsure. It annoys me that she's going to back off trying something just because of

Amanda's obnoxious questions. Who gives her the right to control what her friends do?

"Will it take a long time to dry?" Cami asks.

"You should leave it alone for an hour," I say.

Amanda shakes her head in disapproval.

I rummage through my supplies. "I have white henna. It dries instantly—no mess."

"OMG, I love white henna," Cami shrieks. "Natasha, you have to try it. Amanda, you too."

"No thanks," Amanda says, and walks off.

Cami and Natasha stay behind to get their white henna tattoos. I take care to make sure they're extra beautiful and even add some glitter. It takes a lot of guts to stand up to Amanda.

"But they're the last ones, because I'm all out," I say to the still-growing line. "Sorry, I don't have any more henna paste left. Thanks for your donations!"

Noah helps me get the folding table and everything else in the trunk of Navdeep's car, and we walk back to the soccer field to watch the last few seconds of the first half.

During halftime, the players mill around, hydrating and chatting with family and friends; everyone's waiting for the adoptable-dogs showcase, which will start soon.

"Hey, Simi." Teá has an orange slice in one hand and a bottle of cherry Gatorade in the other. She makes a face as she takes a swig from the bottle. "We're behind," she says.

"Only by a goal," I say. "The good news is that running

around on the field has given you a beautiful rosy glow. I bet Ethan noticed."

Right on cue, Ethan walks over with a few of his teammates.

"That was a great goal," he says to Teá. Praise be to the gods of soccer; he seems more comfortable hanging out with her now. I pump a fist mentally and leave them to it and go find my grandparents.

Navdeep is sitting with them, chowing down on a samosa. Next to him is Suraj, and seeing him here with my family makes my heart do a little flip. I haven't talked to Jassi, but I know they went out. That means I shouldn't be sneaking glances at Suraj, but I can't seem to stop myself.

"This is huge," he says. "Great turnout."

I smile. "It's even better than we hoped."

I'm suddenly conscious of my rumpled Buddy Dog T-shirt, my muddy Converse sneakers, my messier-than-usual bun. I was so focused on seeing Woofstock through, I didn't think about what I threw on before coming. Maybe I should've gone home to get cleaned up, like Noah. He didn't suggest I change, though, so I *think* I might look all right.

"You play soccer?" I ask Suraj, tugging the hair tie holding my messy bun together. I shake my hair around my face. Best I can do at this point.

"Not at their level," Suraj says, nodding at the field. He turns back to me and flashes the sunniest smile.

I've been surrounded by people all day, so why does it feel like he's the first person who's *looked* at me? It's unsettling, but not in a bad way.

Would it be weird to ask him how it went with Jassi? I mean, I am a matchmaker, after all. I have a professional responsibility. I try to think of a casual way to inquire— one that won't make me look nosy. Or desperate.

So did you and Jassi hit it off?

I hope things are going well with you and your match?

Please don't like Jassi too much.

Argh. Better to stay out of the whole messed-up thing.

"Simi!" Noah's running toward me from across the field.

"What's wrong?" I ask, snapping out of my Suraj trance.

Noah's out of breath. He motions to the right.

I turn, and lock eyes with the icy-blue glare of Amanda Taylor.

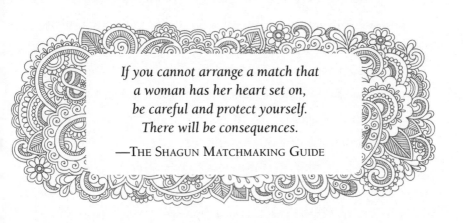

chapter twenty-five

*A*manda's gaze passes over Noah and me, then fixes on where Ethan and Teá are sharing orange slices and wedges of watermelon, surrounded by their teammates and a few dogs. Her face is the same shade of pink as her manicure.

She grabs Cami by the elbow and marches across the grassy field toward Ethan.

"What is she going to do, tie him up and brand him?" I ask.

"Whatever she has in mind, it can't be good."

Unfortunately for Amanda, the adoptable-dog showcase is in progress in the middle of the field. She hollers, pushing the pups and their handlers out of her way.

But karma's onto her, because the wind catches her pink baseball hat and sails it right off her head. It tumbles over and over across the grass, the sun glinting off the rhinestones spelling out her initials.

"My hat!" she shrieks as she chases after it.

She's caught the attention of about five shelter dogs, who think Chase the Hat is a fun new game. A prancing corgi is the first to break formation. It takes only five seconds before Amanda's being chased across the soccer field by a frolicking pack of dogs.

They overtake her easily, pouncing on the hat—and her. They're drooling all over her as they attack her with doggy kisses. "Let go, you mutt!" she shouts, grabbing the bill of her hat. But she's never going to win that tug-of-war. Navdeep, Noah, and I collapse on the grass, laughing hysterically. The crowd is cracking up.

The Buddy Dog handlers have treats and squeaky toys on hand and call back the escapees. "Vito, Peanut, get over here!"

Amanda sits on the field, covered in mud and slobber. Her pink hat's been chewed and drooled on. Her furious scream echoes across the field as she holds it at arm's length.

Teá, brave soul, approaches her. "Are you okay?" she asks, offering a hand.

"I'm fine!" Amanda snaps.

"Too bad about the cap, but that stuff will wash out. Trust me, Neva's drooled on basically everything I own."

Amanda drops her hat on the grass. "I'll never wear it again."

Ethan can't keep the grin off his face. Teá flashes him an amused look.

"Who set up this game, anyhow?" Amanda hisses. "The dogs are going to ruin the field. Who said this was okay?"

"Mr. and Mrs. Nunez and Principal Pinter," Ethan says. "But it was Simi's idea."

I flinch at the sound of my name.

"Simi?" Amanda interrupts. "I thought she just did the flyers."

I take three steps back, hiding behind a few spectators. Noah gives me a worried look.

Mr. Nunez blows his whistle. Mrs. Nunez waves to the players, gesturing for them to get back on the field. Half-time's up.

"Oh, got to go," Teá says. "Game's on."

Amanda stomps back to the bleachers.

The teams troop onto the field. I find Noah grinning. "That was priceless," he says.

"But she's livid!"

"Who cares? We needed a laugh, Simi. And a win. This was both!"

On Monday, Noah and I sit in the lunchroom, looking over the *Mayfield Mirror*. We're dressed in Hawaiian shirts and sunglasses because, according to the Spirit Week calendar—brought to you by the worker bees of the Spirit Club—it's Mahalo Monday.

"Look at all the pictures from Woofstock! They even have one of Amanda chasing the dog to get her hat," I say with a laugh. It's so wrong to find this funny, but I can't help myself.

"When do you think Amanda's going to lose it about us setting Ethan and Teá up?" Noah asks in between bites of his sandwich. "She must assume they're the product of Matched!, right?"

"I don't know," I say, uneasy.

"I mean, no one has ever challenged her before. And she's never *not* gotten what she's wanted. I feel like we've got a big fat bull's-eye on us, especially after she was embarrassed at Woofstock." His eyes go wide as he looks toward the entrance to the cafeteria. "Uh-oh. She just walked in, and she's staring right at us."

Amanda's eyes sear me like hot lasers.

"Relax, Simi. Act normal." Noah peels a banana and takes a bite. "I mean, what can she do? It's not like we control the matching algorithm. It's not like we threw her silly hat to the dogs." He pauses, his face turning pink. "Oh no."

The hairs on the back of my neck stand up. It seems as if a sudden hush falls over the cafeteria. "Tell me she's not coming over here," I hiss at Noah.

He says nothing.

That familiar, petulant stomp warns us that trouble's on the way. I can already see Amanda's flower-power Docs in my head before she actually appears. And she's mad, as expected.

"Simran Sangha." Amanda's tone is as sugary as neon cotton candy, and just as fake.

I turn around, ready for whatever she plans to throw my way. I mean, we're in the middle of the lunchroom, surrounded by people. Principal Pinter is over by the door chatting with Ms. Furst. What's the worst that could happen?

"Yes?" My palms are clammy, but my voice is cool.

"There's no point tiptoeing around something like this, so I'll ask you point-blank. Did you set up Ethan and Teá?"

"Why do you care?"

"Because if you did, I've got a big problem with you."

"Well, I didn't. Matched! did. It's an algorithm that pairs people based on how they answer the quiz questions. Simple as that."

"But you wrote the quiz questions," she counters. "And you must've known that I'd want to be matched with Ethan."

"I don't control who gets matched," I say. "And as far as Ethan goes, it was up to him whether he wanted to explore his matches. Obviously he did."

"You ignored my emails. They deserved a response!"

I set my jaw stubbornly. "It's a free app. It doesn't come with customer support."

"But you were using it as a tool to break people up. That's the same as bullying!"

My jaw drops. "What are you talking about?"

"Amanda," Noah says calmly. "No one is bullying you."

"Ethan and I are supposed to be together. We *were* together, until you interfered, Simi, and we were working on getting back together before your stupid app launched." Amanda points a finger in my face. "Setting him up with that new girl was totally disrespectful!"

She has to be kidding. There is nothing left between her and Ethan—except in her own head. As Nanima says, it's impossible to clap with one hand.

I fold my arms in front of me. "The app is for single people. If someone's in a relationship, then they shouldn't be using it. So why was Ethan? Why were you?"

"If it was a *good* app, it would put people who are clearly perfect for each other together, not pair them with the worst people for them," she says. She's not hearing me; it's almost like we're not speaking the same language.

I pick up my tray and push back my chair. "We're just going around in circles. I'm done with this conversation."

"Good," she says. And then, ominously, she adds, "Because I'm done, too."

She storms off, her hair extensions swishing with every heavy footstep.

"She's bananas," I say as Noah and I walk to the counter to return our lunch trays. "But she's also *really* mad. I almost feel like she's threatening us."

"Simi, maybe we should press pause on the app?"

"No way. Most people think it's fun and useful," I say. "She liked it, too, before the Ethan and Teá thing. Why should we delete it because she has a problem with it?"

"You're right," Noah says. "Most people know our intentions were good. Too bad it didn't work out for Amanda. Maybe it would have, if she'd kept an open mind."

"Good point," I say. "She's missing out because she refuses to see beyond Ethan."

"So Halloween," Noah says, swapping topics—good, because I'm tired of thinking about Amanda. "Can I come over and help hand out candy at your house?"

I paste on a smile, but I can't shake my worries.

Amanda's up to something; I can feel it. Problem is, I have no idea what.

During the next week, a string of weird things happen.

First, I find my locker door's been pried open. My mehendi cones have been ripped to shreds, and mehendi paste is smeared all over the inside of my locker. Even worse—my sketchbook is missing.

I'm devastated. All my creative visions are in my sketchbook.

I consider reporting the incident to Principal Pinter, but I'm worried about the retaliation snitching might bring. Maybe if I pretend nothing happened, it'll end here.

Except it doesn't. When I go to pull my super-fancy algebra calculator—inherited from Navdeep—from my backpack, I find its screen shattered to bits. My lunch account is hacked, and suddenly there's a negative balance. My favorite painting from art class, the one of the vase I broke at Jolly's store, has been ripped from the wall. Ms. Furst apologizes but says she has no idea where it went. And while I'm walking out of school at the end of the week, *finally*—texting Noah, who left early for a doctor's appointment, about the endless pranks—I go flying.

Someone tripped me!

As I crash onto my hands and knees, my phone careens through the air and smashes facedown onto the concrete. I can't even reach for it before Amanda stomps on it—on purpose. A few people see her do it, but they just keep walking. The power of Amanda Taylor, Class President, leader of Spirit Club, School Bully, in full effect. She laughs, does a haughty pageant wave, and keeps on moving.

I scramble up, examine my skinned knees, and then beeline for my phone. The case is cracked. It was a gift from Preet—a picture of the two of us from when I was little. The screen is grayed out—and it won't reboot, probably because of the shards of screen glass that are popping out. I blow on it, shake it a bit, anything to try to revive it. But no luck. I even make a quick appeal to Wahe Guru before I hit the power button again. "Come on," I mutter, but nothing happens.

I want to toss it right back on the ground and stomp on it myself, but I don't. Then it blinks and wakes, asking for my pass code. I exhale in relief, counting my blessings. With any luck, it's still under warranty and I can have the screen replaced. Navdeep will know what to do. Right now I'm just thankful that it's alive.

Now I know exactly where I stand with Amanda. Like it or not, it's on.

chapter twenty–six

*T*he next morning, crack of dawn, the house phone starts ringing.

"Someone pick that up," Navdeep yells down the hall, piercing even my Saturday-morning sleep-fog. Glancing at my alarm clock, I see it's only 6:30 a.m. Seriously?

I groan, bury my head under my pillow, and try to fall back to sleep.

The phone rings again.

Sweetie runs up and down the hall, yipping loudly, excited and upset about the early morning commotion.

"Hello? Hello?" I hear my mom on the phone downstairs. "They've hung up again. Third time."

A warning bell goes off in my head. I drag myself from my warm, cozy sheets and stumble downstairs.

"What's going on?"

"Phone's been ringing since five. I know it's Halloween,

but this is ridiculous. No one's ever pranked us like this before," Mom says.

"Did you get the number?" Dad asks. He's furious. Mom shakes her head no.

"Maybe it's from India?" I ask.

"It's a crank caller," Mom says. "I've disconnected the phone for now." She looks around for a minute wondering what to do. "Chai peeyo geh?" she says at last.

The mention of tea is enough to calm Dad's temper.

"Well, we're up, so we may as well all have some chai," he says. "But I should report the calls to the police."

Mom looks over at me. "Go back to bed, beta."

"I'm wide awake now." And my stomach's all in knots. I'm guessing this might have something to do with the app and Amanda. In fact, I'm pretty sure it does. Maybe I should tell Mom, Masi, and Nanima about the app, even though it's still under review at school? No, it's better to wait until the review is behind us.

"We'll get to the bottom of it," Dad says, starting to whistle the tune that plays before the cricket test matches he likes to watch.

"Who wants breakfast?" Mom says, pulling the eggs out of the fridge, along with the other ingredients for her signature masala omelets: chopped green chilies, coriander, and red onions.

She's whipping up the first batch when Nanima comes down, looking bright and fresh, just out of the shower. She never comes downstairs without bathing, even if the rest of us are lounging around in pj's.

"Good morning, everyone!" she says. "Who was that on the phone? India di call si?"

Mom shakes her head and motions her toward the kitchen table, but Nani doesn't sit. She automatically takes over on the chai duty, adding ginger and cloves to the pot, along with loose black tea. I start on toast—whole wheat and sourdough—and set out the jam and butter.

We sit down to breakfast—with Nanoo and Navdeep still upstairs. Despite the early wake-up, my parents and Nani are in good moods.

"It'll be fun to go to a family wedding again," Mom says, beaming. "Preet will make a lovely bride, and Jolly is a good fellow."

She raises her eyebrows when I crack up.

After a few minutes, Navdeep comes downstairs and pours himself a cup of chai.

"How are the essays going?" Mom asks.

"Fine."

"Are you done with MIT? And UChicago?"

"Yeah."

"What about Rutgers?"

"Done."

"What about Prince—"

"Mom, Princeton is a single-choice early-action college. I can't apply there if I'm applying early action to four other schools. Look, I'm on top of my list. Don't worry about it. I really just wanted to sleep, but the stupid phone wouldn't let me!"

"I unplugged it," Mom says.

Dad walks over to the landline and experimentally plugs it back in. It starts ringing again instantly. He looks at the caller ID, lifts the receiver off the handset, and sets it back down. The phone rings again. This time, Mom grabs the receiver from Dad's hand.

"Hello?" She sounds louder and ruder than normal. "Oh? Of course! Simi, it's for you."

"Who is it?" I ask.

"Teá," Mom says, then whispers, "Who's Teá?"

"Hey, Teá," I say, grabbing the phone from Mom's hand. *A friend*, I mouth, then take the phone upstairs to my room.

"Simi!" Teá says, clearly upset. "I tried your cell but it keeps going to voice mail."

"Yup, I haven't had a chance to get it fixed yet. What's wrong?"

"Well, maybe that's a good thing." Teá's voice cracks.

"What? Why?"

"There are rumors. About you and Aiden. All over social media."

"What do you mean?"

"I mean, they took some down already. I reported them. And so did Jassi and the others. But it's getting worse."

"What do you mean?"

"Everything was fine until yesterday," she says. "And then—bam! They started messing with me, like, seriously!"

"Who?" I ask, bracing for the worst.

"Amanda and her friends."

Oh no. It *is* the worst.

"What did they do?"

"Stole my brand-new soccer cleats from my locker," Teá says, a sob catching in her throat. "They're hanging from the top of the school flagpole. The custodian will try and get them down over the weekend—they might need a fire truck. And that's not the worst of it! They TP-ed our yard. Everyone in our neighborhood is stopping by to ask what happened. It's so embarrassing! And we have to go out and pick it all up in front of our new neighbors before it blows all over our street."

"That's awful," I say. "I think they've been prank calling me all morning."

"Me too. It's so crazy," Teá says. "I can't keep hanging out with Ethan if it's going to be like this. I can't go out with him tonight. I can't even talk to him anymore. I won't."

"He asked you out for tonight?"

"Yes." I can hear a reluctant smile in her voice. "But I'm going to tell him no."

"Teá, don't let her win."

"She already has. My parents are freaking out. We didn't move to Mayfield to be harassed. I'm serious about soccer, Simi. I like Ethan, but this is too much drama. It's getting in the way of everything else."

240

"None of this is Ethan's fault, though. You guys are good together. Why would you let someone like Amanda spoil what you have—what you could have? You can't let her do this."

There's a pause on the other end of the phone. And then: "Maybe you're right."

"Amanda doesn't own Ethan."

"Hang on, Simi. . . . What?" Teá's voice fades away from the phone. She's clearly talking to someone in her house now. "Sorry," she says, getting back on the line. "My mom's calling for me. Ethan came by to help with toilet-paper cleanup. That's so sweet of him. I've gotta go."

After she hangs up, I dial Noah's number. He hasn't been on the receiving end of any bullying at school, but if Amanda's been torturing Teá and me through the phone, she may be calling Noah's house, too.

"Yeah, stay off social media. I mean, nobody believes the rumors but . . ." Noah's voice rises a bit. "You don't need to see that."

Maybe I do, though. Or maybe Navdeep can just zap them away before my mom hears about them from the auntie network.

"I've got nothing much to report," he says, and I can hear him yawning. "There were a few prank calls and a couple of weird messages on our voice mail. Nothing like what's happening to Teá. Or you."

"Amanda's lost it," I say. "Noah, you know how you were planning on coming over tonight?"

"You want me to come now?"

"Yeah," I say. "Dad's watching cricket. Navdeep's barricaded himself in his room. Mom, Nanoo, and Nanima are going to gurdwara. I have homework, but maybe we could watch K-dramas and study together, at least until the Halloween festivities start."

I'll feel much better with Noah around.

"I'll be there soon," he says.

By the time he arrives, I've found us a Korean drama to watch on Netflix. Nothing like binge-watching a new series to take your mind off crappy stuff. By lunch, our homework's done and we switch into Halloween mode. My social media feeds are full of friends in costume. The cutest are the couples in matching costumes. Rebecca is a petite Doctor Who in a bow tie and jacket, and Hasina is a giant blue TARDIS with a blinking blue light on her head. Marcus is a pumpkin and Kiran is wearing a π T-shirt. Pumpkin pi. I can even see Kiran's mom in the background in one of the pictures, so I guess they've talked about Marcus.

Nothing from Ethan and Teá, though, at least not on social media.

Noah and I watch a Halloween makeup tutorial on his computer. We've decided to be zombies, and our makeup is going to be epic. Noah has everything we need, from pale white face paint to blood and gore. He does his own makeup first, then goes to work on me. When he's finished, I tilt my hand mirror toward my face. I look totally undead!

"You like?" he asks.

I'm grinning—the most cheerful zombie ever. "It's the greatest thing ever!"

The doorbell rings.

"Simi, please get the door," Mom yells.

Noah and I clatter downstairs and open the door to a trio of Disney princesses as high as our knees. "Trick or treat!" they chorus.

When the doorbell rings again, it's Ethan and Teá and their dogs.

"You guys look great!" Noah says. Ethan is a swash-buckling Han Solo, and Teá is Leia. Even their dogs are adorable, as Yoda and R2-D2.

"I wanted to tell you thanks for talking me down ear-lier," Teá says. "That's why we walked over to your house. You're a great friend, Simi, and you and Noah are excellent matchmakers." She's practically glowing. Ethan grins, show-ing no sign of the nerves that stopped him from talking to Teá a couple weeks ago.

"So you guys are good?"

"Absolutely fine," Ethan says, squeezing Teá's hand.

After they go, Noah says, "They seem super happy together. Totally worth getting a few prank calls."

I have to agree.

chapter twenty-seven

*D*espite how much fun Halloween ended up being, I toss and turn all night, dreaming up new ways Amanda might harass my friends and me. It is such a relief when light filters through my window Sunday morning. I rush to get ready and bounce down the stairs bright and early, thankful that my app-admin days are over. Navdeep's done with his college applications, and he's game to handle the app review we have scheduled with Ms. Pinter and Mr. Wall on Monday. Between my brother, Noah, and me, we have a presentation prepared, one that will explain the app in a well-thought-out way. Navdeep will convince school officials that everything is safe and under control. Just like he zapped those rumors on social media away before anyone heard a peep. Though he saved the screenshots as receipts.

He will, right?

When I get downstairs to the kitchen, Navdeep's up,

dressed, shaved, and looking very serious. "What exactly do they want to see from us?" he asks, his voice crackling with stress. His laptop is open on the countertop, and he isn't eating his blueberry waffle, a very bad sign. "They've been in our system already as users. They've seen everything. This means we won't be able to walk them through the app ourselves and show it in the best light."

"What do you mean?" I push my plate away, too. The usually delicious smell of Nanima's signature suji wala halwa is doing nothing but making me nauseous.

"You know how we check that all the new accounts have a verified Mayfield High email address?"

"Yeah. Did someone get in without one?"

"Not exactly."

"Then what?"

"Teachers have Mayfield High email addresses, too," Navdeep says. "We never checked to see if emails belonged to students or teachers. Mr. Wall opened an account and got approved when he verified his email. He's been in the app and seen everything. I can see his usage stats. It's like following his digital footsteps. He's seen the quizzes, the profiles, the match stats."

"What's going to happen now, Navdeep?"

"Nothing, I hope."

"So when we go over the review, they'll have all the information we have?"

"Exactly. It'll be completely open and transparent," he

says. "May not be a bad thing. Shows them we didn't do anything wrong. I'm going to see if I can talk to Wally. He loves me." Mr. Wall has been the robotics adviser for all four years that Navdeep has been in the club. "I'll go in early tomorrow and see if I can find him. Don't worry, Simi."

I tell Noah about our little hiccup the next morning while we're walking to school.

"Mr. Wall opened an account. He has a Mayfield High email address. All teachers do. So he got confirmed, and he's seen everything. Probably shown Pinter, too."

"It's a good thing we've got nothing to hide," Noah says. "If they make us shut Matched! down, I'll be bummed, but I'll recover."

"Same, I guess."

"Hey, but we did what we set out to do—something meaningful. We got people to get out of their boxes so they could find someone they really connect with. Look at Kiran and Marcus. Look at Ethan and Teá. And there are plenty more pairs still getting to know each other. Plus, you got some experience in matchmaking, experience that'll hopefully help you figure out what the future holds. The app's a success, Simi."

I'm not completely sure.

"Let's just focus on putting our best foot forward with Pinter and Wall," I say.

We're supposed to meet them at noon. I brought the Shagun guide for luck. Let's hope it works one last time.

"Mr. Wall has been showing me some screenshots of the Matched! app," Ms. Pinter says to my brother as we walk through the media center in the library. "Can you confirm that you, Simi, and Noah are the people behind this app?"

"Yes," Navdeep says.

"Were any school resources used in the development and running of the app?" she says, waving toward a bank of computers.

"No." Navdeep stops and frowns in consideration. The library? But that wasn't for the development of the app, and it's not like we depleted a school resource by suggesting people have conversations within the stacks. "No," Navdeep repeats firmly.

"So I'd like to have a better understanding of how the app works and what, exactly, students experience as they use it," Ms. Pinter says.

"Well, you could try taking the quiz yourself," Navdeep says. "That's probably the best way to get an idea of how it works."

"So I sign up by providing my school email address," Ms. Pinter says, tapping her phone's screen.

"Then I approve your account," Navdeep says.

"Then I take the quiz," Ms. Pinter says, focused on the

app. "Hmm, interesting question...This one relates to academic integrity."

She must be on the question that talks about cheating on tests. We had questions about doping in sports and taking people's ideas in art or writing. Aiden probably lied on that one, come to think of it. Mom's right: People aren't always honest in interviews, online or off.

"Done," Ms. Pinter says. "It says I'm an...owl? Why am I green, though?"

"You're environmentally responsible," I explain. "According to your quiz answers."

"Oh." She pushes back her glasses in a pleased gesture. "Accurate. What happens next?"

"We run the match program, and it gives you your top five matches....You have...four very weak matches...and one strong match!"

"You can't match me with the students, Navdeep. That's inappropriate."

"That's all the data we have, and you wanted to experience what the kids see."

"Nevertheless!"

"Don't worry—your strong match is Mr. Wall," Navdeep says.

"What?" Ms. Pinter says, swiveling her head to look at Mr. Wall.

"He started an account this weekend," Navdeep says, also glancing at Mr. Wall, who's been standing quietly beside

Ms. Pinter. "Apparently you have a shared interest in Shakespeare and early American sci-fi. This is useful, actually. I can put you in intro mode and walk you through the next step.... Mr. Wall, did you get a notification?"

Mr. Wall clears his throat. "I did. It gives me a Dewey decimal call number for a book. Another impressive innovation, if I may say so."

"Thanks, Mr. Wall," Noah says.

"And if I may observe," Mr. Wall says, looking at Ms. Pinter, "the measures these young people took to protect the safety of their peers are also impressive."

"I see that, Mr. Wall," Ms. Pinter says.

We watch them head toward the Political Science section. They look at their phones and then at each other. They're ten feet apart, then two. They have their heads together, looking at their phones and talking.

Are they *laughing*?

"Is it me or are they weirdly cute together?" Noah asks.

"I *think* Pinter is single," I say.

"Wall is for sure," Navdeep says. "Guys? Do you think we've managed to set up our principal and Mr. Wall?"

"Somehow I think we're going to pass this review," Noah says smugly.

He isn't wrong.

"Navdeep, Simi, Noah," Ms. Pinter says when she and Mr. Wall return to the table. "Based on Mr. Wall's findings and what I've observed today, your app does not appear to be a problem. In fact, I'm pleased that you've considered your classmates and their well-being so thoroughly. However, I must continue to insist that the app is not used on school grounds, which includes this library. And should Matched! become a problem—should I find that it violates the Code of Conduct in any way—there will be serious consequences. For now, congratulations on its success."

It's free period for Noah and me, so we stay in the library after Pinter and Wall leave.

"We've done it, Simi," Noah says. "We passed the review. We took a risk, and it paid off."

"You're right," I say, grinning. "I'm proud of us! But you know all the stuff we've been putting off because Matched! was so much work? Maybe we should tackle some of that now."

"Like what?" Noah asks. The library is nearly empty, and it's nice to sit at our favorite table by the window.

"Like...Connor?"

Noah scrunches up his face, then smiles an embarrassed smile. "If I tell you about Connor, will you tell me about Suraj?"

"Sure." I can't believe he's ready to talk. Finally! I put away my books and sit facing him in my best listening pose. "You first."

"Okay. So you know how we've been lab partners in chemistry?"

"Yeah."

"We have a massive report to write that's due next week. Connor asked me to come over to his house so we can work on it together."

"You should obviously go," I say. "Could be a good way to get to know him better. That way you'll know for sure if you—"

"Oh, I like Connor," Noah says in a rush. "Like, *like* Connor…" He shrugs and gives me a shy smile. "I don't need to figure that out. I know already. He's smart and sweet and so good-looking. There, I said it! But I'm not sure he sees me that way. It's hard, crushing on someone when you're not sure if they're into you, you know? The only way out of this is to talk about it, but I have no idea how to do that. Is he into guys? Is he into *me*? I could make a complete mess of it."

"At least you're talking about it with me," I say. "That's a start. How can I help?"

"What's your best matchmaking advice?"

"Go work on the lab report at his house," I say. I feel a tiny pang of envy as I say this, and now I understand exactly how he was feeling the night I went to 'Burban with Aiden. Noah always comes to my house to study, but if Connor makes him happy, I'll learn to share. "Worst case, you'll find out he's not as great as you think."

"Oh, he is.…" Noah sighs. "Your turn. What's the deal with Suraj?"

"There is no deal. Suraj and Jassi? Maybe. Not Suraj and me."

"Suraj and Jassi? So over. She told me this morning."

My eyes go saucer wide. "Really?!"

I could say so much more, but I'm flooded with feels and afraid to believe it.

"Yeah. They went out for coffee the other day and had a good time. But Suraj told her he has feelings for someone else and asked if they could just be friends. Turns out Jassi's into someone else, too. Anyway, Suraj went off to Boston for some family thing all weekend, so I haven't heard anything from him. I can't believe you don't know this already, Simi!"

"How would I?" I demand, still not convinced. "When he said he has feelings for someone else, do you think he could have been talking about someone in Boston?"

"Um, no. I think he was talking about you. Promise me that the next time you see him, you'll tell him how you feel."

"Then you have to promise you won't bail on doing the lab report with Connor. Deal?"

"Deal."

We shake hands over *The Shagun Matchmaking Guide*. Then I hold it out before me and clear my throat. "Matchmaker's log: Two months of matchmaking at Mayfield High, in person and online. There have been successes and failures. Breakups and makeups. Drama and despair. What are our proudest moments?"

"Ethan and Teá," Noah provides.

"Definitely. Some might say Ethan and Amanda are perfect for each other...but not according to our app!"

Noah fake gags. "All those complaint emails she wrote... *Simi and Noah I am perfect for Ethan Pérez. We've dated before and we're meant to be. Whhyyy haven't we been matched yet?* Maybe because *we* don't match people; our computer algorithm does. It's not personal." He gives a little shiver, like something just spooked him. "Somehow I don't think she's done with us."

"I mean, what more could she possibly do?" I shudder at the thought.

"I don't know. But this isn't over." He sounds so ominous, I have to laugh. And shake off the thought.

I go back to my faux announcement. "Ethan and Teá, Marcus and Kiran, Rohan and Priya, and Rebecca and Hasina are a few of our finest examples, but at least three dozen pairs are now happy together thanks to our hard work."

A screeching siren cuts through the otherwise silent library.

"Crap," Noah says. "Fire alarm."

I check my watch. "I heard we're having a drill today. We better get out of here."

My backpack is crammed full of books—I don't dare leave valuables in my locker anymore—and I don't have time to fit the Shagun guide in because the librarian is waving people toward the exit. Quickly, I slide the guide between two encyclopedias, where it'll be safe until I can come back for it after the fire drill is done. It looks like it could snow any minute, and I can't let the weather damage the Shagun guide—it's too precious.

"Let's go," I say to Noah, hustling out the door.

I'm freezing out in the field. I shuffle from foot to foot and rub my arms vigorously, but it's not helping.

Noah's freezing right beside me.

"Stupid fire drill," I grumble.

And then I spot Suraj, grinning at me. At *us*. Me and Noah.

"Hey, look. Suraj's back," Noah says. "New England suits him, apparently. He looks like a young Guru Gobind Singh without the beard. Right out of a vintage comic. How about that promise, huh? Now's a good time to talk to him."

"Stop it!"

Suraj is walking toward us.

"His jacket looks super warm," Noah says out of the side of his mouth.

I shoot Noah a glare as Suraj jogs the last few feet to us, pulling his jacket off as he goes.

"Here," he says, holding it out. "You need this more than I do."

It's heavy and still warm from his body heat when it lands around my shoulders. I clutch it to me gratefully, ignoring Noah's gleeful grin.

"I've got to see Ms. Ireland about...a thing," Noah says. "See you guys around."

Even though I'm not cold anymore, the pinpricks on my skin haven't gone away. "Thanks for loaning me your jacket, Suraj."

"No problem." He smiles down at me, then takes one of my hands and rubs it between his. "You're really cold."

"I'm warmer now," I say, giving him my other hand, too. My heart gallops like I'm running sprints, though I'm standing perfectly still. All the people on the field seem very far away.

"So how've you been?"

"Fine, you?"

"I'm fine. But I have to tell you..."

"What?"

"Your matchmaking app isn't always right."

"You and Jassi?"

He nods and steps closer.

"You had a strong match," I tell him. "Eighty-seven percent."

"That's very exact."

I feel the color rising into my cheeks. Why didn't I keep the percentage to myself?

"Jassi and I do have a lot in common, I can see that, but there's something missing. Something indefinable. And things aren't going to work without it."

"I get that," I say softly. After all, Aiden and I were a strong match, too, and we definitely don't have a future.

A snowflake floats down and lands on Suraj's hair. Suddenly, there are soft white flakes falling all around us. I hold out my hand to catch one, and a couple land on my palm.

Suraj shakes his head. "Amateur. You have to catch them on your tongue."

I stick my tongue out at him instead.

He laughs, then looks at the snowflake melting on my hand. "No mehendi?"

"No, I'm saving it for Jolly and Preet's engagement party."

"Hey, I've got one," he says. He holds a finger over his upper lip. It has an orange mustache squiggled on it, like something a very small kid would make. "My ten-year-old cousin did it for me in Boston."

"That's hilarious. It makes you look very..."

"Ridiculous?" he says.

"Royal!" I say. I can't help laughing a little. What's an Indian prince without his mustache?

"Oh-kay," Suraj says, looking mystified. "If you say so."

He shivers, bouncing on his toes a little. Impulsively, I wrap my arms around him—it's the least I can do, since he was gentlemanly enough to share his jacket. He wraps his around me.

And suddenly, every part of me is warm. Especially my cheeks. But I can't stop looking at him. And he can't take his eyes off me either.

"Better?"

"Better." His voice sounds deeper. There's a laugh at

256

the end of it that vibrates through me because his chest is pressed up close to mine. We stand together, keeping each other warm, and it's perfect.

When we get the all clear to go back into the building, I pull reluctantly away. "You warm enough now?"

"Yeah. Thanks, Simi."

"So," I say as we walk toward school. "Was Jassi bummed that your match didn't work out?"

"Not even a little bit. She's had a crush on someone for ages."

"No way!"

"Yep. And anyway, Jassi's cool and everything, but I don't want to talk about her. I want to talk about us. You and me. I think it's way past time to ask..."

"Yes?" I say, tipping my chin to look at him through the snowflakes.

"Will you go out with me, Simran Sangha?"

I smile. "Yes."

He wraps his arms around my shoulders. "Even though your app didn't put us together?"

I don't tell him that I deleted my quiz answers, that I nearly quit the whole matchmaking thing altogether. It doesn't matter if the app matches us—I know we belong together.

"You know that indefinable thing you mentioned earlier?" I say. "I think we have that going for us."

chapter twenty-eight

*T*he next morning in first period, the SMART board blinks on, beaming Amanda Taylor's annoying face into the classroom for morning announcements.

Someone throws a crumpled paper ball at the screen. I giggle.

"Listen up, Mayfield High," Amanda snaps. "Instead of morning announcements, today we have an investigative scoop to share." She stops for a dramatic pause, then presses on. "Ever since the start of term, the school's been buzzing about a certain app that's set friend against friend and caused endless disruption to schoolwork and activities."

What in the world?

"The students behind the app have proudly taken credit for its creation, and so I think they should be held accountable for the problems it's caused. Instead of saying more, we'll let you watch. Roll the tape, Cami."

The screen cuts to a video clip of me and Noah in the brightly lit library, sitting at our favorite table. My voice comes through loud and clear, sounding foolishly happy.

"*Matchmaker's log: Two months of matchmaking at Mayfield High, in person and online. There have been successes and failures. Breakups and makeups. Drama and despair. Some might say Ethan and Amanda are perfect for each other . . . but not according to our app!*"

The shot cuts to Noah. He's miming the complaint letters Amanda sent via the app. He sounds really mean. "*Simi and Noah, I am perfect for Ethan Pérez. We've dated before and we're meant to be. Whhyyy haven't we been matched yet? Wait—because Amanda is . . . absolutely crazy.*"

What? That's not how the conversation went! Noah and I are onscreen, but our words are all twisted. My head is spinning.

The screen cuts back to Amanda's face, which is pained. "You heard them, boasting about manipulating the app to stop people from connecting. If that's not bullying, what is? As president of the sophomore class, I urge the administration of this school to make an example of these students who have toyed with the emotions of their fellow students and undermined the Code of Conduct."

Marcus, who's coanchoring, says, "The Code of Conduct? Amanda—"

She raises a sheet of paper and reads: "*Mayfield High will be a safe and respectful environment conducive to learning.*

Acts of aggression, to include patterns of controlling or threatening behavior as well as sexual, physical, or emotional harassment, whether in person or digital, are unacceptable and will be dealt with according to the school's disciplinary plan." She lowers the paper and gives the camera a smug look. "That's taken directly from the Code of Conduct—of which Navdeep, Simi, and Noah are in direct violation."

Marcus puts a hand on her shoulder. "Amanda, I think—"

But she cuts him off again. "Because the Matched! creators take so much pleasure in orchestrating romantic connections, they won't mind if I help out one of their own. Watch."

The feed cuts back to Noah and me in the library.

"*I like Connor.*"

Noah's voice amplified over the PA system sends a shock through me.

Oh no, oh no, oh no.

"*Like, like Connor. I don't need to figure that out. I know already. He's smart and sweet and so good-looking. There, I said it! But I'm not sure he sees me that way. It's hard, crushing on someone when you're not sure if they're into you, you know? Is he into guys? Is he into me?*"

The screen clicks off abruptly, thanks to Ms. Holland and a sudden jab of her finger. The class sits in stunned silence with their jaws practically on the floor, staring at me.

Then I hear a snicker from the back of the room—some idiot who thinks it's funny to humiliate people.

I jump up and gather my stuff, my heart thudding against my ribs in a classic fight-or-flight adrenaline rush.

"Simi?" Ms. Holland says.

"I'm sorry. I need to go—I need to find Noah."

She holds the door open. "Go right ahead."

I dash through the door into the quiet hallway. Up ahead, I catch sight of Noah rushing toward the front of the school, like there's a hunting party hot on his heels.

I chase him, catching up in time to see him bolt through the door to the nurse's office, fling himself into a chair, and burst into tears. I go in after him, drop my backpack to the floor, and hug him. Nurse Smith, who's super nice, puts a warm blanket around his shoulders and I hold him while he cries.

"How could she, Simi? I could barely bring myself to tell *you* I like Connor, and she's announced it to the whole school!"

"She's evil," I say. "She wants to hurt you. Hurt us. That's why."

"She succeeded."

I want to tell him we can't let her win. But right now, it feels like she *has* won.

"I want to go home," Noah says. His face is streaked with tears.

"I've called your mother," Nurse Smith says. "She's on her way."

He nods and leans on my shoulder.

I sit with him, trying to come up with a way to make

this better, but my brain is numb. It's not long before we hear quick footsteps in the hallway, and a moment later, Noah's mom walks into the room.

She crouches down in front of us. "Noah! Are you okay?"

His face crumples. "I'm fine. Just completely mortified."

She looks at me. "Thank you for sitting with him, Simi. I'm going to take him home for the rest of the day. Come on, Noah."

They get up, grab his things, and leave. I'm left alone, watching the door swing back and forth after them.

I have a feeling the worst isn't over.

"Simran?" Nurse Smith says gently. "Principal Pinter asked to see you in her office. Your mom's on her way. Follow me, please."

I get up on wobbly legs. Random thoughts dart through my head. Like how glad I am that Navdeep's early applications are in. And thank God he's on a robotics team trip and wasn't here to witness Amanda's ridiculous accusations and her humiliation of Noah. My brother may have walked into the Mayfield High TV studio and shaken Amanda until her hair extensions fell out.

That's a strangely satisfying image, actually.

I think I'd like to shake Amanda till her hair extensions fall out, too. But first I have to face Pinter. And Mom.

"Simran," Principal Pinter says. "Come on in."

She shuts the door behind me and points to a chair. Mr. Wall is here, too, sitting across the desk from Pinter.

"Please sit down, Simran," she says.

I sit and clasp my hands nervously together.

"Mr. Wall and I were very impressed with the app walk-through we had yesterday. But there have been allegations that the app was used to manipulate and bully students," she says. "Is that true?"

"Not at all," I say.

"Unfortunately, it's your word against Amanda's," Ms. Pinter says.

"If you don't mind, Principal Pinter, I think I should wait for my mom before I say anything else. I mean, that's what they do on the cop dramas."

Principal Pinter raises an eyebrow, suppressing a grin. "I understand."

I sit, facing off against her and Mr. Wall. It'll be a relief to see Mom.

Five long minutes pass before there's a knock on the door. The secretary opens it and pokes her head in. "Mrs. Sangha is here, Principal Pinter."

She opens the door wider and Mom walks through. She looks like how I feel: worried, panicked, anxious.

"I'm sorry to inconvenience you, Mrs. Sangha," Ms. Pinter says. "But I fear this matter is serious enough to require your presence."

"Is Simran okay?" Mom says. Her eyes search my face. Whatever she sees doesn't make the worried crease in her forehead relax. "What is this about?"

"I'll start from the beginning," Ms. Pinter says. "Please, have a seat."

Mom sits down in the armchair next to mine and looks questioningly at Pinter.

"So about a month after term started," Pinter explains, "administrators heard rumors of a dating app that many students were using. We thought it was harmless fun but set up a review to be sure it wouldn't become a problem."

"What does this have to do with Simran?" Mom asks.

"Simran, Navdeep, and their friend Noah developed the app," Ms. Pinter says.

If my mom is shocked, her face doesn't betray it. "Is that true, Simi?" she asks calmly.

I nod.

"Goodness, when did you all find the time to do it?" She shakes her head. "Navdeep has so much going on!"

"He was able to walk Mr. Wall and me through the app, along with Simran and Noah, and to be honest, it seemed innocent enough. Complex and innovative, in truth. We asked the creators not to let anyone access the app during school hours and left it at that."

"So what's the problem?"

"Well, this morning another student played some clips during morning announcements. Please watch."

Ms. Pinter hits play on the remote she's holding, and that cringey clip of me hamming it up for Noah plays on the monitor on the wall of her office. Mom frowns as she watches.

When it's over, she turns to me. "Simi, I'm surprised. This isn't like you. Or Noah."

"I know," I say. "The clip was edited. We took inspiration from *The Shagun Matchmaking Guide* when we worked on the app. We didn't intentionally put people together, or keep people apart."

Mom nods. "The app Navdeep showed me last year was based on an algorithm, not manually matching specific people. Principal Pinter, this doesn't make sense." She looks at me and, yes—there's pride shining in her eyes. "You really used the Shagun methods?"

"Yeah," I say. "It wasn't much harder than matching people for Shagun. Just . . . more technologically advanced."

"Remarkable methodology," Mr. Wall says, surprising me. "The questions were thoughtful, and it was interesting to see how the algorithm was set up. I'm curious—do the Shagun methods have a good success rate?"

"A ninety-seven percent success rate, and that's going back three generations of matchmakers," Mom says. "I've never been sure about all this digital matching. My company is traditional. We base our choices on in-person interviews, and our instinct and expertise."

"Which is based on a methodology that can be automated," I say. "At least to some extent."

Ms. Pinter clears her throat. "But Amanda accuses you of deliberately breaking up her relationship. On the clip, there's nothing about algorithms, just Noah implying that Amanda would never be paired with Ethan through your app because of your specific actions. If that's true, then what Amanda said about the Code of Conduct isn't wrong. We have to be firm; cyberbullying is a crime. We must take disciplinary action that will go on your permanent record. That goes for Navdeep, too."

They're going to torpedo Navdeep's chance of getting into his dream school because of Amanda's lying? This is too much for flesh and blood to take.

"Navdeep has nothing to do with that clip. And it's been messed with anyway. Amanda's the one who bullies people. She stomped on my phone before Halloween. She destroyed my locker and stole my sketchbook, plus she took Teá's cleats and TP-ed her yard. Last year, she stuck bubble gum in my hair. And look at what she did to Noah today. All because she's angry that Ethan and Teá were matched and honestly are way better for each other than Amanda and Ethan ever were."

Mom's hands are clasped tightly on her lap. I've never seen her look so helpless. "Surely we can come to an understanding—wait, Amanda put gum in your hair? And *what* did she do to Noah?" Her voice has become icy cold with anger.

"Ask her," I say, my voice rising even though I'm trying to stay calm.

Principal Pinter has the grace to look uncomfortable. "Amanda said she was looking out for the school and the kids by playing that clip."

"She lied. She just wanted to hurt me." I swallow hard. "And to hurt Noah. There has to be some kind of law against what she did. She humiliated Noah—and Connor—in front of the whole school. She probably broke privacy laws, too. If I were Noah, I'd totally press charges. Maybe he will."

"Can I see this clip?" Mom asks.

Ms. Pinter shrugs in resignation and presses play.

Mom's hand goes to her mouth in silent horror as she hears Noah talking about Connor, so honest and vulnerable. When it's over, she says, "Unbelievable. This girl recorded something personal and private about a student, then released it to the whole school without his permission, and you're talking to *my* daughter about bullying? Amanda deserves consequences. And she clearly needs counseling."

"Mrs. Sangha, that is a separate matter, and believe me, we'll deal with it with all the seriousness it deserves."

"Really? You're calling her a whistle-blower. You've bought into her version of the story. I didn't see her parents sitting out front, waiting to speak with you. Probably because her parents have been involved with school council, PTO, and coaching for years. And they happen to be white. There is no institutional bias to believe their daughter, I take it?"

Principal Pinter flinches. Yup, Mom played the race card. "Yes, that certainly could be a factor, and one we'll carefully examine. But Amanda has no history of such behavior, and no record of disciplinary action. This is her first offense. And the fact is, the clip looks bad."

"I know my daughter and I believe her. What I'd like to know is how the clip ended up sounding the way it did. Simi, can you remember what you said and when and where you said it?"

I nod. "It was yesterday, in the library. Amanda must have set up a hidden camera to tape us, and she probably waited for the fire drill to get the camera with the clip." And then it hits me. I can't believe how irresponsible I am. Of course she took it. Why wouldn't she take it? Shit. The library. The book. "When the fire alarm sounded, I left *The Shagun Matchmaking Guide* in the library. I never went back to pick it up, thinking I'd grab it today. But if Amanda had me on tape putting it in the stacks..."

Oh no.

"Ms. Pinter," I say frantically. "I need to go check something in the library."

"Now?" she asks. "This is *really* not the time, Simran."

"It's very important!" I say. Maybe not as important as the possibility of Navdeep being disciplined and ruining his chances for college, but to our family, the guide is up there. My heart sinks at the possibility that it could be gone.

"We'll come with you, then," Ms. Pinter says.

"Thanks, Ms. Pinter," I say, then race out of the room with Mom and Principal Pinter close behind.

I run to the library and go straight to the encyclopedia section. I don't see it....

I look at the shelf above and below where I left the guide. Nothing. To the left and right. Nothing. I run to the librarian at the circulation desk.

"There was a book," I choke out. I put my hands up to show the approximate length and breadth of *The Shagun Matchmaking Guide*. "A very old book. The cover is red."

Mom takes a sharp breath. I can't bear to look at her.

"I left it right here in the stacks, yesterday, during the fire drill."

This is the moment I've feared ever since I started borrowing the guide to bring to school.

"Simi," Mom says. "The matchmaking guide is missing?"

Principal Pinter catches the dead-seriousness of Mom's tone. "Is this book valuable?"

"Is it valuable?" Mom says, her voice shaking. "It is priceless. Irreplaceable. Please begin a search for it immediately. I can send you a picture."

"The school isn't responsible for valuables that were brought on campus without the knowledge of the staff," Ms. Pinter says. "You must understand that."

"I understand perfectly," Mom says. "And you must understand that this whistle-blower of yours, Amanda Taylor, is behind the disappearance of our family heirloom. I will be reporting the theft to Mayfield Police if it's not found within a week. And if a student, a faculty member, or anyone else associated with this school damages even a page of our family's precious personal property, you will not be speaking to me or my husband; you will be speaking to our lawyer, Jolly—Mr. Jashan Singh. In court."

Ms. Pinter's jaw drops open at the transformation of Mom's manner.

"And the threat you've made to discipline my son for a conversation he wasn't involved in is shocking to me. I am certain that if the original clip of Simi and Noah is found, it will prove their version of the story."

"She has a point," Mr. Wall says. "Navdeep isn't in that clip. As far as we know, he was only responsible for the technical aspect of the app, which, as I've said before, is remarkable. In my opinion, it would be inappropriate to take action against him."

Ms. Pinter nods. "Very well, Mrs. Sangha. We'll leave Navdeep out of it. But Simran has suspension for the day."

"I hope Amanda Taylor will suffer consequences just as dire." Mom grabs my hand. "Come, Simi. It's time to go."

"Mom, say something," I beg as we drive toward home. "Anything."

She shakes her head as if she can't find the words to express what she wants to say. "It's not that I don't believe you," she tells me when she composes herself. "I'm not even disappointed about the app. I'm proud of you and your brother—though I wish you would have told me what you've been working on. What I'm worried about is how we can prove that you're telling the truth."

The car falls silent again. I'm too miserable, and too busy racking my brain for some miraculous way to prove myself, to try to talk.

"I'm worried about the guide, too," Mom says, at last. "How could you be so careless with it, Simi? Is that all our traditions and history are worth to you?"

"This is all my fault." My voice sounds rough, harsh, and I can't stop shaking. But I have to keep it together. "I mean, really, it's all Amanda's fault. But it started with me. I should have never taken the book in the first place. But it was like a good luck charm, and I don't know, it just gave me this feeling of history, of confidence. Like I come from a long list of women who know what love is, and how to uncover its magic in all those hidden corners. It..." I take a deep breath... "It made me feel powerful, like I was in control. Like I could make things happen." I swallow hard. "But I never should have brought it to school. It's priceless. And it's gone."

"You were reckless—not only with the guide. You also made enemies with a dangerous person."

"She's a bully. I'm not afraid of her. I've had enough of her bossing everyone around, mistreating all of us for no reason. Noah will get over what happened today. I'll help him. Don't you see? We can't let her get the best of us."

"What about the guide? How will we get it back, Simi?"

"Amanda's taken it. I'm sure of it."

"Just like you took it. Without asking permission. And for what?" Mom shakes her head. "You wanted people to know your name? You wanted to prove that your method of matching is better than the traditional method? None of that was worth risking the guide for.... I just don't understand."

I don't know what I was thinking, risking a priceless heirloom like that. I don't know what's gotten into me this year. Everything's changing, everyone's changing. But especially me. Was being popular really worth all of this? How could I ever have thought that? I shake my head. I was such an idiot. But I can't just let this end like this. I have to fix it. I have to explain. But I owe it to Mom to try and explain.

"Noah and I felt sidelined freshman year. We were shy and didn't participate. It bothered him more than it bothered me. This year he wanted to be a part of the action. He wanted to matter. I wanted to help him and ... maybe I wanted to matter, too."

"Puttar, you do matter!"

"I know that now. This whole thing, for all our mistakes, helped show me that. But there's something else...."

"What?"

"I'm really not sure how I feel about being a matchmaker, like you and Masi and Nanima. Maybe the time for traditional matchmaking is in the past. These days, you can look at a picture online, swipe, and find the perfect person without hiring outside help to agonize over your match."

"You don't have to be a matchmaker, Simi." Mom sounds sad and tired. "Maybe our time *has* passed."

"No, but don't you see?" I say. "The matchmaking app works. We put new questions into the survey, sure, but it worked because of your and Nanima's and Masi's methods—they're a part of Navdeep's algorithm! We found people that were compatible by looking at who they are deep inside—not just on the surface. Our generations-old methods do work, even today. They just needed a little... tweaking."

"You just said *our* methods," Mom points out.

"I did, didn't I?" I'm as surprised as she is. "I haven't decided one way or the other about what I'll do in the future, but I haven't ruled anything out, either."

"That's something," she tells me. "But don't think you're in the clear. You still need to tell your nanima that you borrowed *The Shagun Matchmaking Guide* without asking. And that it's been stolen." Mom cracks a smile. "Trust me, if you think I'm bad, just wait...."

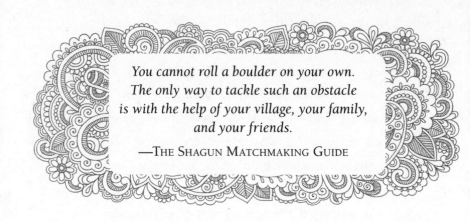

*You cannot roll a boulder on your own.
The only way to tackle such an obstacle
is with the help of your village, your family,
and your friends.*
—The Shagun Matchmaking Guide

chapter twenty-nine

*H*ey, how come you're home early?" Navdeep says as
I walk in. He has his headphones on. I roll my eyes
and jerk my head toward the door.

"Uh-oh," he says as Mom storms inside. "What happened?"

"Amanda Taylor happened," I say. "Long story. Very
very long."

"Nice older brother you are, Navdeep Sangha," Mom
says sternly. "Good work keeping your sister out of trouble."

"Uhh..." he says, clueless.

"The app," I say. "Trouble. Major trouble."

His eyes go wide as Mom crosses her arms and stares him down.

He raises his hands in surrender and says, "Hey, using the app at school was Simi's idea."

"*Chup kaar*," she says. "You could have been in so much trouble today. What if they had given you a suspension? And *expulsion*? And don't think you're out of the woods. No one's in the clear yet."

Navdeep has the grace to look worried. "For real? I just scheduled an alumni interview with someone from UChicago."

"I think they'll let it slide," I say, squeezing his shoulder. "At least where you're concerned. Mr. Wall went to bat for you."

"I swear I'll apply to Case Western, regular decision," Navdeep declares piously. "Wally deserves it. It's his alma mater and he's been telling me to apply forever."

"Forget about colleges for a minute, will you?" I say. He still doesn't know the full story. "There's more. Amanda humiliated Noah in front of the whole school, and she stole the matchmaking guide."

"Wait, what? How? Is Noah okay?"

"I don't know. She recorded him talking about having a crush on Connor and played it during morning announcements."

"What a loser!" Navdeep's been protective of Noah since first grade—pretty sure my brother thinks of him as another younger sibling to look out for. "Poor Noah. He must have been wrecked."

"He was. Went home with his mom and hasn't answered a single text I've sent."

"And she took the guide? You know I've been saying you guys should scan every page of that book and archive it so you have a digital version. It could get wet, or burned, or damaged, or stolen."

"If we get it back, we'll do that," Mom says. "Simi, you better go talk to Nanima. Now."

I look at the family room, where I can hear Nanima's favorite daytime Hindi soap opera blaring. It would be so much easier to let her stay in the dark while I work on a plan to get the guide back, but that would just be another lie. This is probably the hardest thing I've ever had to do, but I take a deep breath and approach her.

"Nanima?" I say.

"Huh, puttar?" Her gray hair frames her face like a halo. "Ki hoya? You're back from school already?"

"There's a problem," I say, and she looks instantly worried. "Not with me; I'm fine. Navdeep's okay, too." I know that would be her first concern, so I put that to bed quickly. She looks relieved. "*The Shagun Matchmaking Guide* has been stolen."

Her face crumples with confusion. "But it's always here, no? In the house. How can it be stolen?"

"I brought it to school, and someone took it."

"But why? It's no use to anyone who isn't making matches. How could your mother say it's okay to take the book to school?" She looks at Mom, who's standing in the door.

"It's not Mom's fault, Nanima. I didn't ask her for permission."

The hurt and disappointment on Nanima's face makes me feel awful. "So it's gone," she says. Her hands shake a little as she pats my shoulder. "So many memories, bachche, all taken with the book."

"I'm going to find it," I say. I don't know how, but I'll figure it out. "I'll make sure we get it back. Promise, Nanima."

"I know you'll try your best, Simi," she says sadly. She looks pale. Unwell. Her voice sounds weak when she says, "It's up to you and Mata Rani now. I hope you'll be able to find it."

"Are you all right?" Mom asks Nanima.

Nanima holds her side and winces. "I have a stomachache. Help me up, will you? I think I'll go lie down for some time."

"How?" I pace up and down the hallway between my room and Navdeep's. He has the door open for a change. "How am I going to get her to give it back?"

"We'll think of something," he says. "What about her friends?"

"Cami and Natasha," I say, waving a hand dismissively. "They won't help."

"Is it worth talking to her parents? Maybe if they know how much the book means to our family, they'll lean on her to give it back?"

I think of how all the Taylors were sitting together at Woofstock and shake my head. Not a chance they'll break rank.

"Does she have a blind spot?" Navdeep asks. "Something we can exploit to get her to give it back?"

I stop suddenly, nearly knocking Navdeep over. "Ethan. Ethan's her blind spot."

"Will he help?"

"Maybe," I say. "But there's no way she's going to admit to taking it and hand it back just because he asks. She's really mad that he's going out with Teá instead of her."

"But what…" Navdeep grins suddenly. "What if she thinks that he and Teá have broken up and he now wants to go out with her?"

"Oh, she'd love that," I say, arms folded. "But there's no way on earth that's about to happen. Ethan is so not into Amanda."

"What if she *thought* he was?"

"Simi," Mom yells from downstairs. "There are some people here to see you."

Both Navdeep and I rush downstairs. I can't think of who would have bothered to come check on me. It's 2:40 p.m. and school's out, so it could be anyone. But I've never been able to count on anyone besides Noah. And I'm pretty sure it's not him.

Crowded around our kitchen counter, tucking into the piping-hot pakore that Mom's just fried up, are Kiran, Marcus, Ethan, Teá, Rebecca, Hasina, Jassi, and Suraj. They're all speaking at once.

"You okay?"

"What happened with Pinter?"

"How's Noah?"

"Oh, these pakore are so good, Mrs. Sangha!"

"You should have *been* there at lunchtime, Simi. Everyone was hating on Amanda!"

I laugh at all the chatter. It feels good to know that I'm not alone in this.

"It's really great of you guys to come. You don't know the worst of it, though...."

Suraj takes my hand. "There's more?"

"Do you remember the big book I held on to in the library on match days?"

"The red one?" Marcus says.

"The one that looked super old?" Teá says.

"The family heirloom you told me about?" Suraj says.

Mom's eyes go wide as she listens to them talk.

"Your friends know about the guide?" she asks.

"Yeah," I explain. "And they're clients. *Satisfied* clients, Mom."

Well, maybe not Jassi and Suraj, but the rest are.

"So the book, what happened to it?" Suraj asks, bringing me back to the problem at hand.

"It's missing. And it's, like, a hundred years old, at least. My nanima is so upset that it's gone. And I bet you guys can guess who took it, right?"

"Amanda," Kiran says. "It has to be her!"

"Except she denies any involvement," Mom says. "Principal Pinter called while you were upstairs, Simi. She says Amanda said there was no book on that shelf and she hasn't taken it."

"She totally took it, Mom—I'm sure she did. I need to get it back. I promised Nanima that I would. And I have an idea. But I need help . . . especially from you, Ethan."

"Anything," Ethan says.

chapter thirty

"What do you mean she had good intentions?" Teá yells.

You can hear a pin drop in the cafeteria. Ethan sits at a lunch table, speechless while Teá shouts at him.

"I can't hang out with someone who thinks that what that pathetic excuse for a human being did was right," Teá says. "We're done, Ethan Pérez. Goodbye!"

"Teá," Ethan says. "I didn't... I wasn't..." His voice trails off as Teá pushes her way through the crowd of freshmen and exits the cafeteria.

Ethan drops his face in his hands, just like we practiced yesterday. I try to keep a straight face as I eat my sandwich, but I'm so proud of the show they just put on. Good thing we figured out very quickly that Ethan could not act to save his life. So, it was all up to Teá to stage a very public breakup. Luckily for us, she delivered.

I just wish Noah was here to see it go down. He's taking a few more days off to recharge at home—that's what the text he sent late last night said. I miss him, but I totally understand. And I can't wait for him to come back and see how our friends have rallied around Connor. Marcus, Kiran, Rebecca, Hassan, Jassi, Navdeep, Suraj, and I surround him at a big cafeteria table. He's exactly as cool as Noah made him out to be.

Across the cafeteria, there's more action.

"Ethan?" Amanda is by his side. Wow, that was quick.

He looks up at her, and she drops a hand on his shoulder.

"I can't tell you how much it means to me that you thought I did the right thing," she says, her voice trembling just a touch. Ethan nods but doesn't say anything. Amanda squeezes his shoulder and moves on. She has a triumphant look on her face as she passes me. I take a page from Ethan's book and drop my gaze, too.

After school, Navdeep, Suraj, and Geet sit at the kitchen counter. They have Bluetooth earbuds and a tiny camera clipped to Geet's scarf. Navdeep's laptop is open in front of him. As they work, Navdeep tells Geet how he nailed his alumni interview for UChicago and is working on his supplemental essays, with advice from Mr. Wall.

"How's the camera setup coming along?" I ask.

"Good," Navdeep says. "You want to see? Suraj, see if it's live, will you?"

They're planning on streaming the footage from the camera directly onto Navdeep's laptop in real time. I can't wait to see if it works.

Suraj clicks something behind the tiny camera.

"Should be good now," he says. "See anything?"

"It's loading," Navdeep says. "Wait for it.... Yes! It's live. Just a second or two of lag, but we don't care about that."

"See! It was simple, right?" Geet says. She is the one who helped them figure out what equipment they needed and borrowed it from her boyfriend.

"Now for the hard part," I say. "We have to get Ethan to ask Amanda the right questions, so we can get her to own up to taking the guide."

"Pity Teá can't do that for him," Suraj says. "That would be so much easier."

He smiles at me. We've been so busy setting up this sting operation we haven't really talked since the day of the fire alarm. I smile back at him.

Geet watches us with interest and turns to Navdeep.

"Are they..."

"Don't!"

"But what's this..."

"Gross. Can you leave it alone?" Navdeep pulls off his Bluetooth and stalks out of the room. "Little sisters don't date," he calls before heading up the stairs. "That's just—it's a *rule!*"

"Whatever," Geet says, laughing.

It's taken a few days to set the sting up, but we're ready.

A very public breakup between Teá and Ethan: check. A couple of innocent hangout sessions for Ethan and Amanda: check. A crash course in hidden camera technology for Navdeep and Suraj: check. Casing possible tables in the lunchroom for the operation: check.

Today's the day. Ready or not, we are a go.

The team's in place. Everyone knows what they should be doing. The most important role, of course, is Ethan's. Can he actually nudge Amanda into confessing?

I look over to the table where he's sitting. If all goes well, Amanda will join him soon and, if we're lucky, he might get her to talk. I'm all the way at the other side of the cafeteria with Noah, so we won't know until after if the operation was a success or a failure, but for now we'll focus on doing our part: keeping Amanda's posse from interrupting the conversation Ethan plans on having with her, the conversation Navdeep and Suraj have wired him up to record.

I text the team.

> Is Amanda there yet?

[Navdeep:]

Almost.

Camera working?

[Suraj:]

Like a boss.

Good luck, guys.

My lunch tray sits untouched in front of me. Noah's is the same. We're on high alert. Amanda's taken from both of us; it's time to even the score.

"You ready for this?" I ask, squeezing his hand.

"Completely," he says with a resolute nod.

Amanda walks to Ethan's table and sits down. No Cami or Natasha in sight. So far, so good.

Someone slides in on the other side of Noah.

Not. Part. Of. The. Plan.

But it's Connor.

"What's up, guys?" He smiles at me, but *beams* at Noah.

They haven't talked since the video broadcast, according to Noah, and I *so* want them to. Just...maybe not right now?

"Nothing good," Noah mumbles.

I want to correct him—*this* is good! Except, I don't want to interrupt, and I've got to keep an eye on Ethan and Amanda.

"Well, that's not true," Connor says. "I got a crush confession the other day—kind of unconventional, but definitely cute—and the guy's finally back at school. I'm kinda pumped, to be honest."

Noah flushes, glancing down at the table before meeting Connor's gaze. "Really?"

"Yeah, I kind of figured it was nobody's business," Connor says. "But it is. Because I like you. And I think you like me."

Noah looks surprised. "Yeah, I do."

Connor nods. "I'm glad you're here," he confesses. "I've been wanting to talk to you, but Simi's so protective—she downright refused to give me your number."

"Oh, um, cool," Noah laugh-stammers. "What did you want to talk about?"

"For starters, I wanted to tell you that I recently broke up with the guy I was going out with back in San Francisco because it wasn't working long-distance. So there's that. Also, I wanted to tell you that what happened the other day sucked. That girl who shared the video of you *really* sucks. But to be honest—I'm glad I know." He grins again. "You're a pretty hard guy to get a read on."

Okay, I freaking love this guy—I haven't seen Noah smile this big in weeks!

"So now what?" he says.

"Now...maybe we can hang out. You know, go do something fun, instead of just studying for chemistry together."

My heart's doing cartwheels. Noah's must be, too—he looks like he wants to jump out of his seat and do a celebratory dance on the table.

Just as he's responding with a resounding "Sure!" Natasha and Cami walk by.

Shoot! I'm supposed to be watching for them—I'm supposed to *stop* them—but I was so distracted by Connor and Noah, I dropped the ball. Now they're headed toward Ethan and Amanda, who are deep in conversation.

I stand up. "Natasha! Cami!" They swivel around to look at me. So do most of the people in the cafeteria—oops. Not Ethan and Amanda, though. Whatever he's saying has got her captivated. Her friends, however, make a U-turn to come by the table I'm sharing with Noah and Connor. They're both wearing skeptical expressions.

"Hey," I say, flustered. It's hard to lie on the spot, and under pressure. "I was, uh, wondering how the henna tattoos I did for you at Woofstock held up."

"Faded away now," Natasha says, "but it was beautiful while it lasted."

Cami smiles, but her eyes are bright with remorse. "I loved mine, too," she says. "I'd love to try the traditional henna sometime, if you wouldn't mind, Simi."

I shrug; she was the one who hit play during Amanda's

broadcast the other day. I'm not sure I want to do something nice for her.

She sighs, a sad sound, then addresses Noah, Connor, and me. "I'm glad the three of you are here—I wanted to tell you I'm sorry. The morning announcements. The video. Amanda had it set up and ready to go. She never showed me what was on it—she just said to play it when she gave the signal. Had I known…"

Noah lets go of a breath. "Thanks, Cami. I appreciate the apology."

"Same," Connor says.

I smile. "Me too."

It feels good to have cleared the air. Cami isn't a bad person—I think that if she ditched Amanda, we could be friends. Same goes for Natasha. They take off, heading out of the cafeteria this time, officially over whatever they were headed toward Amanda for.

Success.

Speaking of Amanda, I look up to find her and Ethan still in the midst of an intense conversation, which has to be good news for Operation Fake Out. I scan the cafeteria for Suraj and Navdeep. They're at a corner table, Navdeep's laptop in front of them, each wearing a Bluetooth ear clip. Suraj gives me a covert thumbs-up.

They've got something on Amanda.

"Play it again," I say. We're home, crowded around the kitchen table, watching the hidden camera footage. Navdeep, Ethan, Teá, Suraj, Noah, Connor, and me.

"It was just so wrong of them to try and break us up, Ethan. We've known each other since we were in diapers. Our moms are friends. I'm just glad you realize it now."

The screen blurs as Navdeep fast-forwards the footage. "I think this is where she says..."

"They didn't care about my feelings and took what was important to me without a thought. That's why I had to get back at them."

"But the rumors about Simi. And humiliating Noah," Ethan says. *"Don't you think you took it too far?"*

Amanda scoffs. "No! I was so upset when they set you up with that girl. Someone so far below you. She's so not worthy. I had to show them how it feels. I had to hurt them the way they hurt me. That's why it was only fair that I humiliated Noah and took Simran's stupid book. I mean, yeah, maybe that was kind of silly, but at least now she knows how it feels when something you care about is stolen."

Navdeep claps Ethan on the shoulder. "Well done."

"I still feel kind of bad about lying to her," Ethan says. "She wasn't mean when we were younger. We spent a lot of time together, because of our families. We were friends. But man, she's so bent out of shape now."

"'Someone so far below you,'" Teá repeats, sounding

disgusted. Ethan squeezes her hand as she goes on. "We should play our video on morning announcements. That'd serve her right."

"No, we have to do this right. We go to Pinter with the footage. Let her deal with Amanda. She'll get what she deserves. And Noah will get his apology, the right way."

The team agrees.

"Please explain yourself, Ms. Taylor," Principal Pinter says, all steely-eyed and stern. Amanda squirms in the chair across the desk from her.

My mom's in the office, too, along with Amanda's mom. We've just watched the footage that Suraj and Navdeep captured, as well as the unedited clip Amanda took in the library. After some convincing from her mom, who is *not* happy, she finally produced it.

Amanda's miserable. "I'm so sorry."

"I had no idea any of this was going on," Mrs. Taylor says. "Amanda's a good kid. I assure you, she's never done anything like this before."

My mom nods graciously, though I can tell she doubts Mrs. Taylor. "I just want our family's book back," she says. "Then you may deal with your child however you see fit."

"I can show you where the book is," Amanda says. "It's here at school. It's safe."

"No time like the present," Principal Pinter says. "Let's go."

We stand and file out of the office. Because school let out thirty minutes ago, the hallways are empty. Amanda leads us to the sophomore corridor. She goes to her locker—just a few down from mine. She turns to the combination, opens the door, and silently removes both *The Shagun Matchmaking Guide* and my sketchbook from its top shelf.

My mother snatches the guide out of her hands and holds it close to her chest. I think she'd kiss it if we weren't all watching. Maybe I would, too.

Amanda hands me my sketchbook. "I'm sorry." She doesn't look me in the eye as she apologizes, but instead at her shoes. "Nothing is damaged. I was careful with both books. I shouldn't have taken them. I realize that now. And"—she hesitates before continuing with a wobble in her voice—"I couldn't read most of the matchmaking guide, but the writing in it is beautiful."

Amanda saw generations of my family's notes on matchmaking and liked them? My brain is not able to comprehend that possibility right now.

"Thank you," Mom says. "It's a treasured family heirloom."

"My mom and my grandmother are really proud of its history," I say. "So am I."

"All right, Amanda, Mrs. Taylor," Ms. Pinter says. "Let's

head back to my office. We have some things to discuss."
She nods toward my mom. "Mrs. Sangha, thank you for
your patience, and for not calling your jolly lawyer."

I stifle a laugh, practically running out of the building
with Mom close on my heels.

After dinner, after the rest of my family has turned in for
the night, I sit down in the kitchen with Mom. She puts
on a pot of chai and tells me that Amanda's mother called
while I was in my room doing homework.

"She apologized. She told me that Amanda's been sus-
pended for a week, and she has to go to antibullying classes.
She also said that she and her husband are going to see a
counselor with her. Apparently, some of Amanda's issues
have to do with keeping up with her extremely successful siblings. There's a lot of pressure there." Mom pauses,
giving me a stern look. "I'm sharing this with you because
I want you to consider Amanda's motivations. What she's
done is very wrong, but she'll pay the price, and hopefully
she'll grow. I trust that you'll keep this to yourself, and treat
Amanda with compassion."

Nanima comes into the kitchen wearing a fuzzy robe
over her pajamas. She knows the guide was returned—she
was just as elated as Mom and I were—but not how it all
went down. I share the details as Mom passes her a mug of
chai.

"How is your friend Noah?" she asks when I've stopped talking. Nanima adores him, as Mom and Masi do. Still, I glossed over the details of his crush on Connor, and the fact that Connor was outed in front of the whole school. Nanima is the best, but she's very traditional in some ways.

"Really good, considering everything that's happened." I take a deep breath. "Nanima, did you know that Noah is—"

"Gay?" Nanima says. "Of course, beta." She puts an arm around me. "He reminds me of my cousin Jaggi."

"Your cousin Jaggi is gay?"

She nods. "He's a journalist. Writes for the *Times of India*, the *Indian Express*, *Hindustan Times*. Such a talented writer. So many stories to tell. Everyone loves him, including me."

I smile. "Nanima, you're the best."

"No, but I do know some very interesting people." Nanima smiles at me. "As do you."

chapter thirty-one

*M*asi's house is decorated with flowers, and her new furniture looks exactly right. There is balance, harmony, and excitement between the sofa, side table, lampshade, and rug—just as there is between the two people who are getting engaged today. Everything looks beautiful.

I, on the other hand, look like a hot mess. I've been running around, helping to prepare for the saghai all morning.

"Simi, go get ready," Masi says. "Take a shower, put on something nice. I want to show off my niece today."

"Okay." I finish stacking the napkins and silverware I've been arranging on the table and walk home.

Next door at our house, things are not so tidy. Our kitchen has been the back end for all the food preparation for the party. The counters are covered in platters and dishes, ready to be warmed up and carried next door at the right time.

It smells heavenly. I grab a samosa off the counter and head upstairs. Sweetie's sitting on my bed, next to the clothes Mom laid out for me—a purple embroidered kameez with a full dhoti salwar and a tasseled dupatta. I get ready in a hurry, listening to bursts of party noise pop up from next door and downstairs—laughter, chatter, kitchen clatter, cars pulling into the cul-de-sac, my dad greeting guests.

"Stop pacing, Simi," Navdeep yells from his room. "Go walk Sweetie or something."

Not a bad idea. I bound down the stairs with Sweetie following me. I pass Mom and Nanima, who are dressed and surrounded by guests.

"Wait for me, beta. I'll walk with you," Nanima says.

I wait for her to lace up her sturdy Bata shoes—she never walks without them—and then we head out into the sunshine with Sweetie. Nanima takes my arm and leans in as she talks so I can hear her.

"Everything has been so busy, but I'm so happy today. My oldest granddaughter getting engaged to a wonderful boy. And my youngest granddaughter is starting to learn the family business. So much to be thankful for."

"About that, Nanima...I'm still not sure that I'll ever be a matchmaker the way you all are. I love art. I'm pretty sure I want it to be my future."

"Then you should not give it up." Nanima thumps her walking stick for emphasis. "No reason why it has to be a choice. Learn all you can about art. Learn all you can from your mother and masi. Do both. And who knows, maybe something else will come along that will make you forget both these things. Be open to possibilities."

"I've never thought of it that way." I'm not sure when matching and art became such an either/or situation in my head, but talking with Nanima has lifted a weight from my shoulders.

"I know your mother and masi have decided to start using the quiz software for the business," Nanima says. "Growth is important. But I wonder, do you think there is a place for what we do in America?"

"Yes," I say. This is something I'm sure about now. "The quiz is a tool. One of many we can use to help us match people. It will let us expand the number of people we can help, because the more people we have in our database, the better matches we'll be able to find. We can get so many more people to share their information if they can sign up online instead of coming in for a face-to-face interview. People from all over the country! In fact..."

"What, Simi?"

"I don't think we should limit our clients to Desis. People are people."

"And love is love." Nanima runs a hand gently over my head and smiles. "I'm tired now, Simi, and I want to save some energy for our party. Let's go home."

The party's just getting into gear as I finally make my way down, two hours after the actual start time. The yard is strung with glittering lights against a sunset-streaked sky, there's a wooden dance floor laid out, and a bunch of settees—little couches brought in by the party planner—for people to perch on scattered throughout the fenced-in space. The November chill hasn't quite settled in yet, so people aren't even bothering with coats over their Desi finery. The DJ is blasting "Sadi Gali," a Punjabi song from the movie *Tanu Weds Manu*. It's one of my favorites.

I spy Noah in the crowd, wearing one of Navdeep's glitzy old sherwanis. He looks way more comfortable in it than Navdeep ever has. He did my makeup earlier, then helped me practice for the bridesmaids-versus-groomsmen dance-off and came up with random dance moves for the spontaneous boliyan that will likely happen today. Noah loves a good party. He does a little spin and hop—his version of bhangra—and then I realize he's actually teaching the moves to Connor. They lift their arms like they're screwing in light bulbs, then Connor grabs him and spins him and I can almost hear them laughing over the thump of the bhangra music. I knew tonight would be the start of something beautiful—but I thought it was Preet and Jolly.

"Simi, there you are! Can you start doing some mehendi?" Masi asks. She points to a bunch of cones and some patterns for people to pick from. "We have one mehendi artist working on Preet and another to work on guests, but she's swamped. Go help her, puttar."

There are at least ten women and girls waiting for mehendi. "I'll take someone," I say, sitting down next to the artists Masi hired. Kiran plonks herself down in front of me.

"How's it going with Marcus?" I ask as I get to work.

"Fine." She smiles. "Better than fine, actually. Did you know my dad coaches the Mayfield Mathletes?"

"No!" I know her dad only as the granthi of our gurdwara.

"Yeah, so he already knows Marcus, and I think he loves him more than anyone." She grins, doing her best impression of her father. "'Bloody math genius, that boy, I tell you.'"

"That's great," I say.

"All thanks to you, matchmaker. Oh, hey, Jassi!"

I put the finishing touches on Kiran's tattoo, then glance up to see Jassi in line, waiting for her turn. "It looks nice," she says, studying Kiran's mehendi.

"Thanks! You're up." I offer her my design book. "What do you want? Flowers? Paisleys?"

"Robots?" Navdeep says, leaning over my shoulder.

"As if!" I elbow him, and he skips away, laughing.

"Okay, yeah," Jassi says, shrugging. "I'll try something robotic."

"Um, are you sure?" I ask, cone poised over her palm. She nods.

I make a quick sketch of Navdeep's current robot, and she giggles. I add a few dots and zigzags around him. "Cute, huh?"

"Yeah," she says.

Nanima peers over my shoulder. "Beautiful," she says.

"Jassi, have you met my nani?"

"No." She smiles at Nanima. "Namaste."

"Jeete raho, jeete raho," Nanima says, her eyes twinkling. "Simi, add some hearts to that robot, no? It will suit!"

"Okay. Jassi, you want?"

"Sure," she says.

I squiggle a few on. Then: "Done!"

A smile lights up her face as she examines her hands. "I can't wait to show it to Navdeep!"

That was random. I frown at her back as she hurries off.

Or... was it? I turn to look at Nanima, my jaw dropping at the thought that...

"These eyes may be old," Nanima tells me, "but there are some things I can still see clearly."

"Oof—Navdeep and Jassi?! Some matchmaker I am! I missed a possible pair that was right under my nose."

"Sometimes you have to step away from things you're very close to, or it's hard to see them clearly," Nanima says.

"It's just so hard to believe that someone might like my rude, annoying, obnoxious, scruffy big brother. . . ."

"He's not so bad!"

"No, he isn't," I say. I'm going to have to do something about Navdeep and Jassi. Now that I'm thinking about it, they'd be great together.

I busy myself finishing mehendi designs for as many people as I can. Mango-shaped paisleys, peacocks, lotuses, suns. There're a bunch of women around me with mehendi-ed hands, asking for drinks since they can't pick up anything until the designs dry.

When I've gotten through the line at my table, I sit down next to Preet. Since she's the guest of honor, mehendi designs swirl over her hands, arms, and feet.

"Simi, you should get mehendi done, too," Preet says.

The mehendi artist I was helping earlier has a lull in people waiting for her. She holds a cone over my hand and looks at me inquiringly as I pick a pattern—sunflowers. The DJ chooses that moment to blast "Mehndi Laga Ke Rakhna," from *Dilwale Dulhunia Le Jayenge*.

There's a commotion at the door, and a deep dhol drumbeat interrupts the song. Everyone jumps up and rushes to a window. The groom's party has arrived. And in style!

Jolly and his family have a couple of professional dholwale—traditional drummers—with them, and they're

300

singing boliyan, old Punjabi folk songs. The dholis' colorful fanned turbans add four inches to their height. Everyone is up on their feet.

"*Baari barsi khatan geya see…*"

They start the call-and-response wedding song. Except,
being Punjabi, you have to respond by dancing, not singing. Each verse calls on specific members of the bride's or
groom's family, and if you're called on, you have to dance—
no wallflowers allowed!

"*Khat key liandhi GAA…*"

"Get my mom, quick." Preet nudges me, because *Gaa*
can only rhyme with *Maa*.

I run off to grab Meera Masi and get back just as they're
finishing the boli.

Yup, Preet was right. And Meera Masi has some moves!
She spins and sways, hands up, shoulders skipping to the
beat as a circle forms around her with everyone clapping
along. Dad sticks his fingers in his mouth and whistles as
people *wah-wah* the performance.

"Simi, look at you, so grown-up!" An auntie pinches
my cheeks between her fingers. I'm holding a drink in my
free hand, so I can't do anything to defend myself.

Help me, Wahe Guru!

"Sat Sri Akal," says a boy's voice coming from right
next to me.

"Suraj!"

He's dressed in crisp chinos and a blue button-down

shirt. His hair is a little bit overgrown and curls over his collar adorably. I wonder how he would look if he grew out his hair long like a keshdhari Sikh. I think it would look really beautiful on him.

The auntie lets go and pinches his cheeks instead.

"Suraj, you're so cute!"

Thank you, I mouth at him. I think he just rescued me.

"Suraj," someone yells, "they're calling you to dance! Go!"

He doesn't hesitate to step into the circle to dance. Jolly doesn't have a brother, so that makes Suraj, his cousin, the default brother—"cousin brother," as my mom would say. Also, this brah can really bhangra, because he's killing it on the floor. Go, Suraj!

When it's over, he returns to me. "That was embarrassing." My heart does a loop de loop as he grins sheepishly. "I'm not usually a dancer."

"You were great." I offer him the unopened Limca bottle in my hand. "Drink?"

"Thanks." He takes it and opens it with a quick twist.

"Simran, there you are!" Mom says. "They're calling you out to dance!"

I peer at the dance floor, and there's Geet, dancing alone and awkwardly, looking desperately for me.

Oh, right; I count as a sister, too!

"See you in a bit!" I throw my arms up into bhangra hands and twirl onto the dance floor with Geet. Not to brag or anything, but I rock this. I jump and shimmy to the dhol's beat, and I can't wipe the grin off my face.

After Preet and Jolly have exchanged their rings—they're now officially engaged!—everyone helps themselves to the buffet dinner, squishing in wherever there's a spare seat. But for some reason there's no one at the little table Suraj and I find in a quiet corner of the garden.

"It's a nice night," he says, leaning toward me and smiling. "No flurries recently, huh?"

My cheeks warm and I smile back. "Not a single flake," I say.

"You know, we haven't gone out yet. I asked, you said yes, but we never got around to going anywhere."

"There's plenty of time," I say.

"Right. Sooo, next weekend?"

"I have to work on Saturday, and my grandparents are leaving on Sunday. Saturday's going to be huge. We're rolling out the Matched! quiz to Shagun clients."

"No way."

"Way," I say. "But maybe I could meet you for dinner. There's the café in the new bookstore that just opened up. I love it there."

"Perfect. I'll pick you up around six thirty?"

"Just let me ask my mom first."

"Ask your mom what?" Mom says—I didn't hear her coming up behind me.

"Um...can Suraj and I go out for dinner on Saturday?"

"Is anyone else going? Or is this a date?" Mom doesn't even try to beat around the bush. She is so, so cringey! This is payback for me not telling her about Aiden, I think.

"It'll just be us," Suraj says. "If that's okay with you, Auntie."

"It's fine, beta," Mom says. "But Simi has a curfew."

"I do?" I ask. That's news to me.

Mom smiles. "It's nine."

"Can we make it ten?" I pout. "I'll still be home in time to hang with Nani and Nanoo before they head to the airport, promise."

Mom nods. She's happy—I can tell. She wanders off toward my dad, leaving Suraj and me at our little table.

"Let's see your mehendi," he says, turning my palm up. My hand is warm in both of his. I wonder what he'll think of the design I chose. He glances up at me, a sudden surprised smile on his face. "A sunflower?"

I nod.

"I love it," he says softly. Gently, he pulls me in toward him for a kiss. Except I'm so surprised, I knock over my cup of ginger ale before our lips can connect.

"That's not fair," I grumble, dropping a wad of dinner napkins onto the spill. Being a klutz has trained me to always grab extra napkins. "You have to warn a girl first, otherwise she dumps her soda everywhere."

He laughs. "Is that the way it's done?"

I shrug, taking a deep breath. "Maybe try again, but go very slow?"

"All right. Incoming, in very slow motion..."

Slow. Delicious. Sweet like atte-ki-pinni.

Even in this quiet corner, I think a couple of aunties may have spotted us, but right now, honestly, I don't care.

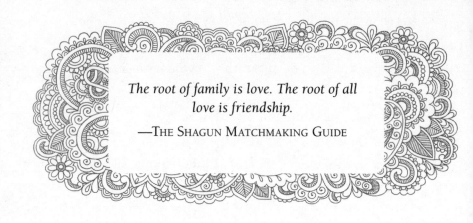

The root of family is love. The root of all love is friendship.

—THE SHAGUN MATCHMAKING GUIDE

chapter thirty-two

Saturday morning, we're all up early for breakfast. The kitchen is fragrant with the sizzle of aloo parathas and steaming cups of masala chai and buzzing with conversation, mostly about the engagement.

"Such lovely photos."

"So much wedding shopping to do now."

"Food was fantastic."

"Manju, keep me up to date with your computer quiz, dheek hai?"

I sit in the middle of the action, soaking up snippets of conversation and basking in the warmth and affection. It's great to just listen to my crazy family chatting and laughing around me. I have a mehendi cone out, and I'm working on a project that I know Ms. Furst will love. It's my drawing of Nanima and Nanoo by the angeethi, but I've traced the line drawing onto wood and I'm going over it in mehendi. I'll weave in a border of swirling paisleys and change the smoke rising from the angeethi into paisleys, too. It's going to be perfect.

"Stop looking at those corny engagement pictures and check out my scans." Navdeep is so over the posed glitzy family photos everyone's gushing over. "I worked hard to get the whole book digitized before you left, Nanima. Here, see?"

Nanima and Nanoo admire the digital scans of *The Shagun Matchmaking Guide* that Navdeep completed over the past few days.

"They're better than the original," Nanima says. "You can zoom in and everything."

"Nothing is better than the original," I say. I hold up my mehendi-on-wood masterpiece. It took me months to think this project up, but hardly any time at all to do it. "Ta-da! I'm done."

"So beautiful," Nanima says. "I've never seen anything like it!"

"Navdeep," Mom says. "I need to talk to you, puttar! Come to the office and explain what you've done with the feature I asked you to build."

"How come I don't get paid like Simi was?" Navdeep complains good-naturedly. I laugh and follow them into the Shagun office.

"We're going to pay your college fees, no?" Mom says, and then she points to her laptop. "I need to be able to compare just a few selected profiles. I can't do full batch runs for every new match—it takes far too long."

"I know; that's why I set up the individual-match tab," Navdeep says. "You can see how any one profile matches up against another you've picked out."

Mom sighs. "Simi, will you run a test?"

"Sure," I say. I grab Mom's laptop, head upstairs, and plop down on my bed. I stare at the Matched! admin page. Who should I pick to match against each other?

You are logged in as Simran Sangha. Pick a profile or profiles to match against, the screen prompts. Oh, the program's set to reveal the data from Mayfield High—not Shagun data. I can still run the test Mom requested; I'll just use my classmates instead of her clients.

An idea occurs to me: If I retake the quiz, I can use my own profile to run the individual match Mom asked about.

But do I really want to be matched again?

I click on the drop-down menu to show available profiles.

Four hundred and twenty-five Mayfield students are in the database.

Why not add one more?

I do it—I retake the quiz, answering the questions exactly as I did the first time, so the data remains accurate and unbiased.

When I finish, there are four hundred and twenty-six available profiles. My MI is the same—a silver unicorn.

I scan the names and icons and giggle as I think of who I could try to match myself against.

Marcus? I bet we'd have, like, a 6 percent match.

Ethan? Probably even lower.

Amanda Taylor? We'd probably break the system and end up with a negative match.

Then one name leaps out at me.

Suraj Singh.

My fingers hover over the keyboard. He's already asked me out, so there's really no point. And I'll be bummed if we're not a match, or a weak match. There's a part of me that's always wanted to know, though.

My hand shakes as I click on the selection box next to Suraj's name and his MI, a golden owl.

Run Match?

I close my eyes and click *Yes.*

The little wheel goes round and round as I tell myself it'll be okay if we're a crappy match. There can be only so much an app can predict. It's only as smart as the people who made it, after all. Mom calls the app a tool, not a soothsayer. And anyway, Suraj and I have that whole *indefinable* thing going for us.

Match complete. View results?

Wow—so quick.

I hold one hand over my eyes as I click to see the report. Peeling two fingers apart like I'm watching a horror movie, I take a cautious peek at the screen.

Classification: strong; 97.8 percent match.

Whoa.

We've set a new match record—Ethan and Teá were 96.5 percent.

I jump up, do a quick happy dance, and then call downstairs, "Scanning for individual matches works fine, Mom."

"Okay," she yells. "Thank you!"

Not a second later, Navdeep appears in my doorway. He stands there, arms folded, a quizzical expression on his face. He's regarding what's on the screen of Mom's laptop.

"Oy, you must've cheated on that quiz," he says. "Ninety-seven-point-eight? Yeah, you totally cheated."

"Did not!" I say. "And guess what? The next match I'm going to run is you and Jassi."

"What? Simi, don't you dare!"

"Watch me!"

I throw a pillow at him, then slam the door before he can step through.

He bangs on it, but I've locked it.

"Simi? Simi!" And then I hear his footsteps retreating.

Ha, he gave up far too quickly for that outrage to be real. Nanima was spot-on.

I pick Sweetie up for a quick twirl around my room. I can't wait to see Suraj tonight.

Stretching my arms out wide, I smile at my hands. The twin sunflowers on my palms shine back at me. The mehendi has darkened over the last couple of days to a rich wine red.

Outside the sky is blue, cloudless. Warm yellow rays slant in through my lilac drapes and light up Sweetie's fur.

It's going to be a sunny day.

acknowledgments

Many thanks to the following for making this book possible!

Mum and Mausi, for their stories and their chatra-chaya, which, to my lasting sorrow, I lost midway through the writing of this book. This book is dedicated to them.

Papa, for the lovely story about Mum and the angeethi, which ended up in the book as Nani and Nanoo's first meeting.

My three sisters, Minni, Ruhi, and Anuja—I wouldn't be who I am without you.

My writing family, including my current and former critique groups, the quiet magic of the Writers' Loft and the fellowship of Lofters, SCBWI New England, and the Boston Authors Club.

Wellesley Books, for giving me something to do when there was nothing to do but wait (and price)!

Sona Charaipotra, Dhonielle Clayton, and CAKE Literary

for the amazing concept, for their patience when personal loss slowed my pace, and for their long and careful midwifing of this project.

Victoria Marini, for selling it in short order.

Nikki Garcia, for believing in this story and for her insightful edits. And thank you to the entire team at Little, Brown for their hard work behind the scenes: Natali Cavanagh, Stefanie Hoffman, Sasha Illingworth, Savannah Kennelly, Katharine McAnarney, Annie McDonnell, and Valerie Wong.

Finally, my husband, Chandra, and my kids, Ravi and Anika, for their patience, love, and support, and Yogi, Bikky, and Zara for being the best companions a writer could have.

Just like raising a child, a book takes a village. I am thankful for every one of you!